Arrow

Arrow

Asa Foley

To order additional copies of this book, contact:
Xlibris Corporation
1-888-795-4274
www.Xlibris.com
Orders@Xlibris.com
59204

Contents

Note:

All proceeds from the sale of this book are donated to Sharing Love: They gather and distribute crutches throughout the world so others can walk with dignity and pride.

sharinglove.com

Acknowledgements

It takes a village to write a book—this was no exception:

Thanks to my wife who carried part of the load I dropped while working on this project, offered kind words of support, made my life the great treat that it is.

Thanks to my kids for helping in every aspect of this book and taking care of other chores while I worked on it.

A special thanks to my daughter Angelica for editing the book during her spring break, instead of having fun.

A special thanks to Sri Michael Owens who inspired this topic through his always thought provoking discussion of life. Michael is an amazing writer that creates from a fertile mind insightful theological discourse of life experience on many levels, a true renaissance man. http://www.thewayoftruth.org/bios.htm

To all of those who proofread, offered ideas, encouragement and supported while getting this project from mind to paper.

Teachers—without which I could not have written this book—without which you could not read this book. Most of all for those teachers that allowed me to see ways of doing things beyond what everyone else was doing, challenge new concepts and try things when they were not mainstream.

Deep respect, love, admiration to Rita Foley, my mother, who took the time to read to me as a child, challenged me to do better, encouraged the best in me. Thanks mom.

0

ARROWS

"From gravity's silken pocket came a silver chain."

Arrows are curious creatures.

Resting in the bow, nervous, unsettled, created for this moment, created to vanquish fear, anger, fill a belly, follow an order.

When the arrow is pulled from the quiver, after hours of creating, scraping off the bark, wrapping of feathers and tip in sinew, there is anticipation, excitement, worry.

Was the job well done, were there unseen flaws in the wood, is the target worthy of all this effort.

Then the bow is drawn, the archer pulls the nock of the arrow beside his cheek, they become one, single in purpose, strategy, destiny.

Energy vibrates through the string as the archer's muscles strain under the pressure.

One shot, it must be right, too high, no wait, too low, will the target move to a better angle, how much, wait, wait, wait.

The fingers unfold, the archer becomes irrelevant, inconsequential to the outcome.

No putting the arrow back in the quiver, it is not possible to feel sorry, remorse, regret, none of that, the fingers unfold, history is made, no matter what your desire, motive, hunger, passion.

As the string vibrates in the archer's hand, the archer changes from master to spectator.

There is such beauty in an arrow being set free, when the first slap of the string hits it there is a slight bend, different in each arrow, its own unique flexing motion working through the air.

Effortlessly gliding up to the sky, the feathers establishing a stable base, the tip, yearning for meat, flesh to rip apart, eager, impatient.

Between the tip and tail the elegant body of the arrow dances, twists, captivates, on it's one and only remarkable journey.

Freedom is a myth of philosophers and poets, nothing is truly free, the archer must follow the rules of nature, the arrow looks to have broke free.

Released into the sky the arrow streaks toward the heavens, for an instant it looks as though it will dance among the Gods.

Gravity has no friend or foe, it takes no lover, hates no thing on this earth.

From a silken pocket gravity pulls the silver chain, a simple tug, it ends the dance, skyward the arrow has swiftly flown, now, in gravities embrace, the arrow must descend to find flesh, a thirst, a desire for blood becomes its only motivation, duty, need, demand.

From growing on the tree, being harvested, crafted by hands, pulled from the quiver, held taught upon the bow beside the archers cheek, its one flight of freedom, this has been a long journey of care, nurture, craftsmanship, elements.

The end of the dance is so different, short, powerful, deadly.

A single impact, a final breath, a deed done, a life ended.

Hands grasped at the arrow, clawing, tearing.

Anger, fear, pain, the shadows of death, the hands were wild, untamed.

As the hands finally grasp the shaft, sporadic yanking, twisting, crying, terror.

The archer had placed upon the arrow tip small barbs, so that it could not be so easily removed, now the barbs ripped deeper into the flesh, caused more pain.

For the archer it was joy, good, a job well done.

Momentarily, the hands, now covered in blood, made a final strong pull on the shaft, the arrow was almost free.

Lubricated by the dying man's own blood, the hands slipped, then released their grip, fell, even the occasional twitch stopped.

A final breath, they called it the death rattle.

The arrow felt no remorse, its long journey from seed, to tree, to arrow was purposeful, this death was just exactly what it was meant to do.

This arrow was a proud accomplishment of the archer, hone the wood, collect sinew from the animals, feathers from the birds, forge iron tips, bone for the string nock carved just right. The feathers placed in a slight bend so the arrow would twist through the air, fly straighter, farther, hit harder, be more deadly.

The man that lies with the arrow now should admire the technology, innovation, skill, tradition that went into his death.

Following orders was all that had happened here, everyone following orders.

A two day walk away, in a field of deep green, an old woman sat down heavily upon a small stump beside a slow moving creek.

The arrow had pierced her heart, she needed no political speeches or banner waiving, no great oratory from a king praising her son.

A single tear fell upon her cheek, her craftsmanship, her creation, was gone.

While the tree was a seed so was her son.

While the tree was growing in the forest so was her son.

Together, the archers crafted arrow, her crafted son lay as night closed in, cold, worthless, used, forgotten.

The old woman cursed God, the king, the archer, then stood and walked on.

Grief was a luxury for the nobles, all peasants had were sons and arrows to give.

1

SO IT BEGINS

"Killing those with nothing was a redundant insanity of war"

Some men find who they are during great conquest, building monuments, leading great nations, on battle fields, too much strong drink, the supple flesh of a lover, in distant lands of dangerous beauty.

Through tests, conquests, retribution, King Philip was forged, built, accepted himself, until he abandoned what others desired, his true self, good, bad, smart, clever, shallow, philosophical.

King Philip had heard a calling from the church, fighting for holy lands, taking back what was God's from the Godless, leaving his wife, two young sons, royal duties.

It was by royal decree that horses, men, ships, all traveled great distances, rid a distant holy land of heathens, die, suffer, kill.

At first the crusade inspired dreams, visions of new worlds, glory of God descending on beams of light in radiant divinity to proclaim his love for a servant in performance of God's will.

Souls are immortal, powerful, virtuous, when in service of God.

During the crusades dreams failed, hardships cut through illusion, hunger made hard men abandon faith for the realities of failing flesh, the thirst for plain water destroyed a thirst for conquest.

Glory in the name of God became profanity from the lips of broken men, corroded with the ugly truth written in blood, tears, hunger, thirst.

Priests that traveled with the crusaders lost their regal air of pompous arrogance.

At home the religion peddlers were ensconced in a church, holy, sanctified by ritual, purified by vulgar displays of wealth, robes with golden thread.

All men in the face of battle, fear, bleed, empty their bowls like common farm boys.

Holy warriors became cowards, dropped their prayers to God, seeking cover, trembled like any other mortal man about to meet God in person.

In the heat of the first battles professional warriors were strong, fierce, confidant, organized, unstoppable.

As the villages, towns, small cities learned of the crusaders approach the heathen males would escape to the hills. The enemy were those left behind, women, children, old men too feeble to hold a blade, heathens would throw stones at the well armed warriors in a pathetic attempt to show anger at the loss of all they had.

Taking the lives of those who had nothing was a redundant insanity of war.

Killing those with nothing took more from the man thrusting the blade than those impaled upon it.

Priests urged the warriors of God on, forward, killing the unholy, taking the life of those God did not love, when dead they would find God, be converted through death to love God, how great the glory of God to accept the Godless.

The men who traveled with King Philip became brutal, lacking compassion for the enemy, frustrated, unorganized, killing was a sport, wagers made, death accepted, woman, children, old men tortured for information at first, were later just brutalized as a pastime.

Through the orgy of fear, violence, animal lust, monstrous actions, a truth came to King Philip.

Taking some of these men home after making them animals would destroy his kingdom.

A sword in the forge can become a farm tool.

A farmer forged into a tool of war will never be made farmer again.

There is no forge so hot as to take the violence from a man with a taste for it.

What was to become of those that had served Philip, protected him, rode at his command, each night the question brought Philip awake in cold perspiration that soaked his night clothing.

Vespers retrieved no answer from God, given that King Philip was doing God's work yet was offered no council or guidance from God himself.

Moving back up the coast Philip, his men, caravan of wagons, came to the gates of a small city. The outer walls were fortified with youths throwing sticks, rocks, small pots of stinking oil, down upon the warriors of God.

The loss of dignity created frustration, anger, rage grew at the impedance to the campaign, the crusaders had evolved from being warriors for the one true God, to a rabble of vulgar, drunken, murderers, rapists, blessed by priests for the most unholy of acts.

Through the gate the crusaders rode, a boy stood by the door of his home, protecting his mother from King Philip, firm in his hand the boy had a sharp stick, more than a child, far less than a man.

Without thought King Philip's blade ripped through the boy's small body, tender young flesh as easy as water, slowly the king removed his blade, watched as the boy called out his last words to the wrong God.

Could it be that this child knew something deeper than the priests about the need for the true God?

King Philip had been told never to question God, the test of faith was lost at the point of a sword.

A young boy, courage, determination, honor, who could call to a false God when the life drained from his eyes.

The priests abandon their God at the sight of a war they wanted fought, how powerful could such a God be to want a war upon one so young?

With the vivid memory of the young boy's brown eyes closing slowly, the color fading from his face, the horror of his mother, tears moistening her fragile features, King Philip rode on, it was not enjoyable, it was a mission to be completed.

At the far edge of the small city King Philip found a garden, first among the plants was an unusual tall bush with thin silver leaves, the tip of each one being bright scarlet red.

Lifting his sword from the scabbard King Philip was struck by the way the plant's leaves resembled his own blade, colored with the young boy's blood at the tip.

Messages from God were often in the eye of the beholder, a gift, a curse, blessings, damnation, acceptance, destruction, fragile, always powerful.

When God talks it is best to be very quiet, pay attention.

This was the last campaign, last conquest, no more would King Philip kill in the name of God, destroy life to find his own place in heaven.

If this destruction of so much was God's plan for King Philip, then God would have to tell him in person, no more from the cowardly priests.

Dropping to one knee Philip prayed as a common man.

From down the coast came news of ships entering an inlet.

King Philip thanked God, rose, rode, understood.

Fearing an attack, the men, priests, hounds were stopped from further pillaging, gathered, they raced for the ships.

There were three ships, small, damaged by a reef, the ship's captain was abandoning the largest, changing cargo.

King Philip had no problem descending quickly on them, taken, it was two days of moving cargo, altering the two ships to take the men, plunder, dignity.

An escape from this land, back to home, soft beds, soft flesh, strong drink, good stories to tell, lies to grow with each telling.

Horses were set free, in this land of little water they would probably be dead soon enough, horse dinner for some family by nightfall.

The ships cargo was abandon to make room for precious stones, metals gathered from the halls of sultans, houses of worship, trophies of the holy war.

Treasure or plunder depends on whether you were the taker or the giver of the item.

In the morning the crusaders were to set sail, all plans were made, strong drink had been given at a last feast, many men slept in the intoxicated stupor of joy, telling stories, lies, boasts, late into the night, exhausted, sleeping soundly.

The drunken men never questioned how so many would fit on two small ships, in the darkness of night the crusaders King Philip had selected to return home opened veins in the necks of those who were too brutal, cruel, inhumane to become part of his kingdom again.

A few men had returned to the city, taken women for sex, using their flesh, fear, pain for their own pleasure, in the morning, seeing the ships pushing through the waves on the horizon, seeing the exposed necks of comrades, knowing treachery of a trusted king.

The blade cutting your throat knows not its master, a trusted friend, worthy enemy, faithless lover, it matters not when your deep red life is running in the dirt.

At home the cargo of precious stones, metals, religious documents were exchanged, priests demanded all bounty for the church, in the end church leaders settled for a small portion of the plunder.

Returning crusaders used the money for building estates, livestock, seed, prosperity was enjoyed in the kingdom.

Rumors flew of the night holy crusaders had cut the throats of comrades, no one would dare ask King Philip, many warriors had died, it was war, it was hell, many brave crusaders had died was all that King Philip would ever say.

Widows of the dead were married off to others, children adopted, in time no questions were asked, no more lies needed.

It is not treachery to make a man an animal so that he will fight hard for you, then kill him when not needed anymore.

If not treachery, then why do the dead come to you each night in dreams to voice objection.

Perhaps it is just merciful to abandon a well-used tool, it could be that the beast was within each warrior all the time, just fertile ground allowed it to bloom, nurture, grow.

It will diminish a man to kill a beast that was once a friend.

War ended many a good crusaders ability to sleep a full night in peace.

Potted in the courtyard just outside the royal chambers King Philip spent hours looking at the plant with long slender silver leaves, red tips, he had never cleaned the boys blood from the tip of his own blade.

Over the years King Philip lost memory of the names of those who died in service to the throne.

The church, feeling cheated by having taken a small cut of the plunder circulated rumors of King Philip having his own men killed.

After years a truce was reached, elders of the church agreed to never discuss the king's treachery, a new cathedral was built for the church on a hill within the castle walls

If used wisely, the truth is a superior tool to gain great wealth, either from speaking it, denying it or crushing it.

No one was the same, no one was better, no one was worse, a stone engraved with names honored all who fought, the monument did not help those that lived sleep at night.

A rose planted at the base of the commemorating stone bloomed bright red, vivid flowers, fragrant, succulent, beautiful, then the petals withered, shriveled little balls, the corpse of something God had made so beautiful fell on the ground, became irrelevant dust.

It was God's simple plan for each of us, warriors, kings, boys that protect their mothers, the end was all the same.

Dust.

2

SILK PILLOWS

*"Soft kisses are deadly weapons in the art of love, they dull the mind,
entice the heart, vanquish all reason, savored by those they destroy."*

Douvan was a village girl, she walked between the rows in the field, bending down at each weed, pulling hard, moving to the next, with full arms she walked to the edge of the field, placed the weeds in the large hole, just like every weed, on every day of every week, of every year, since she became old enough to work.

Men took buckets from the small creek to the field, dumped each bucket, walked back to the creek for another bucket load of life giving water.

It was best not to think, imagine, wonder, just do one more weed, one more bucket, until it was done, of course, it was never done, the goal was always more.

Someday Douvan would be pregnant, then she would be a village woman, no more field work, she had watched birth, painful, screaming, something inside of her desired it, yet every waking thought she had of birth made her terrified of it.

As Douvan reached the edge of the field she could see a movement in the woods, along the trail, something with bright reds, greens, yellows was moving along the small path to the hamlet.

Squinting, the shape running through the woods, a man, a horse, he was riding in Douvan's direction.

Huge, white, proud, dancing more than running this horse was a work of art.

Army horses had come on the trail, they were, dull brown, kind of like the plow horses of the village, this was no army horse.

Dressed in bright silk fabrics the rider of dark complexion was young, tall, thin, he rode straight in the saddle, leaning forward the rider whispered, the horse broke into a dead run, they raced past Douvan only inches away.

A few lengths they went, then the rider leaned way off the horse, grabbing a yellow flower from the ground, pulled hard, the pair whirled around with billows of steam in each breath, the front hooves launched from the ground clawed at the sky.

Racing back to Douvan the young man jumped from the still moving horse, dropped to one knee, held out the flowers, bowed his head down, proclaimed that while unworthy, he would love her faithfully with each breath until he breathed no more.

Douvan's heart raced as she reached out to take the flowers, the boy took her hand, soft kisses on the back, a shiver down her spine.

The young man stood, much taller than Douvan, his soft lips brushed against her cheek, he smelled of sandalwood, wild flowers, roses.

Wagons were moving in the woods now, a string of horses followed behind, the young man leapt onto his horse, raced to the wagons.

Until one of the men with a bucket yelled at Douvan, she simply watched the wagons move down the trail to her hamlet, her heart racing, soft feel of his lips upon her cheek.

Illusions were like that, tricky little lies one tells in the middle of a days work to play with sanity.

Reality was like that, tricky little lies one tells they look, feel, smell so much like illusion.

That night, trading, eating, a celebration in her small hamlet, few traveling caravans came this way, most were lost, this group was moving from one port to another, horse traders from far off, learning, exploring along the way.

Large tents were pitched in a field across the small stream, wagons pulled into a circle, the young man that had kissed her cheek was called the Sultan, not royalty, just a nick name.

As the feast went on Sultan would look at Douvan, smile, eyes flashed, sharp, focused, it was as if the first time anyone had truly seen, understood, wanted, desired her.

Douvan would blush, look away, then look back to see if Sultan held her within his gaze.

Men of the caravan and hamlet sat around the fire, drank golden liquid, told stories, lied, laughed, thick cherry scent wafted through the air from the fire smoke.

Douvan went to her hut, listened, when the sounds died down she snuck out, creeping to the end of the caravan tents, she went to a large tent that the young man had entered earlier.

Opening the flap of the tent Douvan felt fear and calm, changes lay inside the fabric walls.

Douvan did not know what she hoped would happen, a bold step in, her eyes were adjusting to the little candlelight.

Four men sat in a circle on large silk pillows of bright colors with vibrant tapestries sewn in. A thick fog of smoke from incense hung in the air, a man called out, the young man they called Sultan came from behind a long silk cloth hanging from the ceiling.

Sultan took Douvan's hand, she followed him behind the drape, the old men filed out, remembering their youth.

No words, soft lips upon her hand, his breath on her cheek, a plate of dates, small glasses of sweet honey wine.

Sultan removed Douvan's clothing slowly, each lace undone, cloth slipped over her wide farm girl shoulders, he lifted the cloth from her breasts.

Douvan moved slowly, lay back, her body opened to him.

He kissed her lips.

He kissed her neck.

Soft kisses are deadly weapons in the art of love for they dull the mind, entice the heart, vanquish all reason.

Douvan lay upon the pillows, surrender, acceptance, desire, lust, safe, warm, kind.

Soft manicured hands moved over each inch of Douvan's skin with tender strokes, she reached for Sultan, her lips upon his, not soft, hard, demanding, wanton, inexperienced, crude, desire ripped through her.

Sultan pulled Douvan on top of him, she was writhing out of control.

Laying Douvan back on the soft silk pillows, smell of incense mixed with the dates, more honey wine.

Douvan was so young, tender, Sultan took her again, hard, powerful, controlling her moves, making her his prize.

Morning light came in shafts through the trees that danced in shadows on the tents colorful walls, it was like being inside of a beautiful lamp.

Waking to kisses, nothing could ever be this perfect, Douvan captured each moment in her mind, she could be here any time she closed her eyes.

Douvan did not sneak back to her hut, she was not ashamed, her mother looked at her with disapproval as she dressed in her work clothing, returning to the field to keep pulling weeds, others talked about her, she could not hear them, Sultan's soft skin, gentle lips were with her even in the drudgery of her day.

For the rest of her life Douvan would have, silk pillows, honey wine, the smell of sandalwood, nothing could take that from her.

A month later Douvan was married to a farmer, he was kind, dull, calloused, dirty, of their five children the first was much darker skin with soft blond hair, blue eyes, a smile that was a weapon to disarm the hardest heart, Murad moved with the grace of his father.

While quite young, Murad questioned, why he was different from those in the hamlet, Douvan packed his bag, he walked away, never a farmer, Murad's path was far away.

Douvan loved Murad, she knew he would need to leave her to find happiness.

A year after Murad left the hamlet Douvan laid upon her cot in the dirt floor hut, closed her eyes, transported upon the bright silk pillows, sweet dates, soft lips caressed her flesh, washed down with honey wine, the smell of incense

Douvan could feel Sultan, her dark lover, taking her as a prize, giving herself over to passion, lust, desire, her heart stopped.

They found her, a content smile, life passed so quickly, her husband, a good provider, knew she was happy.

3

FACETS OF POWER

"Monarchy—in all its treacherous splendor"

Kings cannot be human, their subjects must believe them to be Gods if they are to be obeyed, pampered, revered, feared.

King Philip's father, King George, had taught Philip well the role of King, the rules of royalty, demands of the crown, decree of the throne.

The crown is heavy, each facet of each jewel is paid for in blood, sacrifice, pain.

No human man could extract so much in blood, pain, tears from those who grovel at his feet. Each day came a demand for even more payment when a whim, desire, thought required sacrifice in service to the king.

Each morn that the sun rises, the king must demand more, require more, punish those that do not give more.

Armies marched on command, military officers understood sacrifice, for they were the ones that most often bled, suffered, died in service to the crown.

A fair, honest, noble, king was not a strong king, morality was the first compromise that one must make when placing heavy metal crowns upon ones brow.

Compassion was skillfully cut away, hung, burned in a public execution called a coronation, empathy, concern, justice, passion were just faint echoes that came in the night while drifting from sobriety to intoxication with royal magnificence.

Alcohol was the royal drink, for it was the elixir that made the mind function in the quiet dark chasm that was power.

Drinking was the excuse for actions that went wrong.

Drinking was the excuse for actions that moral men could not do.

Drinking was the fertile ground of royal decree, proclamation, command.

At age twelve Prince Philip's father, King George, took Philip to the woods where they shot, gutted, skinned a deer. Holding the warm heart of the animal up for all to see the prince was becoming a man, King George beamed with pride.

At age fifteen King George, took a prisoner to the square, knelt the bound man down, with a huge axe Prince Philip executed him. Philip held the head up, King George beamed with pride.

When Prince Philip was eighteen, King George entered the royal sleeping chamber to find Prince Philip, knife in hand. In the instant before his death King George knew that Philip had learned well the rules of the monarchy.

The king is dead, long live the king.

Cunning is what we do to others—treachery is what they do to us.

The crown, robes, throne are the royal statement, the paranoia, fear, passion are the heart.

If you are not one step ahead, then your head is one step from the axe.

The throne was the seat of power for a kingdom, a wise ruler made sure those close to the throne were capable of protecting him when the royal boot had bruised an ego, created an enemy, or had taken a lover desired by another.

All in the cast of the king's gaze could be bought.

All in the cast of the king's gaze could turn on him.

All in the cast of the king's gaze could be seduced by power.

King Philip selected those close to him, commanded them, sometimes the king would have one taken to the square, beheaded, just to make sure everyone remembered they were disposable pawns.

It was King Philip's two sons, Prince Rogan and Prince Harrow that were the problem, Philip did not select them, Philip could not command them, worst of all King Philip could not trust them.

Sadly King Philip could not have one son executed, when the other needed to be shown how displeasing the king was a bad mistake.

To the subjects Rogan and Harrow were a statement of power, for they would succeed King Philip on the throne.

Young princes could joke, dance, smile, love, trust, once older they would need to change from friend of the people to a ruler of the people.

The princes had to be trained to take power, dominate enemies, assume control, so the peasants would know a good ruler would succeed the current king.

King Philip had to face what his father King George faced, Prince Rogan standing in his bedchamber with a blade, a desire for the throne.

This kingdom was after all, a monarchy in every bit of its treacherous splendor.

The king is dead, long live the king, sounded good to those wanting to be king, not good for the current king.

People of the kingdom hated King Philip, his power, his demands, his army was feared in every corner of the land.

A brutal king was far better than a weak king.

Better to fear a tyrant than fear a weak king not being able to protect when needed.

A solution was required for Prince Rogan and Prince Harrow, a protection that would give King Philip control, dominance, yet appear to the people, and his sons, that he was cunning not treacherous.

Clever was required, devious would be uncovered.

Prince Rogan was the one that King Philip feared, loathed, hated. Of course in public the king made sure to fawn over Rogan, praise, nurture.

King Philip treated Prince Rogan, as if the Prince were a God that had sealed himself in the womb of the queen.

It was Prince Rogan that King Philip had trained to be strong, decisive in all matters before the court.

Prince Rogan was ready for the power of the crown.

Prince Rogan was ready for the orgy of death that was the crown.

Prince Rogan was ready for killing his father to take the crown.

Sending Prince Rogan first into battle would be a story for the boy if he lived, which would increase his power, or make him a legend if he died. Both unacceptable.

An accidental poisoning, spells, potions, would be an obvious thought, too obvious not to be thought treachery.

It was deep within the fitful sleep of murdering ones own flesh that King Philip's vision came, a ship with sails billowed against sunset winds, powerful ships moving silently through the water in foggy lands, along rocky shores.

Conquests of gold, silver, slaves, power, all would be an easy sell to an ambitious young man like Prince Rogan.

At first light two large stallions descended from the castle gates, long riders King Philip trusted, with purses of gold, silver they thundered across the hills in search of ships that could make the wind tremble, sea Gods crawl before them, heavy hulls for carrying plunder, slaves, gold, jewels enough to make a young man forget this kingdom for awhile.

Long enough, King Philip thought, to finish his own reign, die asleep in the royal bed with girls under each arm, let Prince Harrow fight his brother, or find a way to surrender when Prince Rogan returned from the sea.

Docks had to be built out into the sea, expensive docks that required sacrifice of able bodied men, a good portion of the treasury, more taxes.

Peasants were beaten when they complained, killed when the crown felt beatings were just too much work, examples improved productivity quickly.

Those without title or property were taken in chains to the shore where they built long docks into the turmoil of ocean waves.

Forges burned day and night making weapons that were to destroy men, timber sails.

Months passed, lies flooded the kingdom, slaves escaped, others put to death for not working hard enough, patriotic speeches gave way to demands, finally King Philip simply ordered it done, anyone who did not help would be killed.

One crisp day a yell came from the docks, sails turned from the point of land and descended to the new docks.

Yells gave way to screams as word went out among the workers of the impending attack. Some craved death over slavery, others felt one tyrant replacing another would change nothing.

Walking to the end of the docks King Philip stood alone.

Anticipation filled Philip's every breath. His command had been for Prince Rogan to join him, the boy had not come, the first act of rebellion, defiance, power needed to be changed, taken back, punishment was at hand.

Twenty riders appeared upon the hill above the docks, these were not the king's army, doing the king's bidding.

The ships danced upon the water, shore birds sailed around King Philip's head asking with each cry if the plan was sound.

There was Prince Rogan, oldest of his sons with the riders, from King Philip's own seed came his own death, on a black stallion Philip had given Rogan as a gift.

The ships leveled off with the docks, gracefully swooped in, the landing of eagles upon prey, fetching up in their talons the evil intent of the riders.

On shore the riders were armed, young, fearing nothing, they were the new rulers of the kingdom, one last thing to do, remove the old king.

From the ship stepped two of King Philip's most trusted long riders. Behind the riders were seasoned killers of no loyalty except money, which was all the loyalty required.

As the sun shown down, waves made jewels dance in the foam, the ships crew would kill any breathing thing, for a price.

Prince Rogan and his men stepped from their mounts, with long powerful strides they started down the dock, this treachery would be fast, planned, not a fools boast, real power taken with a blade.

King Philip, ruthless in many wars, knowing fear in men's hearts, souls, stepped out from the long riders that flanked him.

It was quick, half of those riders with Prince Rogan hesitated for a step, then the others, seeing the hesitation stopped, only Prince Rogan stepped forward.

Rogan's hand on the leather of his blade, the blade was not drawn, this was a brave fool, not a glory bound corpse.

Alone, one breath from death, Prince Rogan accepted command of the ships, outfitted for war he stood on the bow as they slipped away from the shore, castle, strength, stability of the life he had known.

One of the twenty riders with Prince Rogan talked of far off lands, adventures they would have, Rogan's blade cut him twice, sent him to the water dogs for food.

King Philip was amazed, by the power of his own cunning.

Prince Rogan was amazed, by the power of his father's treachery.

Prince Harrow was five years less than his brother, Prince Rogan. Harrow was also of a much softer temperament, Prince Rogan knew that Harrow would never kill their father, King Philip, for the throne.

The weaknesses within Prince Harrow was compassion, justice, morality.

Prince Rogan could exploit these weaknesses in Harrow to take back what was rightfully Rogan's.

In control again, King Philip dispensed justice, spent more time in the mountains with slave girls, mistresses, whores.

Without conquests, the killing of prisoners, many in the kingdom had reduced the taxes they were willing to pay, the army was being paid less.

Corruption is a crop grown in the fertile fields of weakness.

To keep control King Philip ordered the death of two fine young army officers, examples must be made of his power over the military.

Mistakes can be taken back when you are a mortal man, as a God, the king had ordered an execution so someone must die or the king would appear weak.

Power demands good men must die, it is delusion to run a country being fair.

On a part of the road to the brothel where King Philip kept his female play things, after a skin of wine, the king's horse slipped over the side, down a small hill. Later that night, when the army officers found him, King Philip's neck was broken.

A tragic accident—the king is dead—long live the king—a day of sorrow was declared.

Even the court jester cried in public, celebrated in private at the loss of King Philip.

Killing a king was not treachery, it was a plan, a good plan, a plan that cleaned out the bad, a plan that the army hoped had brought in the good.

A week after King Philips death, King Harrow ordered the two officers that were to have been executed brought to the square, crowds cheered as the peasants knew that the new king would release them.

Archers stood around the square, not normal for an execution, a new king was in power now.

Army officers standing around with their units started to get nervous, a simple pardon was taking on a tone of judgment.

King Harrow called out to the traitors in the military that had murdered his father, King Philip.

The military officers noticed that the archers around the square were not like those in the army, these carried a different kind of bow, dress, the quiver of arrows was large, full of feathered death.

King Harrow stepped up to one officer tied to the post, plunged his dagger into the young man's belly up to the hilt, then pushed down.

Pungent putrid smells came rushing up, blood gushed across the stage, Harrow leaned forward as if hearing the man's last confession, then stood back, shouted names.

Arrows hissed across the small square, army officers tumbled down to the ground, dead before they saw the archers lift their bows.

Quickly King Harrow stepped next to other officer bound to the post. Before his dagger could rip the intestines from the young man arrows hissed again.

The archers had been commanded to shoot any officer that moved from his spot.

All of the army officers in the crowd had moved, death was coming, trained to fight some pulled swords, moved forward, others turned, ran, it did not matter, all died.

King Harrow turned to the young bound officer, commands were given, low hushed tones to the condemned. Confession was good for the soul, confession to anything to anyone, confession to knowing who killed good King Philip, shouting names of those laying on the ground with arrows sticking from them would bring freedom.

It was promised.

King Harrow promised.

The horror of blood, carnage, agony, before the young officer, his freedom was assured.

Screaming the names, the young officer screamed out the names just like the new king . . .

The dagger went deep into the young officers belly, life gushed onto the square, his eyes rolled back, life ended, the blade had punctured a lung, no air to proclaim the treachery.

Slumping down, the ropes binding the officers hands held him up as a spectacle for the amazed crowd to behold. Two young strong men slumped against the posts, heads down as if looking at the wounds to their bellies.

King Harrow held back the young officers head before he died, proclaimed the evil one. The crowd cheered.

Those the young man had grown with,

Those that the young man had helped in times of need,

Those girls that the young man had danced with at parties,

Those boys he had wrestled with and called friend

Everyone cheered when the evil was killed.

Everyone cheered, because it was him, not them, cut open in the square.

The moment was not lost on the dark riders that took off through the gates the next morning. Paid handsomely for information, they traveled for over three months to find their true king, Prince Rogan, who had been cheated from the throne.

When the ships had broken port, moved into the ocean Prince Rogan had a plan put into motion. Create great wealth from pillage, plunder, return, take back his rightful throne.

Prince Rogan was now Captain Rogan, ruthless, cunning, treacherous.

Captain Rogan's men feared his every breath, gold, silver, women, skins of wine made for a loyal crew.

Rogan's fleet were not pirates, there was no code, this was a kingdom on the sea with one ruler who killed when he wanted, rewarded loyalty well, praised treachery.

In distant lands Captain Rogan's crew was culled from the strongest they found. Two ships were not enough to build an empire, some ships joined for the bounty, some from fear, all sailed under one command, death or glory were the only options.

4

LONG RIDER

"The hone of a sharp blade takes many slow patient
pulls along a perfect stone."

Birth in a village involved everyone, women ran from hut to hut shouting orders, each duty ordained, gathering needed items, bickering, supporting, nurturing.

Village men sat at fires drinking, as far from the madness as they could get.

Congratulations to the father for his hard work were often unheard because a smart husband was so drunk that the connection of sounds to words could not be made.

Screaming was just part of the process, a baby was more precious because of the pain, sacrifice, hope, lust that went into making it.

Confusion lifted like a fog as the moment drew close.

Buckets of water heated, wagers on which sexual organs, fresh clean cloth brought, laid upon the bed, whispers of the midwifes, procedures to follow, based on generations of folk lore, stories, beliefs.

Pink, slimy, wrinkled little pouch of skin connected to a head that screamed was the end result.

An elder man, Madras sat at the fire with the village men, gray hair flowed down over the fine all black clothing, clean shaven, two swords crossed upon his back, a huge stallion stood quietly behind him, untied, the horse never moved.

Madras, had told the Stallion to wait, so it waited.

It was clear Madras, was no farmer, when his eyes settled on the horizon, far away, distance, another place, an emptiness filled his face, longing, desire, a thirst for any place that was not here.

Madras was one of King Harrow's long riders, legends of myth in human form.

Village men asked Madras questions, only a smile in return.

Words of deeds done did not improve the man or the deed.

There was no way to describe the life of a long rider to farmers, often Madras did not believe it himself, like a mental journal, he kept the stories of his life locked away for private moments.

Life before now was only the lessons learned, use the good to improve life, lessons help a long rider stay alive one more day, tricks of the trade, tools for survival.

Madras had questions he could not or would not ask, the new father, strong big man with farmer's hands, calloused, rough, the mother tall, fair, smart, quick of wit, hard worker.

Screaming, loud, large lungs, Madras looked upon the pink skinned infant, ten fingers, ten toes, black curly hair, squirming, screaming, the child was truly clay in raw form, still, it was good form.

Madras smiled, nodded to the new mother, she smiled, he walked from the hut, in one stride he stepped upon the back of the stallion, the partners stepped gently, quietly, the night enveloped them.

The pink wrinkled pouch of skin that screamed was named Zorn.

A long rider had been born, for ten years Madras and others would ride to this village on large black stallions, look in, note the boys progress, see his skills, perhaps give him a bow to pull, show him how to run, for ten years Zorn would be tested.

If the strength of the father, wit of the mother were within him, at age ten Zorn would be taken to the castle, worked hard, trained even harder, treated well, obedience demanded, humility required, duty, honor, loyalty expected.

The hone of a sharp blade took many slow patient pulls along a perfect stone.

To hone a blade quickly destroys the blade.

A long rider is the strongest blade of perfect hone, or the entire kingdom could be lost.

All kingdoms had caravans of goods traders that went off with products of the kingdom, returned with products the kingdom needed.

Caravans were easy targets, even with a good complement of army for protection, slowly they lumbered along roads filled with goods that could be stolen, converted to cash.

Generations ago the kingdom had started creating a force of men upon large swift horses who could move quickly, quietly though dangerous areas with goods, return with required goods, if one was taken it was not an entire caravan.

Each long rider on a stallion followed by two strong swift pack horses, four large hounds ran scout, front, sides, rear, signaling with barks or whelps they kept the rider, and more important, the cargo, safe.

Long riders were trained in languages to converse with all they met, medicine for themselves, horses, hounds, reading to contract with others, math to keep records, values of stones, to judge the purity of gold, silver, steel.

Each day required running miles, lifting heavy weights, building a strong body to carry out the deeds of the strong mind.

While extremely disciplined, the long riders were able to make judgments in the field, speak for King Harrow, cunning, diplomacy, smiles, romance, even treachery were tools of the trade.

At age eighteen, after training and hard work, those accepted were given a black stallion, two pack horses, four hounds to care for as their own. All long riders agreed this was the greatest day of their lives.

At age nineteen, each rider was given his two bows, short, stout, heavy, for use from horseback, short range, hard hitting, ten arrows on each bow. Day and night bows were fired from standing, sitting, laying, on horseback, running, until fingers bled, muscles ached, the pain was better than a missed shot causing your death.

Long elegant bows were for long range, delicate hunting, these short bows were for defense, stiff bows that took the incredible fiber of each muscle in unison to pull, hold, aim, fire.

Four round nets were also given, the width of a man when extended, made of supple tendons, dipped in oils, soft as a thread, very strong, tied around the edge were small metal balls with spikes.

Six months later came the most important long rider tool, his back plate, upon which were kept two long thin swords, for use from the tall stallions, these blades were quick, deadly, thick soft handles, straps around the wrist kept them from being lost.

The tip of each sword was designed to break away, exposing a new tip, this way a rider did not have to stop to pull the sword back, a quick twist, keep riding, bring treasure back to the kingdom.

On either side of the swords were held two small iron spikes, short with sharp tips, thrown or thrust the tips could pierce heavy armor.

The rear plate itself was the best tool, hard leather on the outside, soft sinew woven tightly on the inside, it would stop most arrows, yet was comfortable to wear, many a long rider had holes made from assassins arrows in his back plate, he lived to tell the tale.

Back plates were statements, from its wear, arrow holes it was possible to tell the age, experience of a long rider, from the holes it was possible to see how many times archers had tried to take his life.

Saddles were leather and sinew wound tightly to reduce weight, keep a good airflow, just behind the saddle pouches held small amounts of food, nets, two bows rested on them, within quick reach.

On Zorn's twentieth birthday a dance was held, It started in the throne room with King Harrow giving Zorn a small sack of gold for trade, a ring with the royal crest for placing sealing wax on documents in the name of the king.

Once mounted Zorn passed through a gauntlet of experienced long riders.

Each rider stood beside his horse, two swords drawn, the new rider would come from around the castle wall, at full speed with a sword in each hand, touch the tip of his sword to all other long riders swords, tradition was important for moral.

Through the castle walls, two draft horses, four hounds, Zorn's personal team, first to his birth village, to say goodbye, then to the horizon, a new long rider would travel for a month to find goods for the kingdom.

It was a test, Zorn's first, most important, paper, pens, sealing wax to gather treaties, trade agreements, gold for goods, trade, merchandise, weapons for protection, weapons to enforce agreements.

Zorn rode swiftly through the castle walls, found trails to his village just beyond the close hills. Kisses, tears, proud of his accomplishments, sad for the loss of seeing him, fear of never seeing him again.

A small pouch of mother's cookies with some fresh vegetables, father gave a bottle of wine.

Night closed in, Zorn, horses, hounds all walked along roads beyond the far hills, further than he had ever gone, to a small clearing, sleep, four hours of sweet restfully sleep, hounds kept watch, moving slowly in the deep woods around the camp.

Awaking quickly, Zorn called the hounds in, kept watch himself, a small bow in his hand, the hounds slept by the fire, bellies full, as darkness was broken by small shafts of blazing sun breaking through trees heavy with foliage the hounds began to move.

Zorn saddled his horses again, gave them each a few bites of vegetables from his village, first real day as a long rider was to start now.

Avoiding roads, following back trails, animal tracks, creeks, streams, offered the best protection, the hounds were always within hearing range, working through the underbrush, quiet, smooth.

One hound, an old bitch was far out ahead, Zorn would catch a glimpse of her up on a hill watching his direction, changing her path to pace his.

She had been the bitch of another long rider, older, wiser than Zorn, one day the horses, hounds, treasure had returned to the castle, the long rider they belonged to was gone, never returned.

As long rider custom dictated the horses, hounds, equipment were split among the new riders, the old bitch given to Zorn, after two years she never considered herself a part of his team. It was fine with Zorn, having a good scout far out was safer for all of them.

Late at night, the darkness covered them, a small stream beckoned, the hounds scouted, Zorn kept his eyes shut for a short time, when he awoke the hounds moved in to be fed.

The old bitch carried a baby deer in her mouth, Zorn built a small fire, cooked the hounds some meat, a little for himself, full bellies, the hounds slept, the young rider moved into the cover of the bushes, kept watch over his team.

Hanging from the saddle was the knotted cord, each day a knot was tied to track the days, without conversation, duty, work, the days blended, lost, became a maze within the mind that could play many tricks with fear, loss, anger. Each knot held a bead, every seventh bead was a red one.

It had been the first red bead day that Zorn realized the loneliness of the long riders, the empty feeling, the desire for a joke, words, conversation, an exchange, or even just the company of another human.

Anticipation of excitement, adventure, trade, barter, had given way to the drudgery of endless riding, finding camp, sleep, moving, transient, unsettled.

Very proud of the honor of being a long rider, Zorn knew that the craft would come through this test, to hear another voice, a kind word, see a smile, would be most welcome.

Lost in his thoughts Zorn moved through the woods along a trail that was wider and more used that he would have liked, the old bitch suddenly cut across just in front of his stallion on a dead run, it meant that he was to follow.

Spurring the large stallion they broke into the woods at full speed, seconds later a loud thud hit Zorn's back and stung, an arrow, from the trees.

The old bitch barked, ran to the left into heavy brush, horses broke right back up to the trail, when clear enough Zorn grabbed a bow, just as they broke back to the trail another man with a bow stood to one side of the road, a drawn arrow kissing his lips.

Before Zorn could nock an arrow a dark gray hound grabbed the archer by the arm, pulled him to the middle of the road, released, the hound ran for the woods, Zorn's stallion was upon the bewildered archer in a instant, crushed him under the thundering hooves.

A movement from the tree ahead, unidentified, Zorn fired an arrow into the shaking leaves, a man's hand fell limp from the tree.

Turning a corner, a few strides later, four men with large sticks could be seen standing in the road to block the team.

Before Zorn could lift his bow hounds raced from the close underbrush, attacked, Zorn could see the old bitch with teeth sunk into the crotch of one man who was flailing about trying to get free.

Zorn's arrows dispatched two of them, horses blasted past, the goal was not to fight, keep moving on, a duty to perform.

Later, farther, safe, the team stopped, drank, ate, Zorn checked all the animals for injury.

The old bitch had a slight limp, Zorn lifted her in his arms, she growled a little then licked his face, then growled a little more, onto the back of a pack horse, pulled up the sides, she earned a rest.

An arrow hung from spot just above the V of the two swords, good marksman, Zorn's first hole, a mark of honor, he noticed another small hole toward the bottom of the back plate that carried a small arrow head, very odd, he wondered when that might have happen.

As sleep came Zorn had to remember that he was alive, most of those who tried to kill him were not, a test passed.

Zorn thanked all those who trained him for his life this night.

Attaching the second red bead Zorn decided to find people, start making contact, trade, these were new routes, new people, care must be taken, trade was important for all.

It was two days before Zorn found a road of any substance, a small trail just to the side of the larger road was followed for four more days before seeing a small village.

Most villages looked much like the one Zorn had been born in, watching the village for a full day and night from the hill Zorn wanted to see what came, went from it, when satisfied, he moved in.

Zorn rode into the village with empty palms up, the hounds had been left upon the hill, only the old bitch accompanied him.

The villager's wary eyes locked on Zorn's every move, he went to the well in the center of town, pulled up the bucket to drink from before anyone spoke to him.

Farmers with fields to tend, annoyed by strangers, fearful of one armed so well, wanting to trade, needing to get gold for barter in the cities, security, Zorn chose his words carefully, cautiously, no demands, many smiles, talk of his own village in their language.

As night fell food was shared, a bed offered, accepted, a young girl kissed Zorn's cheek, later she crept in the darkness between his covers, escaped quickly back into the darkness.

After four hours Zorn awoke, sat beside the horses while the old bitch slept.

Heavy breakfast, wild meat, some bread, all the village had to trade were foods that would go bad before Zorn could get them back to his kingdom.

Then the villagers offered farm implements that were made from crude hands, unrefined, Zorn declined.

An elder stepped from the main hut, made a wave, Zorn followed, head bowed in reverence.

In a clearing stood a herd of the largest cattle that Zorn had ever laid eyes upon.

The cattle were milling about as if confused, upset, Zorn could see they had eaten all the grass and were looking for more food.

Twenty-five big cattle cheap, they were eating the village's food, giving good milk, not as much as they ate.

Meat was easy to find in the woods, wild meat was good, did not diminish the crops as much as these beasts.

The story was told of a ship, crashed years ago with four calves onboard, careful tending had rendered the heard . . . Nice story, not needed, price was the only question.

For only a few coins Zorn got the herd, a young man to help tend them on the trail.

Sadly all of Zorn's speed would be gone, with good tending these cattle could be good milk, meat, hides for the kingdom of King Harrow.

The young village boy gathered the herd while Zorn filled the pack horses with dried vegetables, meats, moving out the old bitch was sent into the hills, brought back the hounds.

Two red beads the herd moved slowly thought the main roads, this ride was another of Zorn's tests, he worried that in his greed he had failed, moving so slowly with these cattle made them an easy target, they might not return at all.

Night camp was when it happened, the village boy woke Zorn, hounds scuffled with something in the brush just outside of camp, moving slowly with sword drawn Zorn made his way through the darkness, in his black clothing he was almost invisible.

In the woods a man stood to Zorn's left, only an outline in the moon's pale light.

Another man approached from the right, the hounds had stopped fighting, now the forest was very silent.

Two men were now on Zorn's left, some conversation, then the two on his left walked away.

The one man to Zorn's right was close, a quick thrust into his neck, Zorn stepped behind the man, lowered him to the ground, alive, unable to breath, speak, quiet, Zorn held him until death came.

Zorn moved slowly, silently, he could see the outline of a man facing the herd, sword in hand, ready for attack, the thin tip of Zorn's blade slipped just under the back of the robbers skull, a twist, the tip broke off, Zorn moved on.

Something was close beside Zorn moving fast, dropping to one knee, a blade swing was close to his head.

Zorn thrust up, into the belly of a fat man who was hidden in the bushes.

The hounds began growling, barking, going crazy, the sounds of children's voices, screaming, terrified, one was screaming loudest, then no sound at all.

A small hovel made of branches was filled with terrified children, the hounds circled, teeth bared, two children lay in front of the hovel not moving, covered in blood, eyes wide open, the work of the hounds, well trained, efficient, not discriminate.

One whistle, hounds stopped, moved back into the woods.

Crying, an older girl fell from the hovel on her knees begging forgiveness, milk was all the men had tried to steal, food, bad men, stolen chidren.

The three men's intentions were no longer the issue, dead men have no good or bad intentions.

Zorn checked on the herd, all was right, the young village boy tending the herd was scared, wanted to move on.

Pulling some meat, vegetables, a hide of milk, Zorn returned to the hovel, placed the items on the ground, ten or more children were standing outside now, more were inside the shelter.

The girl knelt at Zorn's feet, thanked him, the dead men were going to sell the children like animals, she begged for help, the rider took her hands, pulled her up, walked away.

Hardships were everywhere, long riders were traders, hard men, focused, the hardest part was helping only as they could, never compromise the mission.

Two days later Zorn found a small village, told them of the children, where they were, their need for help, the villagers said they would find them, help them.

Zorn prayed that night, his first talk with God in a long time, not for the children, not for his mother or father, Zorn prayed for the strength to be a hard man so that he could stay a long rider.

Villages along the way offered many things to trade for cows, pretty stones of no value, objects of metal that looked like gold, not precious.

Close to Zorn's last set of hills a larger village offered him many military weapons, a war had been fought close by, left behind many weapons that were useless to farmers.

Long riders were cautioned against taking weapons, as they were often substandard metals or construction, swords that broke, armor that was too heavy, too easy to pierce.

These weapons appeared well made, a test shot from Zorn's bow did not pierce the chest plate as it did shooting at the chest plates worn by King Harrow's army.

Zorn noticed a stick with a tube on top of it, almost as tall as he, the warriors that had left it were raiders from far away.

The stick did nothing, like a child's toy, click when a lever was pulled back on top, then another lever was pulled on the bottom, Zorn traded a cow for some of the best weapons, included were a few of the sticks, some bags of metal balls.

As the long rider was getting ready to leave, the oldest villager, one who had watched the war, talked of the sticks, black powder, a ball put inside caused it to bellow smoke, a trick to scare the other fighters.

Zorn's sixth red bead was on before he could see the walls of the kingdom, success, home, another ritual dance, long riders assembled to welcome the new rider home, when Zorn saw the line a wild bolt of energy shot through him,

At full speed Zorn burst through the castle gate with both swords waiving in the air above his head.

Tips flashed when the swords struck each other, the line when Zorn was leaving was silent, this line screamed loudly as a sign of respect, the shouts also acknowledged that all of their work in selecting, training, trusting, Zorn had paid off for the kingdom.

Never again would Zorn be saluted, never again cheered, never would he be acknowledged for doing his job. Code of the long riders, celebration of duty reduced the profound glory of the accomplishment.

This night in a tavern with amber beverages that make men stupid Zorn would tell stories of his first trip, each detail, encounter, choice, thought, how his animals worked, what he did well, what he should have done better, tomorrow an elder rider would offer him suggestions.

Never again would Zorn speak of his deeds, boast, remorse, dream, regret.

Stories diminish the deed, what you will do, is all you are.

The arrow holes in Zorn's back plate were shown to all in the tavern, marks of the long rider on his first ride, all whished him well.

Each long rider kissed the holes in the back plate, it was a way of thanking the Gods for not having the arrow shot higher.

Morning briefings were normally very short, more of a pat on the back, a couple of riders had seen smoking sticks belch fire, thunder, these were the first returned to the kingdom, sadly no one knew how they worked.

In the stable area the blacksmith who made armor had stated the lighter breastplate protectors were not strong enough, the protectors were put on posts, arrow after arrow slid off the curves, slick smooth metal simply pushed blades to the side without a dent.

Captains of the military who watched the demonstration, each grabbed a breastplate for their own protection, the blacksmiths claimed the old armor they made was better.

A heavy purse was handed to Zorn, two days in his village, return the young man who cared for the cattle, find everything about the fire sticks, return with the skills to make them work.

As the sun edged into the sky six long riders, all on black stallions were at the gate, arrows fired high into the air all dropped into a circle, the only rider not included was Zorn who was to follow his old path.

Following the way of your arrow, each of the six riders went to the center of the field pulled his arrow, holding it over his head he rode off in the direction that his arrow dictated.

Whether you believed in one God or many, it was God that made the breeze that dictated where your arrow would land, dictated a path for your life.

The unspoken words were powerful, camaraderie, glory, power, love, trust, duty, yet in the end the words could not convey the power what existed in each mans heart.

5

FORBIDEN LOVE

"Love is always the hardest path, the views are incredible."

Small villages functioning outside protection of the King Harrow's castle were called hamlets.

Each hamlet was different in its own way, some showcased the magnificent work the Gods had done creating the world, lush green fields furrowed in straight lines that the abundant earth repaid with large harvests of food, water rolled through streams or swollen rivers teaming with fish, forests provided game to fill the larders, logs for sturdy huts, fires on long winter nights.

The ideal beauty of the country required hard work that comes in little groups surviving together, clean, strong, free, independent, community goals replaced individual accomplishment.

A few hamlets were superstitious dark places of fear, distrust, hatred, run by cruel leaders, those hamlets did not last long, infighting, distrust, anger, all produced reduced work, crops failed, the forest would not yield to them bounty.

One hamlet sat upon a bend in the river, backed into the mountains, slowly the workers had cut into the forest, deep lush crops that were worked constantly.

In a hamlet work was a most valued virtue, hard work brought praise.

Children grew in straight rows like the crops, manicured, tended to, planted with care, birthed with joy, fed of mother's milk, laughter, a village full of love.

While very young the boys were separated, some went to the fields with fathers, uncles, brothers to learn the craft of farming. Other boys, who had a keen eye, sharper reflexes, or could run further, were taken to the forests as hunters.

For the girls life was simple, marry the man her parents selected, make babies, the training was simple, cooking, cleaning, washing, scrubbing, taking care of the man they married so he could work harder, follow his commands, do his bidding.

Each night when the sun fell, light faded, darkness brought shadows across the land, citizens of the hamlet would gather to thank the Gods for another splendid day, good food, good children, good life.

In each crop of children there were always ones that were not be suitable for life in the hamlet, one that did not work in the field, another did not have the skills of a hunter, there was always one girl that had a temperament which could not be brought under control with hard work or a light lash, to remind her of her place.

One girl named Cozet had raven black hair, piercing blue eyes, soft supple brown skin, she had been worked hard, never failed to finish early, then start problems, strange obstacles that made it hard to find a family willing to marry a good son to her.

It stared with Cozet's questions, why so many questions, it was not possible to answer them all, questions about Gods, following laws of nature, mountains, fish, rain, babies,

Cozet could not accept that everything was the work of the Gods, no other answer could or would be given that she would accept.

When Cozet was quite young she started with the stories, lies, fibs, about monsters in the woods, fierce creatures in the mountains, a dragon in the river who came in the night to kidnap children.

Cozet's stories were cute at first, then other children would gather round her, soon she would scare them so badly they could not sleep, always imaginative stories, when she should have been focused on work, cooking, cleaning, the virtues of a good hamlet woman.

The lash had been laid upon Cozet's back so often that some worried she would scar, she never cried or declined to make more trouble later.

Once, the men met to find a way to get water to the new fields up higher in the valley, while the men met, discussed, talked, contemplated proper procedures, drank wine, Cozet went high on the hill to the stream, put stones at odd angles, creating a deep pond.

From the base of her pond Cozet put stones that sent the water cascading down, at the bottom a large flat stone was placed to spray water out over the furrows in the field taking water to the new crops, the work of men.

It took days for the men to remove what Cozet had done, a woman, in the field, destroying the plans of men. Fingers were pointed, the lash applied, Cozet never cried out or complained, stood, walked away, laughed, told more stories.

Some talked of trading Cozet to a merchant for pots, pans seed, others laughed when asked if their sons would marry her.

At last a young man known to be slow of wit, cruel, was selected as her husband, Cozet was to marry him in two days, she screamed, cried, carried on, demanded the marriage be stopped.

Cozet yelled at her parents, she would select her own husband, be a good wife to him, how stupid her tears were, it was forbidden to marry any other than the one selected by the parents.

Much to her parents surprise, fear, loathing, anger, Cozet ran from the hut directly to a young hunter that was returning with game over his shoulder, demanded that he marry her, he stood with his mouth open, eyes wide, confused, startled, overwhelmed.

The young hunter named Wolf had often laughed at Cozet's stories, laughed when the lash was applied to her for disobedience, joked with friends how some fool would be stuck with her for a wife, headstrong, willful, demanding, she would be a curse for any man as a wife.

Wolf's parents had selected a beauty for him, yet the power of this wild, untamed girl was overwhelming. The other girls were obedient, kind, soft gentle, with supple figures, large hips, the makings of fine wives and mothers.

A smile came to Wolf's lips, he stood silent, Cozet looked at him very frustrated, with passion, yearning, no girl the hamlet had passion or showed very much emotion.

Then Cozet told Wolf that he would never regret having her for a wife.

Wolf laughed, she slapped him, he kissed her, she held him, she cried, he kissed her, she kissed him hard, ran her fingers to his long soft golden hair, pulled him to her, it was desire, lust, frustration, tears, hope.

Love is always the hardest path, the view is incredible.

When Wolf told his parents of the wedding the next morning he was ordered into the forest, his parents would not talk to him, or even look upon him, in all his life there had never been such anger in his mother. the next morning Wolf crept back into the hamlet, an elder married him to Cozet, no family present.

Cozet went with Wolf to the forest, days they walked, hunted, she tended camp, he scouted for signs of an animal to kill, take back, a peace offering for disobedience.

The newlyweds made love in a meadow beside a small waterfall under a sky of stars, the moon sat upon the hill so close it could be touched, stars shot from the heavens in brilliant hews of reds, blues, oranges, soft lavenders.

Exploring each others bodies, playing, touching, kissing, tickling, Cozet with a quick wit, showed Wolf a soft gentle side that was hidden as a child, taking him on top of her she cried out for all that she knew would make her a woman, found in his embrace her true self, joy of all that was within.

In the morning, together, under the blanket they were hidden from the deer that came to the clearing for water, food, mating, Wolf's first arrow was a mere twenty paces, deep in the animals side, the deer staggered.

The second deer turned to look, another arrow, farther away, caused the second deer to step back, then regain its feet.

Before Wolf could call for Cozet to stop, his new bride ran at the closest deer, hooves flashed, horns swiped through the air, she screamed, her voice echoed across the valley floor, the terrified deer took a step, gathered his feet, the girl, his wife, leapt upon the stunned animals back, wrapped her arms around its neck.

The second deer that was farther away was staggering back onto its feet, then fell again. Wolf fired another arrow, just under the second deer's chin, with an angry scream the deer collapsed.

Trying to regain for a second shot on the first deer Wolf realized that his new bride was upon the animal's back, an arrow might hit Cozet also.

Grabbing up a knife Wolf ran at them, the deer panicked, tried to run, Cozet's weight was too much.

Wolf came up behind, stabbing wildly into the animal's rear flank, with a mighty kick Wolf's ribs caved in, sprawling across the deep green grass Wolf was now unable to breath, all he could do was watch helplessly.

The deer reared, kicking wildly into the air with Cozet hanging on, she gave no quarter, no fear, she did not scream or cower.

At the clearings edge the deer laid down, unable to fight any longer, Cozet spoke softly to it as the life drained from its body, blood ran down into the green grass, her words of comfort, thankful that the animal had given his life, to show her parents the forest God had blessed her union with Wolf, the hunter.

Cozet ran back to her husband, held Wolf in her arms, for two days she lay under the blankets with him, ribs healed, she made him laugh, it hurt, she seemed to enjoy his being helpless, at her mercy, she cleaned the animals, they made love, again and again.

Wolf did demand, he demanded sternly, commanded over and over again, he tried to demand, that Cozet never do anything like that again, attack a wounded wild animal.

Cozet never agreed, yet Wolf demanded, ordered, pleaded, in the end she kissed him, kissed him again, he demanded, she kissed him, he never said another word.

Never was anyone in the Hamlet told of the events in the field, their marriage was tolerated by both families, never accepted by the hamlet citizens.

It was important for breeding to keep the children focused on the work at hand, disruptive forces like Wolf and Cozet, disobedient children, would destroy a community quickly.

At the edge of the hamlet, closest to the forest, an old cabin was given to Wolf and Cozet, dirty, dingy, without table or chairs, they were sent to live.

During the first rain Cozet had told Wolf they should move outside, it was dryer, the thatched roof seemed to gather water to bring into the cabin. She carved a plaque for over the door calling her cabin waterfall.

Cozet returned to her parents cabin only once, for a large cotton cloth that they had held for her, a present from long ago when she was a good child, an obedient daughter.

The huts only had holes for viewing, cold in the winter, hot in the summer, wet in the rain, damp on foggy mornings.

With rough deer hide for blankets, bedding, under, it was fine, most people in the hamlet slept in clothing to protect their skin.

Cozet placed the cloth folded between the layers of hide, no clothing was needed, Wolf was a fortunate man to feel his wife's warm tender flesh entwined with his each night, her soft breath upon his neck, her love to warm him, her passion to be expressed so freely.

An obedient wife was not how any would describe Cozet.

Wolf was a quiet man who accepted the gifts he was given without demanding more.

Other hunters would joke about Wolf's wild wife, he would point out that he was a hunter of wild animals, not barn yard pigs that slept in their own shit, got fat, ate too much.

After twelve full moons some questioned if Cozet had allowed Wolf to mate with her, she was not with child yet, perhaps she was too wild to be a real wife.

One good friend of Wolf's even demanded to see his manhood, the hamlet had decided that when Wolf had tried to mate with Cozet she had bit off his manhood, cooked it in a pot, eaten it.

6

TWO COME

"Would a warrior fear a beggar, less the hawk fear a mouse."

In a kingdom, a long weary journey along trails, over mountains, through cold streams, from that of King Harrow sat a castle of old rock, large strained timbers creaked in the cold, groaned when warm.

Rock by rock, walls grew in fear to protect the people who inhabited the castle.

Two old men sat upon a short outside wall, just in front of the gate of the lowlands castle.

As the old men discussed issues of the day they bent from years of toil in the fields, years of servitude, beaten physically, mentally, emotionally.

Not much more than ragged beggars clothing covered their leathery brown skin, yet they were engrossed in the conversation at hand, as if the rest of the world did not exist.

As the two men talked knights approached from the forest, watched the walls, movement, a glint from a spear tip, defenses coming against them, the knights encouraged along the knights in the mist behind them with small waves of the hand.

At the edge of the clearing, a hundred lengths or so from the castle wall, the other riders stopped in the tree line, waited, anticipation, nervous.

Two scouts in fine silver armor were sent on to find a weakness worthy of exploit, a way through the walls, captives taken, gold plundered, women to satisfy lust, to the victor goes the spoils.

No movement inside the castle walls made the scouts nervous, their horses could feel the tension building. A few strides before the old men on the wall, the horses stopped, calls made, no answer was given by the old men.

Again a call was made to the two old men, as if they were deaf, blind, indifferent they jabbered on about this, that, nothing.

The youngest scout hoisted from its scabbard the fine blade that he treasured. Not too heavy as to slow down his swing, yet not so light that it deflected on heavy armor or bone, deep pride this knight had holding such a blade in his hand, it gave him an incredible feeling of power, invincible, a skilled warrior.

The other scout was just starting to pull his own blade when he realized that the two old men had jumped up, they were standing on the wall, each was holding a bow by his side, relaxed, easy, without fear or anger to propel the arrow, they were harmless.

Dressed in strong armor the scouts were not afraid.

Would a warrior fear a beggar, less the hawk fear a mouse.

The scouts laughed, how stupid the show, arrows would simply bounce off the armor, fall harmlessly to the ground.

The old men's bows snapped to position, drawn, aimed, with each sinew of muscles stretched to the limit, just a finger flick sent the arrows away.

Each arrow went through the holes in the knight's faceplate's slits for vision.

Despite the beautiful shine on the armor, the elegant steel of the swords, the heavy steeds that carried the knights into battle, or even the army waiting in the woods to attack.

Perhaps the hawk would be wise to fear this mouse.

All of these great preparations for war were for naught, a slight shaft of wood with some feathers, a sharp rock at the tip bound in animal sinew just ended the war before it started, it was unjust, not fair, violated the code of honor.

Standing on the wall the two old men dropped their tattered robes, the bodies of young brash muscular men were revealed.

Cunning or treachery depended on your side of the clearing.

It was only two men on the wall with simple wooden bows, any group of well-armed knights could defeat them.

Four riders broke from the woods on command, racing across the clearing, thundering hooves shattered the peaceful day, it was a sight to behold, strong steeds straining under the weight of men, armor, anger, across the clearing they charged.

White puffs of steam flying from the horse's nostrils announced each breath, hot sweat poured off the steeds backs, flying out over the riders in a white foam.

The archers on the wall simply waited with the bows down, outnumbered they must surrender, there was no other choice.

On the wall arrows were nocked slowly on the strings, the limbs flexed, powerful arms held fast, at twenty lengths the riders stopped riding a weaving course, all knights closed in for the kill.

At the same instant the first arrows snapped from the bows in a gentle rhythm, each arrow found its mark, the two inside riders felt their horses buckle under them, it was the horses, at close range, in the neck, hooves faltering when not able to breath, first onto bent knees, leg bones shattering, then crumbling down to the ground under the weight.

Second arrows were strung, the two remaining riders had closed to ten lengths, at five lengths the shots hit each rider in the face-plate, even before they could swing the shinny weapons they put so much faith in.

Two knights tumbled from their horses with armor, arms, shinny steel crashing together in a heap.

The two men on the wall laughed as the rider-less steeds raced past.

Arrows strung, archers relaxed, waited, death was a patient mistress.

The first two horses shot in the throat with broken legs were crying out in pain, the bold, brave, elegant knights that had pushed them forward were now just trying to stand, with bent amour pressing into their flesh it took great effort.

As expected, six more riders broke from the trees to give aid to their brothers in arms, protect those soon to die, revenge for the dead.

The new riders thundered across the open area, a commander shouted for them to stop, anger, pride, frustration are blocks to the hearing of young men.

Trained killers can count on the failure of youth to understand the true nature of fear, survival, even simple patience.

Youth is not just impetuous, youth believes itself immortal.

The knight's horses thundered faster, harder, righteous fools with a code of honor are easy prey for those with no illusions of grandeur.

It was not possible for the knights to stop, the cards dealt, from the ground the archers had the angle they needed, just below the chin of the horses, just above horses breast plate, how powerful, yet fragile, a weapon the horse is.

Dropped as if commanded, the last falling within ten paces of the two archers.

Even light battle amour gleaming in the sun, great workmanship, was more than a man could lift just after taking a hard fall from a dead horse at full gallop.

Pulling the swords off the first fallen brave knights the archers dispatched those closest to them.

The thrusts were not to end life quickly, the desire was for a scream to roll across the countryside first, a hundred riders watched as two men cut down their finest, bravest, most impetuous, foolish, brave young men.

Finally the commander turned his horse, walked away, older, fight a more worthy enemy on another day.

Crush their minds, their bodies would falter.

Destroying a man's will is more gratifying than simply ending his life.

The last two riders had gathered enough strength to stand, one last stand for the glory of war, camaraderie, honor. The blows came, down they fell, the riders in the trees were gone, kicking their steeds for freedom, life, hard lessons learned.

The two men turned, walked back into the castle, a laugh, a joke, a good day.

Inside the castle walls were many dead bodies laying around, tied to things, the two men had come in the night, moving quickly, they had taken the wall guards before the guards knew a fight had started.

The castle was prepared to defend against gleaming silver armor, large horses, a hundred men.

Two old men in rags had simply walked in, taken life all night long, with almost no resistance.

Women were taken last so they could watch their children die before their last breath was stolen, tears soaked the mothers blouses.

The two killers had asked for nothing, taken nothing except life, there was no joy, anger, sadness, each life taken without word or emotion.

Leave money, it has no value,

Leave swords, they have no value,

Leave horses, they have no value,

Leave the dead, they are a canvas for the glory of God,

Another castle, more blood, a nectar of the Gods, someday, enough would die that God would praise the two brothers, take them up to heaven, exalt the servants of God.

This was a revelation born while watching a mad man burn a witch at the stake, death brings God glory, it must be, the old man chanted it while their mother pulled at her ropes, screamed for mercy, no salvation on this earth for their mother.

Sinner or saint is determined by who holds the other end of the blade, the dead were unworthy in the eyes of God, the ones that lived must have loved God more.

No requests for mercy, if you believed in God, it was destiny that you were dispatched to be by his side, if you did not believe in God, you needed to die anyway.

Warm sun kissed the two men's journey, it was God speaking to them.

The farther from normal, the more we must think ourselves normal to survive.

A mind must destroy that which is not functioning properly by creating a reality that explains our insanity, to believe ourselves insane is not something mind can comprehend.

Truth is that we are all mad, nuts, off our rocker, we just share the common illusion of reality, to justify life, love, affection, self esteem, respect, without the illusion of sanity comes the devil for our soul.

7

THE HUNT

"Joy to frustration, to anger, to hatred, to revenge, a fast journey, minds were dangerous creatures when not tended properly."

Blue sky is fantastic, the rays of the sun come down for warmth, making crops grow, light, small bits of water drifted in a dance with the winds that the sky God brought.

Sunsets that streamed the most beautiful shades of reds, pinks, oranges, were a final gift of the sky God for a hard days work.

Beloved God in the sky could also become so angry, vengeful, demanding, large gashes of fire would rip across the beauty of God's glory destroying all within range.

Yelling could be heard from the sky God, deep rumbling of a voice in a language no one in the hamlet understood.

Confusion often came from trying to understand the Gods needs, arguments started over how to worship the Gods of sky, earth, forest. These were powerful Gods that could give a wonderful life, destroy the entire world, punish those that did not offer proper sacrifices.

During the last hot season the focus of the hamlet was praying to the Gods of the sky for more rain, the God of land was thirsty, crops needed more water, yet the land Gods had demanded sacrifice to keep the crops safe. It was the forest God that had felt betrayed.

For ten days the hunters had not been able to find fresh meat, larders were low, what meat was remaining had a rank smell, most families had given it to the hogs, chickens.

Desire for food pressed the hunters deeper into the forest. A very small deer, was all the forest God had provided them, a sign of his power, a sign of his anger.

The hunter, Wolf, had made a great shot to take this small deer, it would only feed them for a day or two. Some hunters demanded they not eat of the deer, offer it instead as sacrifice to the forest God.

Normally a very cohesive group because survival depended on each other, the hunters were now arguing, complaining, worst of all blaming each other.

Questions were asked, who had not given the proper sacrifice to the forest God during the last years celebration of the hunts, who held back a rabbit from the alter or boasted his hunting skill, a skilled marksman could only shoot a deer offered by the forest God.

After a day of accusations, grumbling, ill thoughts followed into the darkness, around the embers of a small fire the hunters agreed to move deeper into the forest at first light for a larger deer.

Later, it was understood that this decision had angered the forest God.

The forest God started with small movements in the darkness just outside of camp, then it sounded as if a hundred men were moving as one, a bush pushed aside, trees shaken to their roots, men shaken to their souls.

Forest Gods do not appear to men unless very angry, this one took the small deer, lifted it in huge jaws, as a single meal, the limp animal was shaken, thrown to the ground, huge claws swiped into the air, teeth the size of daggers flashed in the darkness.

Most hunters screamed, ran, cowered down in submission.

Only Wolf lifted his bow, single arrow, the scream from the forest God shattered men's souls, broke their spirit, destroyed their confidence.

Crashing through the woods the forest God allowed them to live, took pity on them, left some of the deer for them.

Perhaps the hunters were not to have killed this deer, it was like others they had killed before, this one had been a favorite of the forest God.

In whispers there was talk of having to kill the one that shot an arrow at the forest God.

Wolf was the one that had hurt their God, made a God run into the woods.

As the fire died down, before the sun rose to fill the sky, a small dagger ripped through Wolf's cover, all the hunters stood in silence around the body, sad, yet knowing that those who shot a God must die so the hamlet did not suffer the wrath of a God.

Wolf's body was placed at the edge of camp so the forest God could see how the hunters would never shoot at the forest God again.

Only a short distance from camp a large buck with the biggest horns ever seen in the hamlet walked within a few yards of the hunters, stopped, sniffed the air.

Arrows flew swiftly, the beasts legs wobbled, the buck dropped to his front knees, before the animal could move again, another set of arrows pierced the hide.

Praise to a merciful forest God for understanding, seeing, testing them, showing them his mercy.

In each hunters heart, in stories around the camp fires, in legend of the hamlet, the evil of shooting at a God was shown to bring doom, unless the hamlet took action to show the God their love, devotion, sacrifice was hard, assured harmony with the Gods.

While the hunting party never returned to the hunting camp, it was a good thing, Wolf's body no longer lay at the edge of the clearing, drag marks from its resting place to the small stream, blood trail, sitting upon the rock tending to his wounds, anger in Wolf's eyes, fear knowing every fiber of his being.

Wolf's own friends, his own people, hunters, brothers, stabbed him in the darkness, placed his body for sacrifice at the edge of the clearing.

Deep in Wolf's right side the blade had missed vital organs, blood loss was critical, made him weak, faint, soft, easy target.

Unarmed, alone, shunned, sacrificed, Wolf lay upon the rocks in the sun, rested, healed, plotted revenge, dreamed of revenge, let revenge consume him.

Wolf heard the sounds again, just like in the darkness of last night, the forest God was coming to kill him, bushes pushed aside, trees shook, no place to run, hide, escape, if this were the end, let it be that his last breath was stolen by a God.

Wolf pulled a rock from the stream, it would not even be noticed by a God, at least a good fight, that was all Wolf had to offer this God, one good fight.

Limping into the clearing came the God, huge, five times that of a man, black fir matted, dirty, evil black eyes, huge teeth. Standing up on his hind legs, there it was, part of Wolf's arrow in the God's arm, sticking out a few inches above the paw.

Deep slow breaths now, death was at hand, give it honor.

Smelling the air, clawing at imaginary foes, the God dropped to the ground, clawed at the bits of deer the men had left, then walked back slowly into the lush green forest.

Messages were not clear from the Gods at times, this message seemed to be a statement, Wolf was not be to punished for shooting the God, he was now respected by the God.

Wolf was to share the forest with the God, share this place, he was immortal like a God.

Wolf prayed, those that tried to kill him failed, those that sacrificed him failed, those that put a blade in his back must die to appease the forest God.

It was days before Wolf could pull himself up to walk, the forest God provided plants to eat, small fish in the stream, frogs with tender legs, time to sleep safely.

Days later a large rabbit jumped into the field beside Wolf's soft bed of pine needles, a small snare of reeds, a rock, snapped around the terrified rabbits leg, God providing food for the trip home.

Fire burned softly, putting a glow on the rocks, a low fire might not be noticed if hunters returning to kill Wolf again, friends with more blades for his back filled all his thoughts, dreams ripped him from sleep often in the night.

Standing slowly Wolf moved on two legs heading back into the morning sun, each step calculated, falling could open the wound again, pain searing through Wolf's back, sides, mind.

Far ahead, the hunting party returned to the hamlet with the heavy packs of the forest Gods gift to them, each step was hard, worth the trouble to show how they had been favored with the largest buck the small hamlet had ever seen.

Meat would be eaten at a feast, cooked upon the open fires, skins tanned, antlers made into tools, sinew would make rope, hair for thread.

Celebrations filled the night, great fires burned, dancers in bright colors, some pretending to be the deer, hunters, forest God, standing tall, yelling loudly, waiving knives wildly in the air.

Everyone jointed the feast, ate of the large deer, except one woman, who mourned the loss of her husband, a good man, gentle, strong, kind, her lover, friend, how sad to know his archers skill made him evil, an outcast.

Cozet knew Wolf was not a bad man, she understood the need to kill him, she tried to understand, as the darkness closed in, the cold came, dancing died down, try as she might, she could not comprehend the need to kill her husband, a good man.

Laying alone upon their bed Cozet wrapped in a blanket she had shared with Wolf, his stories would make her laugh no more, his flesh would not be her comfort or give her warm security, how could they have killed such a man.

Wolf's bow, knife, bag all lay upon the table. The men who had killed Wolf delivered his things to Cozet, for her next man to use, she was young, strong, a beauty in her own way.

Holding the bow to her chest with one hand Cozet stroked the feathers of the arrows with the other, tears streaked her cheeks, confusion filled her heart.

Cozet desired to strike out in all directions, kill the God, kill the cowards that killed her husband, kill the forest creatures until the God felt as lonely as she did.

No one had come to hold Cozet, comfort her, her husband had shot a God, angered a God, brought revenge down upon them, so she was treated as an outcast among friends.

In the morning a plate of food sat upon Cozet's doorstep, she knew the plate, a good friend, one friend, perhaps Cozet would let that one live.

A woman that would bring only a plate of food was not a real friend, no kind word, hugs, encouragement.

No, this was not a real friend.

Stepping through the door into the light of a new morning was wonderful, wrapped in a cloth under Cozet's arm was the bow, quiver, small bag.

Everyone tried not to notice, as if life could be unchanged, a woman to bathe in the shallows of the river, open water, cleaning herself.

Pretend the crazy woman cursed by a God living among them was not a problem

Just as Cozet reached the river she turned, walking deeper in the woods, just outside of view of the hamlet, she lay upon a stump the bow, quiver, small bag, all she had of Wolf.

Taking the bow in her hand, pulling an arrow from the quiver Cozet was going to learn Wolf's skills, become a hunter as he had been, she had watched, knew the movements, now it was her time.

Closing her eyes Cozet prayed for strength, lifting up the bow with a straight arm, started to pull the string back, arm shaking, pain, fingers curled around the string sent a burst of pain through her arm.

The bow was not even half way back when the arrow broke free from its rest, the string snapped from her fingers, feathers scraped along her arm tearing open flesh.

Feathers then slammed forward into Cozet's hand, slapping her knuckles, blood spraying, the arrow fell to the ground a few steps before her, a scream came through the woods, anger, anguish, loss, suffering.

Falling on the ground Cozet grabbed the injured arm, held it to her body, sobbed, why could she not do this simple thing, would the forest God laugh at her, mock her.

Cozet felt alone in the woods, every day of her life growing in the hamlet she had been with friends, protected, now shunned, tears poured out, she closed her eyes.

Standing with resolve, Cozet took the bow again, pulled another arrow, tried it all over again, the same result, scraping of arrows feathers upon her fore arm, feathers wrapped in sinew driven over the soft flesh of her hand ripping it slightly, pain anger, fear, were her great teachers, friends, mentors.

This second arrow was at the base of the tree, some twenty paces further, not powerful enough to kill, those skills would come in time.

A callous was a tool, arrows were tools, fear a tool, hate a tool, together a powerful weapon would be formed.

One hundred arrows each day, Cozet's fingers bleeding, muscles contorted in pain, she did this without fail, to not suffer she would be failing her husband, a soul not with her that lived in her every breath.

Little notice was given Cozet in the hamlet, the good people were wondering what to do with her, how to deal with this cursed woman, some members of the hamlet felt it might be easier just to have her join her husband, let some young couple have the nice cabin close to the river Cozet had named waterfall.

Some argued that Cozet did nothing wrong, she should be given to a man to care for her, make some babies, let her be taken by a man for she was a good woman, let her live.

In the hunting camp, after Wolf had shot the forest God, Nathan started whispering in the ears of the others, powerful words mixed with fear can be strained into actions impossible for rational men to accept.

Nathan was old, fat, bald, his thoughts were not for the injured forest God, his thoughts were of his own fat wife, Wolf's much younger, full figured, soft wife.

Kill the husband, take the wife, lust was an old motivation.

When Nathan first offered to comfort Cozet his own wife could see what he had done and what he planned to do.

The hamlet did nothing about Cozet, like ignoring a festering sore she lived alone among them.

Cozet had a garden, rabbits, a few chickens. No one offered Cozet part of the harvest, invited her for food, children played on the other end of the only path to keep away from her evil cursed cabin.

Late at night Cozet would pull the bow back against her cheek, just hold it there, days of doing this had taught her to keep a straight arm without a shake, without any motion that would deflect the delicate arrow.

Men in the hamlet also pulled bow's to develop strength, aim, precision, yet they dreamed of shooting a large deer or running rabbit. In Cozet's mind, her bow always pointed at the men of the hunting party, or the coward's that had shunned her.

A cold winter came, dancing drops came through the clouds softly resting on Cozet's roof, bringing a swelling to the river.

Revenge provided all the company Cozet needed in the cold.

Practice was indoors with the small dagger Wolf had carried, swung in small motions, stabbing at air, wood, even killing a rabbit for the pot was done by placing it on a table, moving the knife as if in a fight, then in one swift motion sliding the blade along it's throat, grabbing the twitching body by the ears, in one deft downward thrust cutting open the belly.

It was so easy on a rabbit, would it be so easy on a man, fighting back, swinging his own blade, struggling to keep his life, would a man die as easy as a rabbit.

Only one set of eyes ever looked upon Cozet with compassion, connected to a body that was never seen, love, compassion, desire, fear.

Wolf could not go to Cozet, he had shot a God, she would be better with another husband, a man that could care for her.

Pelts covered the walls of Wolf's cave, death was his business, carving the most perfect bow, making knives from stone chipped away little by little to a sharp edge, arrow tips that were long, stone, designed to twist in, then break off.

Iron tips had been cheap, easy to buy, best choice when in the hamlet, in the woods all Wolf had was stone, so he made the tips like his grandfather had done, long, sharp, lighter than iron so they flew farther.

Wolf's first bows were crude devices of vine for string, hardly the bark nocked off the tree limb.

Those first bows killed the small animals that gave Wolf hide, sinew, bone to craft more complex bows, straighter arrows, more deadly tips.

Bone and stone tips could not pierce armor, any animals in the forest was fair game, even treacherous two legged creatures that walked upright.

A lonely life, solitude requires a change in thinking, revenge must replace friendly thoughts, perhaps madness was the change that was needed, stealth became a friend, accomplishments that would have been shared with a loved one must be rejoiced alone.

Joy to frustration, to anger, to hatred, to revenge, a fast journey, minds were dangerous creatures when not tended properly.

Two young hamlet boys came to Wolf's den one day, through the woods, up the side of the mountain following his footprints, a few drops of blood from a dead rabbit.

Perhaps Wolf had left the trail as an invitation to someone, anyone, share the madness, experience his torment.

The boys were not armed, probably a sling or small dagger, boys of this age were not archers.

The lead boy, first son of Nathan, leader of the hunting party, if not the man that stabbed Wolf, at least one that decided, watched, dragged his body for sacrifice.

Many paces out, steady, coming, pulling two arrows, Wolf held one in his hand, put the string in the nock of the other, took a breath, held it, let it out slow, easy, relax.

Stepping to the entrance Wolf could see the boys were only a few steps away, the bow moved into place, arrow pulled back against his cheek, release.

Small boys were soft, sharp stone arrow tips ripped through the flesh, blood spattered, his killer's first son was dead.

The other boy pulled a dagger, a futile move, running was futile, begging futile, praying futile.

Two bodies, so young, blond hair on one, black hair on the other, someday Wolf would have loved to have a son, someone to teach hunting, fishing, survival skills.

Before the bow released Wolf moved it slightly to the side, the arrow passed within a hands width of the boy's ear, the boy did not flinch, it was too fast, the boy was too scared to twist away.

Wolf and the boy stood in the sad moment looking at each other, life would not be the same for either of them, at least the boy would live to tell the tale, stories for the camp fire, looking into the eyes of a mad man.

Slowly the boy knelt down, kissed his comrade on the cheek, stood, walked back to the hamlet forming in his mind the story to tell, why had he been allowed to live, how the hunter who had shot a God was not dead, alive, killing young unarmed boys in the woods on the other side of the mountain.

Was it a vision, reality, insanity, how could the boy explain being alive. He would lead them back, he would take them to the body of his friend, Wolf would pay for what he had done.

Wolf sat quietly for a long time looking at the boy's body, what had he become, revenge was all that he had lived for after they stabbed him, now that he had tasted the bitter flavor of revenged he cursed it.

All of his bows could do only do one thing, kill, no joy, no life, no wisdom, only end life, Wolf wanted to curse the bow, arrow, string, of course then he would have to curse his arms, fingers, skill.

Wolf went in the opposite direction of the hamlet, simple plan, go around the men who would come to kill him, go to the hamlet to see Cozet one last time, travel to where he was not known, start a new life.

Running at times the boy had fallen on the steep jagged rocks of the mountain trying to find his way back exactly as they had come, cut, bruised, blood oozed from knees, elbows, wrists.

As the boy stumbled into the hamlet, screams went out, panic, story told, men with sticks, a couple with bows, took off running.

The exhausted boy was given water, food, bandaged, then went with a second group of men to kill the evil hunter who the forest God had brought back to punish them.

Nathan's fat wife looked upon him with disgust, she alone knew all of this was his doing, his desire for the younger woman had killed her oldest son.

In the wife's eyes it was not Wolf that was evil, it was the man who would share her bed, who she would cook for, who would need his clothing washed, at night he would kiss her, take her breast in his mouth, the same breast that had fed her dead son.

When Nathan mounted the steps to his hut he found the door blocked, pounding on the door he demanded entrance, nothing was said, he pounded on the door again, demanded entrance again.

Nathan's son was dead, his wife was upset, she would get over it, she was his wife, this was his property, she was his property.

After a long time Nathan's wife's head appeared in the small opening used for ventilation. Nathan demanded entrance, she was gone again, he commanded entrance.

Nathan knew his wife must do as she was told.

The smell the fire, feel of heat, smell of smoke, the screams of a mad woman.

At first Nathan was going to break down the door, save his wife, mother of his children,

Then Nathan realized the function of the fire was just too perfect, she was the only one that had figured out his plan, now she would burn to death, she was fat, old, wrinkled, a new wife would be more enjoyable at night anyway.

Nathan moved animals away from the cabin so they would not be hurt, things were moving in his cabin, alone inside, her own fire, it would be better if she did not suffer, she was out of her mind anyway, blame it all on Wolf, take his woman, younger, firm skin, having not given birth Cozet would feel better to hold at night,

Nathan's wife screamed, he did hope she would die without too much pain, if she screamed less it would be easier on him.

Other women came running, Nathan explained that the door was blocked, there was nothing he could do.

Together the women broke down the door, flames burst out though the opening burning away the eyebrows of a couple women, they fell back, laying on the ground the women of the hamlet were horrified when Nathan's burning wife crashed through the door in flames, fell down the stairs, landed on top of them, burning them also.

Nathan was the only man there, he just looked down, his wife, burned, no emotion, his fat wife dying, no remorse, no grabbing for water buckets, blankets, the women jumped away from the body.

Nathan's wife screamed, alive for one cold scream at death, flames were shooting through the roof of the cabin now.

A few of the women poured buckets of water on Nathan's wife, she was gone.

Nathan never moved, a few of the women spat upon him before they walked away.

She killed herself Nathan tried to explain, he spoke to their backs, had she told these women that his plan had been for a younger woman to sleep with all along.

Flames of the burning house, smoke, screams, some of the men running to kill Wolf realized that Wolf may have been in their own hamlet hunting them, burning down the hamlet while they were in the mountains hunting him, the men turned, ran for home, all they had could be lost.

Hamlet wives met their husbands at the edge of the fields, men tried to tell the wives they were mistaken, no man would let his wife burn to death, his cabin burn down, inside each heart they knew it was true.

Nathan tried to say the truth was not true, he had been respected an hour ago, he was not one of them any longer

Nathan simply turned, walked away, no possessions, no cabin, the life he knew was gone, he cursed his fat old wife for destroying his life, from respected elder to villain when they realized what evil had lived among them.

Careful not to be seen, Cozet had watched, looked on, her bow in hand, quiver over her shoulder, she wanted so, just to let one lose, one beautiful, slender judgment would make her feel so good at that moment.

More important was Wolf, alive, betrayed, alone, the one Cozet loved needed her, old men could face her wrath later, she vowed vengeance with a fierce soft whisper.

8

SAIL KINGDOM

"Lessons paid for in blood were never forgotten."

Prince Rogan's two ships sailing up the coast, selecting small easy targets was profitable yet tedious work.

Captain Rogan wanted, needed, desired more to build an army capable of taking back his kingdom from his brother, King Harrow.

Rogan's fleet added more ships, men, weapons, under the simple plan, join or die.

Simple requests that had two options, one being death, seemed to get the best enthusiastic acceptance.

Ten ships of various make, style, power made a versatile fleet, oars pulled under the sinew of men whipped for motivation.

The small thin black boats swept into the coves, over reefs. The small boats weakness was they floundered, sank in the large waves of the open ocean.

Large bulky battle ships could hoist huge canvas sails to slice through deep oceans.

Battle ships would be cut to pieces on reefs close to shore, never getting close enough to shore for loading of men, plunder, slaves.

Men required food, water, women, strong drink for relaxation. A large crew took great planning to move, provisions, pleasure, staying in one place made them easy targets.

Passing a small point of land jutting out into the rabid sea Captain Rogan looked upon the wreck of another ship, wood, canvas, rope on the rocks, so elegant in the water, flying along under Gods own breath, ships were a vision to behold.

Torn asunder on the rocks the carcass of a ship was just so many pieces of a dream that had died, ugly, broken, twisted, a warning to all that came upon her with dreams of their own, dreams are easily crushed in a sea not treated with respect.

The waves relentlessly pounded the once strong timbers until there would be nothing, in the end men always failed when nature chose to destroy them.

On shore a single old man sat quietly, Captain Rogan thought that the old man would rise, run, flee, puzzled when the old man simply watched. Something was to be learned here, or a price to be paid, alone in a small boat Rogan went ashore.

No pleasantries were passed, mostly the two men said nothing, the old man named Tobias, walked with Rogan, joined, never discussed, there were no options, it just was.

Planning was done for the next conquest, knives sharpened, quivers loaded, it was Tobias who asked Captain Rogan to negotiate with the next village. Trusting so quickly was not easy, done, a chance taken.

Going alone Tobias was humble, taken to the king of the next area to be destroyed, for two days the old man described the ruthless army that would descend upon them, vial beasts in human form made of raiding parties expert in conquest, pillage, rape, hungry, nothing to lose.

There was good news, Tobias explained softly with a note of apology, the king's army did not have to be destroyed, their fields did not have to be burned, the king's power would remain intact.

Provide tents by the shore, food for men, served by women that were entertaining, pleasant, kind, submissive when the food and wine were gone, the beasts would get on their ships, go away, perhaps even consider this village a friend, perhaps help in time of need.

On the third day the ships pulled to shore, tents were waiting, food spread upon blankets, women stood in lines waiting to serve, a small price to pay for survival.

Five days of lust, gluttony, over eating, drinking till passing out, fulfill the crews desires, a tribute was then taken, gold, silver, grain, the ships moved on under the breath of God.

The village would try to find peace with itself, rejoice in having been spared, slowly recover from all that it had given.

Captain Rogan, worried, as captains do, that under this new plan the crew would become lazy, unable to fight when needed, they were raiders, warrior skills were not just needed, without them they all would die.

Each dark cold night with food, wine, women in his tent Captain Rogan would think of his younger brother, Harrow, on his throne, in his castle, making love to his concubines. No excess of food, flesh or wine could erase the need to correct this injustice.

Once a month Captain Rogan would simply kill a crewman for treason, none of his crew questioned, this was what was just done. To wield power took fear, to protect the crew from harming themselves, from anyone truly thinking of committing treason.

Then it happened, Tobias found a village with a strong army, powerful weapons, a resolute nature. This lord did want to fight, allow death of all to protect his village, surrender this time would mean that this village might be willing to surrender every time.

In three audiences with the lord Tobias pleaded for reason, found the lord's ears deaf, the lord's questions had required Tobias to provide vital information, the lord had extracted from Tobias to know the reality of the situation.

Tobias quickly provided a strategy in exchange for his life, at midnight, after wine, food, pleasure, Rogan's sentries in the rapture of being pleasured by woman's flesh, the army swept through the tents, killed over half of raiders before an alarm was sounded.

Blood ran down to the shore, Captain Rogan's remaining men, naked, drunk, unarmed were able to make it onto the two large ships, slipped away in the night leaving the rest of the fleet at the shore.

Sitting silent in the water a few hundred lengths from shore with the sails down Captain Rogan watched as many women were walked to the shore, stabbed to death by the army, better to die this night as a hero than live with the shame of having pleasured a beast man from the sea.

Tobias was last, taken to a point of land, a single blow removed his head, placed on a large pike facing the ocean, he served a final purpose, a warning, we give nothing to coastal raiders.

The flames on shore died down, the two ships pulled sails up, moved on.

Lessons paid for in blood were never forgotten.

Over half the crew dead, eight ships lost, this was a small price to pay for the lesson of weakness, now the question was how to become strong again. This was a terrible thing, yet one of the best that could have happen, for it would never happen again.

When the attack had started, the woman on top of the Captain Rogan held a blade in her hand, hesitated. It was slow, making love to a woman that was bleeding to death, her pain, terror, anger, made spasms of rage flash through her.

Rogan stabbed her a few times in the back, shallow, painful, not fatal, then held her down, used her, grabbing her by the scruff of the neck Rogan very slowly slid the blade between her ribs while pulling her hips up, the orgy of violence was intoxicating more than any other drug.

Silently Rogan stood, rolled her over, looked down upon her wild eyes, each shallow thrust by design, painful, the fury in her eyes told the story.

She was an animal, he had made her like he was, nothing human, beast, savage wanton out of control.

One last thrust through her right breast, just past the rib, making a small hole in the air sack, when the knife was removed she would die. Captain Rogan held the knife blade against her body, admired his work, pulled the blade, watched life drain from her eyes.

The men that made it to the ships were demanding retribution, an attack, war.

A fools quest, wars were always lost by someone, the winner got to write the history, as that lord would for his people. Even more valuable than history, the loser got the lesson.

Fighting for revenge won nothing, fighting in anger won nothing, fighting to conquer was a game of egos.

Captain Rogan had a kingdom that was his, a cunning brother to wage war against, a prize to take back.

The unspoken words were much more powerful

A savage animal kills for food or survival.

Righteous men that kill women to keep them pure, that savage could justify any sacrifice, face any army, destroy himself to vanquish any enemy.

Give moral savages a wide birth, for in being so moral, they have lost sight of all humanity.

There were two blessings in darkness of that night, Tobias being executed, Captain Rogan knew that Tobias had helped them destroy his men, Tobias would have had to be hunted, killed, that was finished now, yet somehow, Captain Rogan felt a loss for Tobias.

Rogan's weak men were now dead, some on shore, some on the ships from wounds, all had lost part of themselves tonight, no more weakness, lazy ways were gone, Captain Rogan's men would now be a strong fighting unit out of blood soaked fear.

Good.

Small quarters on a war ship, Captain Rogan closed his eyes, all he could see was the woman he killed, half crazy, she was looking up at him as he plunged the dagger through her breast.

Killing was not a new skill for Rogan, often life had ended on his blade, his mind was clear, never had a face come back to him. She must have been a sorcery woman, agent of the devil.

She was dead, Rogan was alive, there were no more questions to be asked or answered.

Closing his eyes again she was there, this time Rogan could feel the dagger, the thrusts, cuts on her back as he took her, each cut made her tense, a pulse of rage he fed upon, the sensation consuming him was, was . . .

Rogan awoke to find his own dagger unsheathed, what for, what was his intent, how could she have done this to him. He threw the blade against the bulkhead, went back to sleep.

In the morning the dagger was back in its sheath, Rogan had not put it there.

Captain Rogan had not pulled the blade from the wall, not placed it into its sheath.

Thinking about the taking of her life while raping her at the same time, it had made him aroused, it also angered him.

It was her blade, she was going to plunge it into him, the cold blade was to have ripped open his throat, Rogan had done nothing that she had not planned for him.

Gifts from women often had a price that destroyed men, wrapped in beautiful paper, ribbons, bows, offered as a trinket or bauble, the trap always had fearsome jaws that striped the flesh, ripped muscle to the bone.

No woman is ever enjoyed, the gift delivers a debt that must be paid.

Empty beds make men think of having a woman.

A woman in your bed makes you think of travel, far away lands.

Both are right, both are wrong, both will destroy a man's ability to be a man.

On deck a black day had moved in, rain came from all angles, waves crested down upon the last two ships of the fleet, the sea was breaking along the deck, sending good men to the depths, food for the sea dogs.

Captain Rogan commanded directions blind to their outcome, it was useless, they did not know where they were, could not see where they were going.

The ship upon the rocks was now coming back to Rogan's mind, was his fortune told already, visions were not real, unless you accept them.

A single bolt of lightening gave them a split second of bright light, land to the right, a hard left, out into the open ocean.

Waves might destroy a ship, rocks would destroy their ship, the lesser of evils is the choice of sane men.

The captain's quarters often lay empty as Rogan's body inhabited men's quarters for sleep, the smell was horrid, the snoring was booming, loud sounds filled the ears every moment, the louder the better Captain Rogan thought, drive her image from him, take her from his sight.

Her image talked of time, distance, following the sun or moon, as if plotting a parchment to his doom.

There is a cove down the coast, a good ten day run with full sails, where you can lay in, provision the ships, wait, there are monsters there, head to sea, yes catch the wind, find shore in a distant barren land.

Talking in Rogan's ear, he could hear her, her breath made the hairs on the back of his neck stand on end.

Swatting her, as if a fly, Rogan rolled from the second bunk to the floor, awoke with a crash as the deck came up to meet him.

Looking down from a top bunk a crewman called out to be careful, these bunks were much narrower than the captain's wide grand bunk. The captain's bunk is more suited for a man and woman together.

In a flash Captain Rogan's blade was against the man's throat. The demon in your head leading us to hell, or you sending us to hell on her order, not a problem captain, the sailor rolled over, went back to sleep.

Simple crew, simple choices.

Down in the galley fresh fish was being cooked, every day, all day, fresh fish, it was all the provisions they had left, a hook, line, luck.

The day the sky released its final torrent, the ocean had broken, the last large wave, all went quite on the ocean.

Sky soft, gentle, no wind or movement was upon them, a flat ocean without a current. All of the sails were up, men were upon the deck, the ship did not move.

Nothing was a terrible sentence to live through.

Give pain, fear, anger, a fighting man had to have an adversary, nothing was a weapon they could not fight, a sentence they could not serve.

The woman in Rogan's head must have caused this, led him to this, her revenge was nothing, yet this nothing would surely kill them all more slowly than a blade or pike.

Looking over the aft Captain Rogan could see her face in the water, not the anger, fear, wild animal that he had stabbed in the breast, this was her soft face when she entered his tent, removed her robes to offer him comfort, pleasure, this was her lying, cunning conniving face of treachery that she used to get close enough to plunge cold metal into his body.

Rogan threw a bucket overboard at the face, it vanished into the ocean, ripples extended out, he could no longer see the face, he was rid of her, he had dispatched the devil in his mind.

When the water was calm again she was there, she looked sad, she was calling to him, she wanted him, she needed him, he could jump over the side, be with her, Rogan's dagger was in his hand, he was going over the rail to kill her again.

Two large hands pulled Rogan back.

She must not win when there is a kingdom to reclaim, a purpose in your life.

Soothing as the words were, she kissed him goodnight, woke him in the morning, talked to him each day to help him, lead him, a good guide was required on the path to hell.

9

KILLING FRIENDS

"Others felt that Wolf had moved on, Cozet was alone, worthless, kill her now"

The hamlet was in turmoil, people yelling, panic in the air, how to defend from a man they had wronged. Wolf was justified in this revenge, he had to be killed again.

Cozet, Wolf's wife, heard the men who had found their bows race to her hut, they kicked in the door, things were tossed about, how stupid to think she would hide there, she was going to use the forest now, it hid her on her wedding night, it would hide her how.

A whisper passed Cozet's lips, please let the forest God take pity, help her now.

Tramping of feet, men were running through the hamlet looking for her, Cozet stayed behind a pile of old wood, slipped around some stacked rocks, trying to get to the rabbit pens that would lead out to the freedom of the forest.

Cozet knelt down, crouched, ready to spring, a single arrow in her hand, the quiver on her back loaded.

One man stopped running, the others looked back, it was only one feather sticking up, just one tip of one feather from Cozet's quiver that the man noticed.

Standing momentarily, facing the wall, the man drew an arrow carefully from his own quiver.

Sensing a presence, hearing the foot steps stop, Cozet nocked her arrow, drew the bow back, leapt up, turned in mid air, when she gained her feet the man was there, just starting to draw back his bow.

Her arrow went where she was looking, in the chest of an old friend, one she had shared stories, food, her husband, Wolf, had given extra rations of deer meat, the metal tip of the arrow went right into his chest with a hollow thud.

Screams from a few paces away, running men, another arrow, she ran, stopping just past the edge of a cabin, two men came, the first was right on top of her, bow in hand, her arrow stabbed into his chest, held in her hand like a spear, feeling the violent convulsion of death take him down.

The dead man grabbed his chest, fell upon Cozet, his weight slammed her back into the wall, stunned for a second she was not able to get free.

A second man went two steps past, tried to pull his knife, his was a farmers sheath, more to protect the blade from falling than speed, Cozet pulled hers quickly, as the man stepped forward Cozet plunged the blade into his throat, his hands at his side trying to remove his blade from the sheath.

The other men had gone the other way around the cabin to cut Cozet off, she was moving with all her strength, running to gain distance so the bow could be effective again.

Cozet heard the sound of the sling spinning up, in a small boys hand, she did not identify the sound it quickly enough, the rock spun from its cradle, smashed into the back of her head, spun her over in a summersault, unconscious, shallow breathing, her thick hair had stopped the large stone from breaking her skull open.

Running forward the boy kicked at Cozet, looked at his own father with her blade in his throat, kicked her face, ran back to his cabin, cried in his mothers arms.

In the hamlet crime was not a problem, no jail, no stocks, no use for restraining a prisoner. On a bank beside the river were two large poles planted deeply in the ground where skins were tied, deer hung, blood ran easily down from there into the river, away from the hamlet.

Cozet's hands were tied behind her around the pole, fear gripped the men, talk was, let her go, Wolf would let the hamlet men live, kill her, Wolf might not come, both were strange, kill the freaks to make the hamlet safe.

One man pulled his blade, placed it against Cozet's right arm just below the shoulder, started to make a cut, no arm, no bow, no more killing.

More voices filled the hamlet, elders appeared from the forest, unable to find the hideout or bodies on the mountain they had returned slowly to put out the fire.

Finding so much death, they decided to put Cozet to death now, kill Wolf later when he showed himself.

Calls for mercy, use her as bait, bring Wolf to the hamlet, he would surrender, kill the hunter when he comes for Cozet.

Others felt that Wolf had moved on, she was alone, worthless, kill her now.

Women from the hamlet called out to kill Cozet quickly without pain because her life had been destroyed by treachery, let her not suffer more, Cozet had a sister who cried out for quick mercy.

It was decided to leave Cozet tied to the post tonight, kill her quickly in the morning if she wakes up.

10

DOCK RATS

*"The sea could be an evil cunning bitch when she chose
to kill a sailor who made mistakes."*

Murad's mother was a strong farmwoman, Douvan had taught Murad to work hard, respect others.

Murad's father, a trader from a far land, dark skin, with black hair, piercing black eyes, big smile, nicknamed the Sultan.

Sent from the hamlet of his birth, Murad traveled for days before getting a ride to a port city in a neighboring kingdom.

On the farm Murad had learned that hard work was its own reward, in the city, not much more than a child, Murad now found that hard work done by others was very rewarding.

Murad hid in the hills, sneaking down at night to steal food, trinkets, one night he happened upon a box containing money from the hold of a ship that lay in harbor, there was so much he could not count it.

Hiding most of the money, Murad took a few coins from the bottom of the chest to walk the streets during the day, like a real man, one coin for a fine meal, he acted not as the farmer he was, he was now the sultan he had been told his father was.

A ship was unloading, boxes looked expensive, carved, gold fixtures, another abandon child, they called them dock rats, was paid to steal it for Murad.

Murad soon employed the scurrying rats to do his bidding, they were stealing at night, he sold the items during the day.

Fearing the rats would soon be caught as the thefts continued, Murad purchased a wagon with one old horse, along the road south, trade, exchange, four rats in the wagon to protect his goods.

While Murad sold, rats stole, the stolen goods were then sold to other buyers who they stole even more from, it was a good business.

Murad and the dock rats worked at their craft, in the large city of a lower kingdom they purchased a small ship, only two crew were willing to stay, working for a child captain was considered bad luck.

Working their way back up the coast Murad was now a ship's captain.

The two adult crew that had stayed on exchanged treachery late in the night, kill the kids, take the ship, sell the ship and cargo, live happily on land.

Curious dock rats overheard the conversation, the night before the sailors were ready to strike Murad had provided them a cask of fine amber liquid, in drunken sleep ropes were slipped over the two adult sailors necks, tied tight to a length of anchor chain, over the side the chain went.

The chain took the rope, the rope took the sailors, the waves took them all.

Trust is a captain's tool, without trust the crew begins to splinter under heavy load.

The dock rats were proud to work for Murad because he was a cunning leader, yet the captain remained one of them at his core.

In the open ocean Murad's crew practiced for attack, running ropes, pulling sails, turning hard. Day after day he worked them, each job done again, ropes run, climbing, jumping, cursing the rigging.

Day after day they took the small blades each carried, thrown at various distances each learned to stick on every throw. Practice the tools of the trade, the trade of sailors, thieves, assassins.

Nights were the most fun, hide from Murad, move around the ship in the dark, silent, quick, not get caught, a game, child's play.

Two full moons on the ocean, Murad finally ordered them to turn toward shore, more than seven days of seeking the right port, the right ship, larger than theirs, stronger, more storage, then it appeared, like a baby waiting for her mother, quite, on a small dock, rocky shore, the captain was provisioning her, some of the crew would be ashore.

No time to wait, darkness closing, hard turn, the rats ship ran up against her targets aft, inches away, jumping from one ship to the other, the rats abandon their own ship.

Five children, no problem, no one saw them, like shadows in the gunnels they moved behind rigging bags, masts, barrels.

Like the training Murad had put them through daily, a quick throw, hard thud, a crumpling figure on the deck, forward a few played cards, four died without ever feeling the blade against their throats.

The fifth was trying to understand what he was seeing when a blade passed through his ribs, he looked astonished at the handle sticking from his small vest, fell back, passed on.

Below decks things would be more difficult, closer quarters, faster action, more men, surprise not an option.

Opening the door to the captain's quarters a boy could be seen inside, feeding a large man at the table, no room to throw, a rush, three fast.

The steak knife in the large mans hand just about severed the head of the first one to rush, the second rat drove his blade home just before the large man slashed fiercely at him.

It was the cabin boy who pulled his own blade, thrusting it under the man's chin, blood ran down over the cabin boys hands, arm, chest, blood of the man who tortured him every day, an evil man, it felt good to see his death come from one he had abused.

Standing for a second the dock rats and cabin boy just looked at each other in shock and amazement.

Murad beckoned the cabin boy forward, with them, join in, part of the crew.

The cabin boy pulled a key from the dead captain's belt, a locker, beside the bulk head, huge padlock, fire sticks, forty or more, the rats had never seen anything like it, the cabin boy pulled powder, shot, patches, teaching Murad to load, they prepared ten, only five crew below decks.

Slowly Murad's new crew moved to the back hatch, a door below decks, crews quarters, the cabin boy first, Murad second, a couple sailors in suspended beds, quick thrusts, the sailors feared death, yet it was upon them in their sleep.

Another young boy was in front of them, the cabin boy motioned the boy to step aside.

In the back room three large men were tying knots in a piece of rope, the first man moved fast for his blade, the cabin boy extended the fire stick, smoke filled the air, Murad choked, closed his eyes.

The other sailor was now upon them, blade in hand, a concussion from Murad's fire stick, the sailor stumbled backward, a third stick pushed forward, a thud, all was quite.

Loud sounds would alert the men on shore, quickly the new crew ran to the deck, the two cabin boys pulled up the ropes, ladders, planks from the ships side, Murad's crew reacted to the new ship with all the skill of seasoned sailors.

Sails went up, sailors that had been onshore ran to see what was going on, looked for something to do, nothing, in the blink of an eye their ship was under way without them, just far enough that swimming would not work, besides, those in the water would have been cut down by fire sticks.

Those on shore could only see small boys climbing the rigging, how could that be, boys could not run a ship.

A loaded ship, bounty, fruit of their skill, courage, earned.

Bodies were tossed overboard with a song, scrubbing the decks was done with a song, open ocean, travel, it was only Murad that did not sing, as captain it was his planning, plotting, what next, sell the goods, provision the ship, to what goal, he had not thought that far ahead, things were moving too fast, a few days at sea to think.

The second morning, coming just out of the sunrise behind them Murad could see her, their first ship, abandoned when they took this one, the old crew, wanting this one back.

Keeping their ship going with a child crew, no skilled sailors, a couple of cabin boys, everything was working out just fine.

Out running a ship with seasoned sailors would not be easy, their old ship was lighter, faster, her crew more skilled, sailors, fighters, seasoned on wind, blood, canvas.

By the second day the pursuer had more than cut the distance in half, each hour she was inches closer, some trick would be required to outrun her, stay alive, win.

That night when the wind kicked up, with all her sail set the larger ship was able to spread the distance, Murad made a choice, head for deep water, outlast the smaller ship, more men would require more provisions.

Murad knew the small ship was lacking adequate food, water, facilities for such a crew, they would tire of the chase when their bellies were empty.

All that next day Murad watched, while the smaller ship was faster, her lighter hull could not cut through the heavier waves, more turning than the larger ship was doing to face each wave, spread the distance slightly, open the gap to stay alive.

That night with all lights off the larger ship waited for some clouds, anything to mask her course, nothing, a perfect starry night, clouds be dammed.

Three nights, no squall, low wind, small waves easily bounded by the pursuer, the distance was close, not closing as much as before.

It was the forth night, darkness crept in, a slight change in direction to the left, quiet, quick, all they needed was a half hour of the pursuer delaying the turn, it would give Murad the distance they needed.

Experienced sailors on the small ship had been waiting for a miscalculation by the children, this was it, as soon as the large ship turned she lost part of the wind, by turning at the same time, the smaller ship could keep the wind, gain a perfect cutoff angle.

In the few minutes it took for Murad realized his mistake, the small ship made the cut, he looked up at the sails of his large ship just starting to catch the wind again.

The trick had not worked, within a day or two the small ship would be upon them, close enough for arrows, taunting tactics, perhaps a ram, perhaps fifty men coming over the side to kill six young boys.

A small streamer from the bow line showed the wind to be just to their left, slightly, he turned the ship for a straight run with the wind, use what he had, hope something would be provided to change this chase, the ocean offered nothing, wind, waves, more wind, more waves,

The monotony of death following on a small ship was wearing on both ships.

Murad was sleeping on the deck at night, just behind the boy holding the wheel, it was morning, a brilliant red blazing sun breaking up from over the waves showed the way, calling the boys to the captain's cabin they started taking stock of the items onboard.

Fifty fire sticks, a few long, most small, the cabin boys were expert at loading of the fire sticks because that would have been their job during a battle under the old dead captain.

A plan was developed, waiting for death was not an option, the small ship had only a few short fire sticks taken onshore for protection.

Transported to the aft deck, each gun was loaded with extra powder, two balls each fire stick was then lashed to the rail pointing aft, each gun had a rope tied through the trigger guard.

The clouds finally came and played their part, in the dark the large ship's sails were not set tight, slightly lose, losing wind, the smaller ship was gaining more rapidly now, an hour or two they could catch her, put an end to this chase.

Murad could hear the sailors on the small ship, just aft, orders were being given, the rats and cabin boys were sent aloft, steady, waiting, impatient, ready for this to be over.

It was a simple plan, drop the sails, the overtaking ship would be forced to turn, once the larger ships aft was lined with the side of the attacker let go with all rounds.

As the large ships sails dropped the small ship came close to ramming her aft deck, turning hard the small ship was just able to maneuver away from the impact, a quick pull on the rope, all fifty guns unleashed one hundred balls at the small ship as she maneuvered past.

Only a few sailors were killed, anticipating some kind of trick the experienced sailors were hidden when the balls simply struck wooden planks.

The children were now in the rigging setting canvas as fast as possible, shots rang out from the small ship, aimed, not wild as the dock rats had done, screams came from the rats in the rigging, shot in the leg, fell to the deck, badly hurt.

Another volley from the small ship as it maneuvered to come along side the larger ship.

In the rigging, children, afraid, kept working, enough wind caught the sails of the larger ship for her to turn slightly away, this sucked the wind from her sails again, it was like watching the life drain from Murad's crew.

A shot from Murad's ship, a cabin boy, one loaded, one fired, one loaded, one fired, first the mate on the wheel of the small ship tumbled from a round through his shoulder.

From the deck of the small ship a man appeared to be giving orders, the second shot hit his breast plate, he flipped in mid air as if hoisted by a rope.

Confused for a moment crewmen on the small ship ran for cover, the next round from the large ship was not fired, the cabin boy waited for a target. Waiting was worse than if the cabin boy had fired, no leader, afraid, the sailors waited, it was the break Murad was looking for, sails caught enough wind to run, enough to survive another night.

In morning light the small ship was still chasing, Murad realized the small ship had no choice, without provisions on the ocean the only hope they had was to capture his ship to get the food or they would all die.

The sea could be an evil cunning bitch when she chose to kill a sailor who made mistakes.

Each day the small ship dropped back, little by little, Murad last saw the outline of her sail on a sunset run, turning slightly to catch the wind, the small ship was easily a week out if no one made a mistake.

Murad thought about what must be occurring on the small ship as sun, waves, hunger, thirst, insanity was setting in.

Wanting to turn, to help, offer aid, share some food, water, the truth was Murad could not see any land either, how far behind death would his child crew be to the experienced sailors.

On advice of a cabin boy Murad started heading his new ship to the sunrise each morning, keeping a steady course was hard, at least they felt they were moving toward land.

Many days gone they caught a strong breeze, making good time, the faint outline of a fog bank appeared, excited, thinking land must be in range, Murad sailed right for it.

The dock rats talked of all that they would do when on shore, rich from plunder, fine meals, silver plates, goblets of water like a lord or even a king.

When closer to land the dock rats could not see any fog, long stretches of sand beach reaching all the way back to a land full of sand, hot, foreboding, flat, no game, no life, barren, desolate, disheartening, as bleak as they had become.

A line was drawn on center of the mast, from far back on the aft deck Murad threw a small blade, stuck with the tip on the left side of the line, a direction was chosen, whether it was north, south, east, west no one knew or cared, it was just the way they were going.

Any decision is better than no decision.

11

OBSERVERS

"Making Harrow unhappy could cause the death of a family."

Looking down from the top if a hill above the hamlet, King Harrow's scout watched the smoke, first black, something bad was burning, then white, puffs of billowing smoke up into the sky, it was being put out.

One woman was tied to stake beside the river.

Reporting back to Harrow, a fire in the hamlet they were about to visit, better to sleep tonight, go in fresh in the morning.

This recruiting party was small, twenty men, forty horses, collecting fighters to repel Prince Rogan when his ships docked.

Scouts rode out from camp, looked forward, found routes, after the tent for King Harrow was setup two slave girls were put inside to make the bed for him, get bath waters, oils with sweet smells, rocks from the hot fire were placed inside to keep the tent warm without smoke.

Dinner was eaten early, massage, pleasure, fun, girls were cute, willing, flexible, good slaves, best of all their families were held in cells back at the castle.

Making Harrow unhappy could cause the death of a family.

The scouts were sent out to small camps to protect the main camp.

Removing the scouts from camp kept the sounds from the king's tent private. Begging, screaming, crying, the lash on a ripe buttocks, a hard bite on a soft swollen breast, these were king's pleasures, not for scouts to gossip about.

Drunk, aggressive, willing girls, the night was late, pleasure was hard work, exhausted, Harrow dropped off to sleep very late.

The recruiting would continue in the morning, it would be a late morning, the cook made note, start the fires late, King Harrow hated to be woken by the sound of wood crackling, smell of smoke, taste of heavy meat.

12

SURVIVAL

"Fear becomes speed. Anger becomes strength."

Hamlet men who were swiftest of foot crossed over the mountain, followed the trail, found the boy's limp body, pain, grief were replaced with sadness, anger, frustration.

Fresh footprints were found, leading away from the hamlet, accepting what must be done the hamlet men followed, not a misguided sense of desire for vengeance, this killing must be done, there were no options.

Wolf had moved swiftly down the path, his tracks were, wet, deep, no debris, not far ahead now.

Open running, faster, breathing hard, the two hamlet men were closing, somewhere on the far side of the mountain they lost the track, finding small signs of Wolf, faster, looking as far ahead as they could, find the trail, lose it again, find it, panic.

Having spent years hunting game Wolf knew the skills, plans, smells, shadows of the forest, the hamlet men were farmers, wrong players for this game, they did not know the rules.

High on the edge of a hill Wolf went, the two pursued just where they were led. The thing Wolf had not counted on was how fast they had run, speed removed caution, a failure Wolf could exploit.

Having guessed Wolf's path to the hamlet the men were now slightly up a rise from Wolf, exposed, upwind, stinking, most of all crashing through the brush, breathing heavily they were easy to spot, target, identify in his woods.

The first archer from the hamlet had perspiration running into his eyes, breathing in huge deep gulps of air, arms throbbing from the chase, slowly he lifted his bow, waited a moment for Wolf to show himself.

Wolf stepped into view, stuck an arrow in the ground, while the archer on the hill paid no attention the sound of his own bowstring singing, Wolf could hear the arrow break free of the bow.

Wolf moved away, at this range it took the arrow a blink for the arrow to reach where he had been standing.

This arrow landed a good twenty paces short of the arrow Wolf had placed in the ground, sadly the arrow was far to the left.

Breath control was required to shoot straight.

Returning to the arrow in the ground Wolf lifted his bow, so did the archer on the hill, both strings sang at once.

Wolf moved to the right one step, back one step, the arrow struck short, left again.

The archer on the hill did not move, knowing if his arrow was short shooting downhill, Wolf could not reach him uphill.

Wolf's rock tip arrow was lighter weight, from a longer bow with curved limbs.

The arrow point went into the archer's leg just below the groin, with the downward angle it ripped apart the thigh muscle, vital arteries that fed it blood were ripped apart, the rock tip broke into pieces part way through the journey leaving only the feathers sticking out of the leg.

The second pursuer realized what had happened, stronger bow, lighter arrow, farther range than his short bow with heavy steel tipped arrows, perhaps he could pierce through armor, no armor here, just the thin skin of a man.

Follow, wait, get close, not in range, a child's game that decided on this day who would live, who would die.

The remaining hamlet man would move when Wolf fired, must kill Wolf when he is dormant, unimpressed, not devoid of fear, fear will help him provide a mistake, help make Wolf mortal.

Running now, to get within range, pursuing Wolf, turned a corner at full speed, the archer heard Wolf's arrow hit the tree behind him, gripped his own bow to get ready to fire a kill shot.

The hamlet archer felt a twinge, Wolf was just forty or so paces, in the clear, the pursuer calculated the distance, lifted the bow, started to pull back the string.

A pain spasm ripped through the pursuers chest, he looked down, the arrow he heard hit the tree had passed through his gut, the feathers ripped off while the arrow passed through, sticking from just under his ribs feathers were there, red blood soaked him now.

Sitting back against the tree the pursuer felt life drain away. Looking up he could see the face of Wolf, a friend, hunting partner, child he had spent hours playing with, no apology would do, nothing could be said, life slipped to other worlds, there was no holding on to this one.

His last memory was Wolf giving a kiss upon his cheek, how cruel forgiveness of another is, when we do not forgive ourselves.

Wolf walked quickly now, running would mask the sounds of other pursuers, he needed to stay alive, perhaps a missed step on a rock, a broken leg, Cozet would die before he got there.

Darkness was the hunters hiding place, Wolf slid along rock faces, crawling across fields, the back of the hamlet was in view, small fires burned, waiting long enough Wolf could see movement, they were waiting for him.

Slow, one movement, rest, another, stalking prey, smelling for anyone close, laying on his back under trees to see a leg dangling down, a bow move, a mouth yawn.

Wolf was sure they were tired, because he was, in numbers came confidence, relaxation, security.

Wolf was alone, awake, alert, ready to die, ready to kill, ready to save his wife, if they had not killed Cozet already, these were the friends that had killed him once, now he would repay them.

Along the bank of the river Wolf scouted, no one would be looking for him to come from the river, it was cold, things moved in the water, he stayed silent, waited.

It was just before morning light that Wolf noticed the body hanging from the post, long black hair, they had killed her then put her on display for him, they would pay.

Then a noise, from behind one of the huts, his bow ready, arrow on the string, a woman walked to Cozet, gave her a drink, moved on, Cozet's head hung down again, her arms pulled back, she was in pain.

From hidden places hamlet men were watching Cozet, she was the bait for Wolf, he moved silently back into the forest, faster now, night would soon be gone, drawing the two blades from the archers he had killed, placing them in his mouth, pulling four arrows from the quiver, one on the string, three laced into his fingers, the run was swift,

Fear becomes speed.

Anger becomes strength.

On one knee a short distance from the fire, human forms were clear, each hit, like the patter of rain, four arrows found targets quickly, up running, each body crumpled, Wolf came from behind, a quick thrust of the blade to the throat, blood sprayed.

Back in his mouth, the blades tasted of the blood of friends, Wolf took a breath, looked around, could see no movement.

Running, turning left, right, Wolf knew where the next fire would be, where more friends would be, where blood could be taken again.

The sing of bowstrings came from right, left, trap, move, quickly, twisting behind anything to protect, an arrow struck Wolf's quiver, a shot on the run, Wolf put an arrow into an old friends chest.

Screams, more running, the thud of the arrow into Wolf's leg sent a shockwave through his body, spun him, took him to the ground.

Wolf fired from the ground, not seeing the target in the darkness, hearing the scream.

Feeling the arrow in the dark Wolf got both hands on it and snapped it cleanly with just a stub sticking out, moving again, one leg searing with each step.

Crashing through the door of a hut, women, children down in the corner, hiding.

Wolf wanted to say he was a good man, a kind man, do not hide, this is not my doing, your husbands are trying to kill me, the words did not come out, Wolf was silent, no words could justify him to them.

An arrow slammed into the door, another past Wolf's head, two more through the door, one nicked Wolf's neck.

Screams, children running for the door, the mother hiding, fear gripping her, an arrow went through the chest of the first boy to the door, hurling him back into the hut, falling at Wolf's feet, never had anything shaken Wolf so.

Wolf drew the bow, ran for the door, out with the children, Wolf on one knee, four more arrows, children running, when a large shadow with a bow appeared, Wolf put an arrow in it.

Hard wood log, thick, solid, swung with only the anger a mother could create, her son dead, her husband dead, she had flown from the hut steps to smash the log down upon Wolf's head.

Wolf was dragged to the post, tied beside Cozet, doing what must be done, solace is the last comfort of those believing they are doing right thing.

Some of the men discussed what a good lesson killing these two outcasts would be for the children, a simple lesson, those that were strange, ended life badly.

Decisions were being made about how to kill Wolf and Cozet, a knife across the throat, a blade in the heart, cut the wrists, let them bleed out, shoot them with arrows.

Some wondered which should be killed first, was it harder to be killed first or watch the one you love be killed.

A boy started shouting, riders, many, royal, white horses, coming.

King Harrow looked upon the two tied to the post.

A story was told of the shooting a God, killing hamlet folk, many had died during the last night.

Cozet's sister talked of the treachery done to Wolf, Nathan trying to take Cozet as a lover, Wolf was a good man, Cozet a good sister.

King Harrow appeared sympathetic, stepped down from his white horse, held Wolf's head up, asked a few questions to which most got no response. The blood loss from the arrow in Wolf's leg was great.

Join the king in a great war that was coming or die here on the stake.

Wolf mumbled something incoherent, King Harrow said that Wolf had agreed to join him in fighting his brother.

Wolf spoke more clearly, demanded, his wife, Cozet, be brought with him, the king declined, Wolf said he would rather die here with her than live without her.

One of the men in the village cried out, two of his brothers had been killed by Cozet, she must die.

King Harrow asked how many had Cozet had killed, she did not know, five or six.

A woman ran from the back of the hamlet with her son dragging behind, Cozet had killed the boy's father, it was only right that the boy be taken to the castle, treated as their son, give the boy named Morgan a chance.

Reluctantly King Harrow agreed, Prince Rogan was on the ocean at this very moment planning to remove him from the throne, all were welcome to come fight Rogan.

Wolf was cut down, hauled to a hut by two large scouts, one of the scouts tended to the arrow in Wolf's leg by ripping out the arrow, pressing moss into the wound, tying a bandage around the leg.

Harrow ordered Wolf be cared for, sent to the castle in a week, the hamlet elders reluctantly agreed.

Morgan was hoist reluctantly on a horse behind Cozet, his first life gone, a new unwanted life just starting with the murderers of his father.

13

VIKING PRIZE

"Quiet came the reaper."

Claws dug into dirt as they pulled the large cats, wolves, foxes through the dark woods, hooves pounded across open fields in a spectacular show of flesh, muscle, terror.

Wings spread, pulled into dark sky large bodies that moments ago were quietly at rest.

Burrowing animals, insects, reptiles went to ground, holes deep in the earth to protect them, the fire swept over, air was sucked from the holes, suffocated.

Those that could run, did, most of those that could not run died.

It was on Captain Rogan's lead ship, a dark night, the oceans offered up her prize, a fire, the coastal camp of a Viking raiding boat.

Like a sirens song calling them home, the light shown from the large fire, silhouetted shadows, danced in the tall trees, made a great stage to deliver a death play.

On Captain Rogan's command, his ship was alive with men moving in total silence, trained, practiced for this moment, an army of archers came to the side of the ship, the crew stood on the other side for balance, sails were only part up, a gentle breeze kept them taught, quite.

The second ship kept to her course, watching, double back if needed.

A small skiff departed the backside of Rogan's warship, tar oil rags muffled the sounds, backs strained as they pulled through the water toward shore.

The archers were all fixed on Captain Rogan, two arms up, each hand with three fingers.

Rogan then held up one hand in a fist, made an arch across the front with the other hand.

In unison the archers each pulled from their quivers three arrows, nock upon string.

Rogan snapped up his hand, the archers snapped up their bows, pointed in the direction of the fire on shore.

Rogan snapped his hand down, one hundred arrows were sent to the sky.

Without hesitation another hundred arrows were nocked, pulled, launched, not in perfect unison this time, they were spread in time, space, zenith.

A third flight of arrows danced into the sky, the first set was still in the air while the third set was launched.

The men in the skiff were amazed at the beauty of the arrows in the night sky making a full arch over them, a soft breeze could be felt, a soft hiss came from the skies above, death snakes of the sky, death was in harmony with nature.

Quiet came the reaper.

Arrows with heavy metal tips crashed down in camp, they did not awake the sleeping warriors, the screams of comrades impaled by arrows did wake the camp.

Just as some Vikings realized the situation a second hundred arrows came crashing in, breath, fear, reaction, then the third wave of fine feathered death landed.

Most of the arrows only hit the dirt, stuck in the ground, some of the arrows went into the fire, sending a shower of sparks, smoke in the air that made it impossible to see, breath, escape.

Many of the arrows that hit Viking warriors were in legs, arms, causing pain, not death, some were in chests, backs, bellies, a breath for a prayer before death.

Shouting, the living warriors ran for the woods, some through the fire, burning clothing on the men soon caught the brown grass around them on fire, setting the forest ablaze.

Vikings that wanted to return to camp for a fight were stopped by the fire.

The skiff landed, five men from Captain Rogan's crew ran for the camp to recover as many arrows as they could in the dark, five more tended to the skiff beside the Viking longboat.

The rest of Rogan's men charged the Viking longboat, the prize of the raid, while one chopped at the rope with a large axe, a few started to board her.

Three huge blond men stood on the deck of the Viking longboat, with huge axes they split two of the sailors in half like kindling wood.

Archers from the skiff nocked arrows, ready to fire, a Norseman from the skiff held up his hands, waived for the archers not to fire.

The Norseman shouted at the Viking men on the longboat some strange words, the three looked back in amazement, they did not speak or move, once again the Norseman shouted at the three, one shouted back.

The exchange went on for a moment, one of the three Viking warriors swung his axe to the side, killing the man beside him with a blow to the belly. This was the lookout that had slept through the attack, a price had to be paid.

The two large warriors chose to raid with their new crew, same job, just a new captain. The longboat was the prize, they pushed it from the soft sand, with the help of the two new crewmen they worked the oars, straining muscles, out to the warship.

The longboat could work in shallow water, inlets, rivers, oars when no wind, two new crewmen that knew how to utilize her power.

In the hold of the Viking ship were the spoils from towns they had raided for the last month, it was like allot of work being done by others, Rogan reaped the rewards.

By the time the ships were under way again the forest was ablaze creating an odd orange glow that could be seen for miles.

Captain Rogan worried that the two new crewmen would feel a need to exact some revenge because of what had been done to their comrades, friends, countrymen.

Instead the two Viking men went to sleep, no emotion for the dead, no sadness for the wounded, they were safe, alive, unharmed, that was all that they required.

As the weeks went on Captain Rogan found that feeding to two hulking Vikings was a job unto itself.

Some gifts cost much more than others.

14

THE FAIR

"Youth came to the fair, exuberant, flushed cheeks, strong, swift, youth in all its confused glory came to the fair."

Rolling over the hills, valleys, through the trees, across clear running streams, the music of the castle fair wafted, twisted, bounced, played in fields of bright orange flowers.

Slight breezes would catch the sound, hold it, combined they become a symphony, punctuated by laughter, screams of delight, joy, happiness.

The first spring birds, insects, the rustle of bushes would provide the harmony for the mixture of magic that made smiles break out over all the faces.

Fair was only once a year, a new season starts, babies are in wombs growing, crops are just dreams, seeds in barns waiting for soil and water, a new calf breaks from its mother taking the first wobbly steps, they all fall to the ground with a thud, get licked mercilessly, regain their feet, try again, a ritual as old as time.

Months of rain had washed the villages clean of the muck of man, new again, fresh, bright, sun broke through the fog early on these mornings, dew sat upon the green grasses making them look like shimmering fields of diamonds.

The eyes of children were wide with excitement as jugglers, musicians, magicians, candy makers would ply their trade.

Fair had started as a time to sell seeds for new crops, those that would gamble on weather, floods, sun, soil, early freeze, perhaps they were just dreamers, many just said mad, get a job, work for someone, safe.

The revenue men for King Harrow would walk the streets extracting fees for booths or sales, or because they wanted payment, take a little food, steal goods. The tax collectors were honest thieves in the employ of the king, not welcome, tolerated, inevitable, accepted.

Over the hills vendors and patrons came, walking, with small carts pulled by wifes, donkeys or children, filled with garments, earthen jugs, fine swords, pots and pans forged in the furnaces of larger kingdoms.

Sell, barter, exchange, hook or crook, there was a profit, benefit to the exchange for both, one better than the other, some got nothing at all.

Youth came to the fair, exuberant, flushed cheeks, strong, swift, youth in all its confused glory came to the fair.

It was here that a girl could find a boy, a wench a lad, a lady a lord.

All was accepted for this week in the castle, youth knew no rules of the heart to follow, no wisdom of choice, casting eyes down properly to show a soft gentle side was not required at the fair, take it all in, for it was your time to grasp, hold, embrace, cherish, make memory.

Old men only had tales of days at the fair to remember when youth was gone, so make memories now to remember in the twilight of old age.

Many from outer areas with little world contact traded on the best commodity of the fair, rumors, stories, outright lies, exaggerations, bold boasts, sincere tales of things that had never happened, might happen, could happen, should happen, in the mind of the speaker, in the ear of the beholder all words were true this week.

Games of chance, skill, trickery, slight of hand were offered up to those weak of mind or strong of drink, often a small wager changed hands in good spirits. A boxer, wrestler, fighter, took on all comers, at the end of the fair many had the mark of his knuckles upon their cheek. Some found while nocked out their purses had vanished by magic.

Tents of women were kept down a long path, just outside of town, the path was well worn, the eyes of wives with rolling pins were sharp for a husband on the wrong path, those husbands that were stopped found their purses gone, those husbands that made it to the tents returned with empty purses anyway.

Among the flurry of the crowd there were agents of King Harrow listening for rumors of things that royal court should be made aware.

One cunning young agent culled from King Harrow a stipend to the woman's tents just outside of the castle.

The agent argued that men who drank, made love, relaxed, would be more free with their words, secrets, stories, share with a stranger, stories that the king would seek council on.

For fair week the young agent made love like a mad man, possessed with a purse bearing golden coins he was a favorite of the women when they stood in front of the their tents.

Women would seduce the young agent in with smiles, eyes, lips round, full, hips swaying gently to an unsung song, dressed in small silk, cloth, skin, their bodies showing paradise for the one with coins to dispense.

After making love, quite whispers upon the cot would tell of mad Captain Rogan, sailing ships laden with treasure from village, town, city, with plunder of all worth taking.

The size of Rogan's fleet was from ten to over one hundred, one whore talked of being taken by Rogan himself to a bay where twenty ships riding low were sitting, over five hundred men made fires on the shore where dancing girls draped in gold were strewn about, in the morning the girl said that the beach was empty, all had moved on.

Distance, where were they, headings, weapons, when were the visions, were they dreams that vanished in the mist.

Gold made for visions of more gold.

Passion made for visions of more passion.

Power made for visions of more power.

Drink made for visions empty, void of real conquest, delusions, grandeur.

The final notes of the fair were played, seeds sold, goods traded, purses picked, kisses exchanged behind the sheds.

The young agent returned to King Harrow with reports, Prince Rogan, who had sworn vengeance, was building a fleet capable of exacting revenge, no specifics as to location, direction, intent, dreams or loathing.

Whoring for a week the agent had tried without any luck to find more answers of valid belief, none could be found among the working girls or the drunks that walked their path.

Anger filled Harrow's face, it was simply the mask of fear, kings dare not wear fear in public, kings fear nothing, anger accomplishes fear in others, pain in those that displeased King Harrow.

The young agents bloodstains covered the floor, maids cleaned for days, the stain remained. King Harrow decided that the bloodstains served a purpose, fear was good among agents of the king.

A few days after the fair ended an old agent returned to the castle, questioned about the return delay, he had fallen in with a troop of jugglers and acrobats who danced among the crowds then traveled with them a short way out of town.

The old agent placed his hand on the hilt of his sword, a scabbard was about to be emptied. Harrow was even more frustrated getting ready to tell his guards to dispatch the old agent.

The old agent continued, the jugglers were not good, as a matter of fact they were quite bad at juggling, spent all their time looking at the castle, roads, people, walls, gathering information.

King Harrow sat back, the old agent said nothing, there were no more questions to ask or tales to tell, the attack would come this year or Prince

Rogan's agents would have waited for the next fair, the attack will be well planned, executed, trained warriors, cutthroats, villains.

Men of the sea were nasty to fight, they had nothing to lose, a leaky boat, a life that most would not wish on a dog, rotten food when there was food.

Moral men of city, village, hamlet would have something to lose, nothing to gain, some reason to fight, with what enthusiasm.

Dogs of the sea were perfect tools for Prince Rogan to retake a throne that was already occupied.

Taxes would need to be exacted to build a larger army.

King Harrow's life changed, which changed life for many in the kingdom.

Mornings of sunlight, warmth, beauty, lustful interludes, became tormented sessions alone in rooms of maps, charts, weapons, guards.

If Prince Rogan had agents scouting the castle, could he have paid guards to remove King Harrow before the war could even start, ascension to the throne would be easier with Harrow dead.

Advisors to the court of Harrow were fearful to speak, in rage Harrow had decapitated two advisers just after the fair for disagreeing with him about food rationing.

The executed agents had simply requested more food be given the people, the royal grain silos were being sold for money to buy, something, some weapon, some army, something that could defeat the thousand men in a hundred ships that Rogan had built to destroy his kingdom.

The vision of dogs set upon a newborn calf became King Harrow's dream each night, ripping at his eyes, face, haunches the kicking calf would cry for a mother that was unable to come, lest she would lose her own life.

When would Harrow's people, servants, guards, army, realize that, like the mother of the calf, they could not stop the dogs from ripping apart the calf without losing their own lives.

The first night of the dream Harrow watched from afar as the calf stumbled in the field, heard the dogs, watched his mother walk away.

A week later King Harrow was standing beside the calf in the dream.

Last night King Harrow was the calf.

Screaming, jumping from the bed, cowering in the corner, servants and guards piled into the room.

Rumors.

Castles are built of brick

Kings are built from fear

Kingdoms are built from rumors.

A mad king commands no respect, out of his noggin, whacky as a jaybird, or loon, or some other stupid animal.

King Harrow had been using the rumors for years, now the rumors were not by Harrow, the rumors were about Harrow.

Then it came to Harrow, make his people the calf, make his people feel his fear.

Governors, mayors, council of the hamlets around the castle were called to a great feast.

Orders to those brave lads delivering the invitation were clear, ask, cajole, plead, demand. If the leaders would not attend, kill them, ask whoever replaced them.

God is testing us was the mantra of King Harrow's great proclamation.

God has brought demons from the bowls of hell to find our strength, faith, desire for life that he has given.

In God's name the kingdom must fight these creatures, in God's name we must pay more taxes to build an army.

All within hearing knew the enemy was Harrow's own brother, the only devil was in Harrow's dreams.

Others thought that after the feast, with full bellies, they would take what they could, ride to a new kingdom, new king, sane king, safe life.

This was going to require taxes, allot of taxes, more money than many had.

Through dinner, the wise leaders of the kingdom never said a word against King Harrow's presentation, in fact many clapped, hooted, hollered down the devil, swore to the king they would destroy the demons when they landed on shore.

By the end of dinner all had subscribed to King Harrow's plan, all were ready, pledged, devout, resolute, fists clenched, shouts of demand for King Harrow to build an army, lead them in a fight against these beasts.

The makers of weapons, armor, sellers of horses to the army rejoiced, war was good business.

Priests rejoiced, a war against the demons of hell filled church pews, opened pocket books, morality was a good pontification for tithing more.

That night King Harrow slept soundly, deeply, no dreams, the dogs had been set upon the kingdom, he was safe in his royal sleeping chamber.

Outside the royal sleeping chamber door two guards stood watch, each wondering if he were to enter the chamber, kill the mad king, would the other stop him, neither guard tried, fearing the other would kill him.

15

MAKING ROYALTY

"Rose was alone, except for the cells breaking apart in her belly."

The last shafts of sunlight kissed the waves, people sat to a last meal of the day, a warm summer had blessed them, new thoughts, contemplations, conspiracies would take form in the darkness.

Weeks of riding from King Harrow's castle was the large kingdom of King Alansano, a strong army kept it safe, built on the trade of wine and weapons.

A small castle sat close to the shore with a good view from her towers of the ocean, surrounded by deep dark forests, the only way in or out was a single road with many guards, agents, watchers.

In the small castle the lord's heavy robes had been removed, hung on hooks, laid upon tables, taking with them the trappings of power, the resolve of a ruler, the need for decisions.

Only one purpose was served in these stonewalls, first of the alarms against sea raiders, warning to King Alansano of approaching ships.

This remote castle was also a good place to send a lord that had displeased the king in some way, or untrustworthy for a job of real importance.

As the lord placed the last of his clothing on the table he looked to the bed with lust, passion, desire, none of these filled Rose, the lord's wife that looked back at his bulk, fat, squat body, sad that she would have to suffer the vial love making yet again.

Rose was the cousin of a low lord, given as a gift to King Alansano. When Alansano banished this insipid lord to the watch castle he gave Rose to him as a gift.

Rose had a perfect body, saintly face, as Gods little joke on all men, Rose hated being touched.

As her duty Rose, gripped the sheets, closed here eyes, spread her legs, gritted her teeth till the job was done.

It was Rose's duty, to produce a child that could marry a male heir to the throne.

Each night Rose filled herself with pride, suffered the insult of penetration by this ugly stupid slug, to create a royal child, a lady in performance of her duty.

It was a degrading duty that filled Rose with disgust, remorse, anger for each agonizing moment. Worst of all Rose had to play to the disgusting ego, feign praise, admiration, thanks for the fat smelly troll to extinguish himself with the most hideous faces, sounds, smells between her legs.

Along the road, first of the guard houses, four guards sat around a small table with a bowl of stew, bread was torn from a loaf, a pitcher filled goblets, two dark figures moved though the open viewing holes in the wall as if they were a draft of air.

Two guards fell face down in their bowls never even knowing that anyone had entered the room.

Rising quickly the other two guards tried to draw full swords in the small room, before the blades had cleared their scabbards, daggers ripped into their throats, bodies crumpled to the ground.

Finishing the stew, the two dark figures moved on, darkness was becoming a friend, torches burned in guard houses providing a clear path.

No ships passed, no alarm given, no bell rung, no one left alive to sound the alarm.

Guards at the castle gate were easy, if the two had been passed by all of the guard houses along the road, the two dark men must be harmless enough, perhaps even a message from the king, or religious on a pilgrimage to find lost souls.

The last thing spoken from the captain of the guard was an order to open the gate.

Arrows quick as bees from the hive found their marks. One brave young officer even drew a sword, stood strong, resolute, important, opened his mouth, an arrow ripped open his lungs, no air, no sound, no foolish men with swords to fight.

The walls of the castle contained halls, curious hidden passages, no locked doors, no one felt death was upon them.

At the top of the castle were the lord's chambers, large doors moved softly, quietly, the open door let a small breeze in, the lord turned up from Rose for a moment.

The Lord's blood poured down upon Rose's face from the open vein in his neck.

Fear ripped through Rose, her husband's body fell to the floor, large white breasts with soft pink nipples were exposed.

Death was a passage, done quickly, the name of God, the plan, yet there was a hesitation, new feelings, desires, a hand grabbed, teeth bit down on the nipple.

Grabbing the bed sheets tightly, air filled Rose's lungs, a scream started, cut short when the tip of a blade pricked the inside of her mouth, she closed her teeth on the blade, closed her eyes.

Waves of intense pain rolled through Rose's body as the small figure ripped at her breast, bite down, then let her go, then bite down again.

The killer pulled down his pants, Rose guided him in, he knew what he wanted, it was crude, mean, hateful, powerful, disgusting.

He stood, walked away, brother was cleaning up, Rose closed her legs, wept.

Alive among the death, morning sun showed the true cold brutal world as if a canvas painted in pain, blood, anguish, despair.

Rose was alone, except for the cells breaking apart in her belly.

King Alansano's guard came two days later, fell upon their knees, prayed to God, asked forgiveness, found the only survivor, took Rose back to the castle.

Rose was to be one of Alansano's special guests, nights were long, cold, lonely affairs. Arraigned marriages to queens that lacked attraction, passion, lust, special guests could make the life of a king bearable.

Husband dead, pregnant, Rose was grateful to be a special guest of the king, her attitude now more receptive to the king's needs.

Desperation creates desire.

Nine months later, her life settled, Rose gave birth to a girl, Ivy, taken as a lady of the court the new child was treated as nobility, a royal child.

Ivy's father knew nothing of creation, sex, passion, lust, after that night in the castle he often took females when the two had found a house, village, castle, anything with people to send to God, food to eat, those he had taken, who did not resist him, were allowed to live, some wished they had not.

16

LONG RIDER—SMOKE STICK

"Every free benefit was paid for, some of the best intended were very expensive."

At King Harrow's castle gate six long riders prepared to travel, find fire sticks, Zorn took off on his old path, return the boy who helped with the cattle.

Arrows rose from the six riders bows, high into the sky, slight breezes, the twist of a feather, slightest motion of the wrist, six arrows hit at the same time in the circle. Each rider rode to the center of the circle, rode in the direction of his arrow, past the arrow, kept riding to glory.

Zorn spent a few days in the village of his birth, eating well, served as if an honored guest, long nights of wine, sleep, stories, hounds getting fat, lazy, board, fighting among themselves.

The team crept out in the darkness, avoiding long goodbyes, tears, admonishment of trips home.

From the village who had given Zorn the first set of fire sticks the old man suggested that he follow the coast, sticks came from foreigners who traveled the seas, it was the best place to find the men who made them, knowledge of how they worked.

In the young boy's village they welcome the return of their child, a welcome guest, food, drink, stories, smiles, tears, strong drink for the men at night.

The girl who had crept to Zorn's bed last time walked boldly to him this time.

She took Zorn's hand, walked him to a hut at the edge of the village, she removed her clothing, candle light, soft skin, tender kisses, small waist, thick hips, strong farm woman.

A young scared girl on Zorn's first trip, now carried herself as a woman.

They bathed with water from a warm bucket, slowly dripped oil scented of wild flowers, letting it fall on the stone floor.

As the candle flame went out they slept, soft, content, holding each other.

Morning light, the girl knelt beside Zorn, looking into his eyes, she no longer found the hunger for her.

Nothing of the nights passion existed, Zorn's eyes were already over the mountains, trails, being a long rider had taken his heart again.

She demanded he love her more than who he was.

Zorn's eyes were now full of pity for her, she held him, it was ok, it was fine, she knew he would not be hers, her lover would never stay, she accepted that, she wanted him to return someday.

Every free benefit was paid for, some of the best intended were very expensive.

Feeding Zorn each bite of food followed with a soft kiss, she smiled when he walked out the door.

She lay upon the bed all day crying, laughing, holding the soft leather bedding against her face to have that last smell of his scent, that was life, accepted, unfair, what was done, was done.

Rumors, fairytales, folklore, stories, lies, all based on hope, believed long enough they became the truth. Zorn worried that he did not know which truth he followed.

On a point of land Zorn found a beautiful small castle set alone, a lookout upon the ocean, they would know of ship traffic, tell him a direction to follow, perhaps traders from other lands had even stopped here.

The army officers at the gate kept a close eye as Zorn approached, arrows appeared in small holes in the wall waiting for the archer to distinguish any reason to fire.

Zorn kept his palms up, smile, soft voice, the hounds closing in to protect their master made the officer that stopped him more nervous.

As Zorn stepped from the stallion an arrow flew from the wall between the rider and officer, immediately the officer held up his arms to stop any more mistakes.

Zorn offered short simple descriptions, a simple trader, trade of goods, information, a meal, no harm, the officer was nervous.

Then the officer told the story, all killed, all inside dead, two men, old, ugly, cruel agents of the devil. Castle walls were to keep out evil, once evil was inside, the castle was a chamber of death.

Few pleasantries could be exchanged after the story of what had happened here, arrows were pulled from the walls, gates open slowly, trepidation, strength, a prayer under Zorn's breath.

A courtyard full of mounds, buried in the middle of the castle, no one would ever live here again, a graveyard.

Magistrates were nothing more than those that did jobs no one else wanted, this officious round-faced fat man was counting bodies, identity of those they could make, swords were grave markers for soldiers.

The papers of the magistrate were full of marks, many just lines for each body in the common grave, men, woman, small blond haired girls, boys with blue eyes that loved to run, all were just a mark on the paper.

A pile had been made of things of value, loot, burying it would change nothing.

The magistrate pulled Zorn into another room, the kingdom would take the loot, hard to hide, sell some cheap, gold coins would be easier to hide.

Fearing loot of the dead would bring him bad luck Zorn declined, again the magistrate insisted opening a large chest full of many items such as hair clips with pretty stones, a sword caught Zorn's attention, the make was not of this land, jewels imbedded in the handle were of great value.

Searching the box Zorn pulled a few items, a very short fire stick, unlike the others this was very decorative, valuable jewels were imbedded all along the wooden portions, heavy, a holder for the balls along the handle, a pouch of powder tied to it.

The magistrate argued for five coins, Zorn offered one, the magistrate settled for three, the rider offered one, the magistrate demanded two, Zorn offered one pointing out that one was better than none, the magistrate agreed, muttered under his breath, there was more gold in the sword than Zorn had just given in the coin.

Slowly the horses, hounds, rider moved out of the castle, grateful that the meeting had ending without more death.

Moving down the coast Zorn changed pace often to keep anyone following his patterns, laying in wait, establishing a good attack point.

Armed men in uniform could be seen upon the various roads, appeared to be searching, looking for trails, viewed from the hills they were easy for Zorn to avoid, also easy for two killers to avoid.

In the dark, up a small hill from the hounds and horses Zorn was keeping watch, long days, careful moves, weary, Zorn closed his eyes for the slightest second.

A blade touched upon Zorn's throat, startled, awake, he jerked up his hand, a hand clasp upon his arm, held it firm, a voice talked of his impending death.

Another voice came from the hills above, alone, they knew Zorn was alone.

On the other end of the blade the uniform was tattered, worn, dirty, the blades holder had sharp eyes, strong physique, the blade held firmly, confident, professional, a man to be reasoned with.

Zorn's move was quick, pushing up just enough, inches from his throat, the military man thrust the blade forward, a simple grab of the thumb, twist back, the blade fell free.

Zorn's foot into the knee sent the military man back a step falling on his ass, thud, a curse, anger.

Quickly Zorn grabbed the sword, holding the handle out to the startled officer, hands up, the long rider surrendered, when it was on his terms, if they were to fight, it would be a fair fight.

The woods came alive with armed men running at Zorn, the hounds were racing from the field, a whistle, the hounds all sat, angry, growling, wanting action, denied.

Taking his sword back the officer called back his men.

Zorn took a knee, hands open, empty, a smile, diplomats tools.

Telling of the visit to the castle, Zorn knew of their mission, men moved in around them, a hound growled, the man close to the hound drew a sword, Zorn reached for a pike, the officer stopped the man, Zorn returned the pike.

Reaching out a hand Zorn waited, two men, dark forest, missions, orders, respect, the hand was taken, strong, solid, relaxed, joined, trusted.

The military man removed a ring, safe passage for Zorn upon these lands, this was a lord, these were his lands, his men.

Questions about the fire sticks, enough die with the weapons they have, better weapons mean more death, the lord knew of rumors, knew they were coming.

If you find them you may want to not have found them, better ways to wage war are not always the best thing to have.

Why so obvious a show of hunting on the road during the day, a simple plan, drive the hunted into places like this so they could be taken easily at night, just as they had Zorn, indeed a good plan.

Inattention had allowed a sword to be placed against Zorn's throat, perhaps as his training had so carefully impressed upon his stubborn thoughts, leave the memories, focus on the job at hand, each smell, movement, change in breeze.

A city appeared on the horizon, up a small bay, there were sails at port, many buildings.

Zorn hung back, looked on for a day, night, a few carts with horses moved into the town, lights at night stayed on late, music wafted through the air.

Moving into the city at morning light Zorn was slow, this was his first real city, of traders, gamblers, whores, drunks, men wanton for cheap money will do evil things.

Huts with small doors lined muddy streets, a blacksmith was pounding already, small boys covered in dirt moved the large bellows up, down, up, rhythmically, one after another in a monotonous drone of air blasting hot coals. Embers showered down with each hammer blow, a rainbow of sparks fell upon the blacksmith's heavy leather apron.

Close to the docks, a corral, a large black stallion, two pack horses, Zorn looked astonished, a long rider, one of his own, the packs were upon the horses, this rider had not cared for his animals.

Care for your team, or they will not care for you.

A small hut next to the corral, Zorn called out, no response, hounds whined as they approached the hut, whines, whelps, barking of hounds in the hut, how odd, in the corral they could protect the horses, no long rider would do this.

Only one conclusion, this rider was in trouble, needed help, unfriendly territory, a sword in one hand, pike in the other.

Zorn found an old man who motioned him over, all they wanted was to get the drunk out, the old man walked into the tavern with Zorn in step close behind, ready for ambush, treachery.

Laying in the corner was a figure dressed all in black, long blond hair flowed down onto the floor, curled in a ball, perhaps sick.

Zorn knelt beside the body on the floor, hand on the shoulder, word in the ear.

Like a flash the body on the floor spun around, a hand grabbed back for a sword that was not there, connected to a back plate that was not there, the smell of the mans breath, vomit, mixed with bad food, heavy drink.

The old rider pushed away Zorn's hand, stood on his own, wobbled, leaned against the wall, the tavern owner appeared with the back plate, swords, pikes.

The end of the swords were red with blood, weaving, the old rider put on his back plate, walking out of the tavern, staggering, not yet sober, gathering himself.

At the corral the old long rider introduced himself as Dracon, sobered up quickly, a story, why, how could he do this to himself, judgment of the young was harsh, righteous, pious, wrong.

Dracon was now somber, slow, the explanation, information took communication with sailors, sailors in port drank, whored, gambled, so Dracon drank, whored, gambled with them to get the information that he needed.

Dracon had taken a ship from the kingdom of King Harrow to this port, the plan was to start riding once informed of what he was looking for.

Better a planned informed ride than setting off lost without a plan.

Zorn understood, he had lost so much time on this ride already.

Fire sticks, no, Dracon knew nothing of fire sticks, he was looking for Captain Rogan to inform King Harrow of his brother's movements.

When you live among drunken sailors it is easy to become a drunk, understand, empathize, do not go down with the man.

Where was Captain Rogan, evil demon of the sea, he was coming, all Dracon knew was that the wind was blowing him up the coast as they spoke.

Dracon upon his stallion looked more like a long rider, the two rode to a farmhouse, large barns, many cattle milled around in the lush green pastures.

Behind the largest barn a corral stood, sheltered, hidden, all horses were released into the pasture, the hounds all headed for an overhang, young maids came to curry out the horses, two more brought food, water, pets, hugs for the hounds.

Hounds from hell, demonic, purposeful, suddenly looked as pups, soft, cuddly, happy in the arms of a young maid with a treat in her hand.

Hounds and men had many things in common.

Inside the barn a hidden staircase led to a room, long, open, books lined the walls, a huge bed at the end, at the side of the bed another staircase led to the roof, a lookout, ships coming could be seen for miles from there.

Two maids returned with a tray of food, pitcher of milk, the girl with the tray appeared to not be leaving, sitting on the bed, talk of having done her milking for the day.

At night the sailors would be at the taverns, time to see them later, information was more important, trade could also be done with a captain willing to claim that some of the cargo had been lost overboard.

By morning information would be plentiful to those awake enough to listen to a whore or bartender with a few coins in their pocket.

A maid took Zorn's hand, she could help with a good days sleep, in the maids room ten small beds were laid out.

The milkmaid washed Zorn all over with a rough farm scrubbing, treated more as a bovine than a man, he did not complain.

The maid who had just washed him, dressed in long night clothing lay beside Zorn, he seemed uninterested, she worked to make him interested.

Light faded before Zorn started to wake, the maid helped dressed him, kissed, touched him, led him back upstairs, Dracon was reclining on a large chair with the girl who had stayed with him.

Work was at hand, they would eat in town, drink, buy drinks, listen, steer conversations, smile laugh, buy a whore or two for any sailor with a story to tell.

Walking into town Dracon explained that he bought the land, barn, cattle to employ the girls, most were working in the brothels in town, hated the life, so he hired them to tend the cattle.

Zorn kept thinking how Dracon was violating so much of what they had been taught, stealing from the kingdom to drink away life in debauchery, disgusted, quietly Zorn followed along, skills to learn.

An ugly hut, girls milling around outside, the girls ran out to meet them, Dracon held each one, kissed them all, smiled, rubbed their breasts, pinched their butts, asked about sailors that had visited, sailors they had as customers, where the ships were, any good stories.

Oldest of the girls stayed, Dracon kept her tight beside him, gave her some coins, she exposed a breast, Dracon sucked it long, hard, the girl started protesting, then pulled the back of Dracon's head, as Dracon walked away she swore any lover that night she would be thinking of Dracon, no matter how much her other lovers paid.

Disgusting, wretched to watch, Zorn was not walking beside Dracon any longer, trying to distance himself from the evil lifestyle this lost soul lived.

Laughing, Dracon called Zorn closer, a ship was in, new, landed today, from the east, carrying travelers from the far east, a caravan that had been to China, filled to the gunnels with silk, trinkets, treasure.

Demanding they go to the ship directly Zorn was invigorated, Dracon laughed again, go on that ship, they hit you on the head, they have a new deck scrubber. Let them go to the tavern, loosen them with amber liquid, information would flow.

The first tavern was no more than a few tables, wine, food, girls came to the table, questions of ships in harbor, then sent away.

A Second tavern was more lively, drinks, games, yelling, pats on the back, Dracon motioned to Zorn, a tavern down the street had the ship's master, crew, stick close, learn.

Entering the third tavern a fight was going on, swinging wildly blows were landed on anything close, no finesse, Zorn pushed a drunk back into the mix, made his way to the back where a distinguished man sat calmly watching the fight.

Dracon was buying drinks, hands on the shoulders, laughing, jokes, a song or two, the man beside Zorn asked if he would like to bet on one of the men fighting, Zorn took the bet, a second later Zorn's fighter was flat on his back, payment.

Questions about fire sticks while Zorn paid the bet, it was fast, to the point, no friendship, no drink, the man not only knew about the fire sticks, he had a shipment of a hundred below his decks.

Zorn's eyes about popped out of his head, his words were quick, strong, demanding, payment for the sticks, how to use them, do some business, a sale, pay handsomely.

Quickly the ship's master nodded to two large men by the door that had been watching the fight, they trouped out of the tavern to the ship at port, large, dark, smelling of human decay, waste, urine.

Onboard it was quick, the ship's master tripped Zorn, the large man behind hit Zorn over the head. Into a cell below decks, his back plate hung on a wall in the captain's office with his heavy purse.

Many hours later Zorn came around, head pounding.

In the cell beside Zorn a man, thin, tanned, weathered, beaten, lay on the floor, four years in this cell, hit on the head, taken, held, working when at sea, in this cell when in port.

The first morning light started to break when Zorn heard shouting, sails creaking up the mast, the ship was rolling from side to side as it pulled away from the dock.

Two hours out the first mate came down with a few large sailors, the two men were pulled from the hold cells up into the bright sun, at the back of the ship they were given buckets, brushes, a taste of the lash to make them work.

Scrubbing a set of boards where the men's poop would stick before being flushed off. Land was in site, too far to swim, the sun beat down, Zorn accepted his fate for now, when time presented he would get free.

Sailors surrounded the two captives, a fight started, the first mate grabbed Zorn, a twist of the arm, shove, over the side Zorn went, a small empty cask followed, grabbing at the wooden cask Zorn was able to stay afloat.

The other prisoner was grabbed, a quick thrust of a blade between his ribs, a large piece of wood struck his head, the body was tossed overboard on the other side of the ship, two tried to escape, on killed, one drown, a good story for the captain.

A back plate was tossed over at Zorn, before the waves consumed it he was able to get one hand on a strap.

Kicking to shore Zorn could hear shouting on the ship, soon arrows struck the water behind him, then it came, a thud, clap of thunder, over his shoulder Zorn could see smoke rising from the ship, a fire stick, then another pop followed by a clap of thunder, water sprayed from something hitting the water just next to him.

They had lied, all lied, the information he needed was on that ship.

Kicking for all of his worth Zorn took hours in the water to fight his way to shore.

Crawling up on the beach, half drown, proud of surviving, Zorn realized he was miles from his team.

Back at the tree line, in the shade, a drink in hand, Dracon sat with four young girls in various stages of undress, the horses were tied just behind them.

Zorn half crawled to them, the girls quickly removed his wet clothing, fed him, poured him drinks, kissed him.

Dracon lifted a glass, a toast to a first mate that loses at the tables, throwing Zorn over the side paid the debt, not only did Zorn live, a valuable lesson.

Young riders like to learn by being told, Zorn was angry, intended to hold a grudge.

A camp out on the beach that night, drink, made love, eat fruit, cheese, meat, made love more, animals, uncivilized, taking pleasure in being alive.

For two weeks Zorn stayed in the milk barn, worked the taverns at night, learned to gamble, drink, make friends before asking questions, milkmaids by morning, lovers when the milking was done.

Late one night Dracon pulled his young protégé out of a whores bed, over, change, time to move, Captain Rogan's fleet had been seen a week out heading this way, good seas, a few days, there was work to do.

In the morning the maids were not making love, feeding him, offering flesh for his pleasure, they were packing small items into wagons attached to the larger cattle, casks, buckets, clothing.

Two wagons headed to the hills, two went to the town with Dracon in the lead, Zorn wanted to ask questions, Dracon was full of purpose, conviction, prepared for work.

In town Dracon called out on each street for people to come down to the port for a meeting. From all around, huts, taverns, brothels, shop keepers went to the port.

An army coming, many ships, no money, they will take, kill, destroy, rape, to the hills, if the fleet passes we return, if the fleet pulls in the bay, burn the town to the ground.

The ships must be stopped, no food, no water, the fleet must leave here hungry, thirsty, tired, unsatisfied.

No one questioned, everyone moved out, gathering meager possessions, wagons loaded with casks from the taverns, clothing from brothels, homes emptied, a trail of people walking up into the hills.

Dracon was not among those heading to the hills.

Gathering Zorn, taking goods from his packhorses, a small ship in the harbor, Zorn refused to leave, Dracon demanded, warn the kingdom, the captain and few crew watched, listened, curious.

Dracon was deliberate, he would burn the city before Rogan could use it, not a scrap of food, not a drop of water, not one whore for pleasure, no cow to eat.

Dracon was focused on Zorn's eyes, under the center of the barn, a mans height down, a chest, dig it up, build the city if it is gone, an order, request, pleading, death was likely, it was Dracon's legacy to keep this port as a place of information along the coast.

Before the ship set sail Zorn could see milkmaids unloading torches from the wagon, off to the four corners of the city, the ship hoisted all of its sails, a mass of canvas buckled under the wind, this was not a voyage, a race, out of port, fear gripped the captain, any ship the approaching fleet could grab would be commandeered or sunk.

Turning out of port the ship's captain kept watch behind them, unable to catch site of a sail did not reduce the captain's fear.

Just after sunset small dim lights could be seen, lanterns, a city unto itself, so Rogan's fleet did not hit each other, lanterns hung from each bow, stern, port, starboard.

Close to morning the lights behind them were all gone, the small ship had sailed away from them, outrun them, faster than the army on water.

Perhaps, worried, it was possible that the army had headed into port, fresh water, food, relaxation, it would be hard to pass up before a long voyage to attack the kingdom of his brother King Harrow.

Small thuds could be heard across the water, the Gods were angry, thunder, perhaps the Gods were helping Dracon.

While Zorn feared for the safety of his mentor, he also felt anger at his own judgments of Dracon, brave, courageous, smart, Dracon had done more for the kingdom in this one selfless act than Zorn would ever do in his life.

Two days out Zorn was called on deck by the captain, on a table lay a long wrapped pouch, a gift from Dracon, a deed to this ship, it now belonged to Zorn, a valuable gift, Zorn was not a passenger, he was the ship's master.

From the pouch the captain pulled a fire stick, black, engraved gold ran along the parts, pouch of powder, pouch of balls, a bag with flints, screws, a mold to make more balls.

The captain taught, gave many lessons of loading, making balls from melted lead, the lessons went quickly, first balls hit the water beside floating boards, in the end most hit the wood on the first try.

The fire stick would not replace the bow or sword, the explosion of power was fun, exciting, thrilling to shoot.

Just approaching darkness on a calm day with sails waiting for a puff of wind, two large sails were hoisted on very thin fast boats hidden in a small bay.

Once the boats hit the open water they could produce speed, these ambushers were already in the wind, they could get close before the wind made it a fair race.

On the attacking boats archers moved to the bow for a better shot, it was a mistake, forcing the bow down removed the balance, the two boats slowed.

On Zorn's ship the captain and his men raced below, returned with two large fire sticks each, men were setting up their equipment, the captain turned Zorn's ship right into the ambushers.

While far off the fire sticks were pointed high, into the sails, loaded with two balls, a small chain between them, they ripped gaping holes in the sails, unable to harness the wind, the ambushers slowed.

Zorn waited until the small boats were close, thump, an archer grabbed his chest, fell, the young rider grabbed another sick and fired into the crowd of archers now trying to move back, one brave archer lifted up his bow, released the arrow, proud of his power, skill, courage.

The arrow fell short of the ship, catching the wind now, just starting to move, the ship's captain called for another volley, the second boat was closer now, an archer got an arrow into the ships sail, most just hit water, the next volley from the boat would not be short.

Swinging the rudder around hard the ship's captain took aim at the back of the lighter craft, his fire stick was larger than the others, a dull thud came from a billow of smoke, flame, thunder, as the stick erupted, everyone stopped to look as the captain of the small boat, one moment had a head, the next he did not.

Gathered from other lands the archers were superstitious, some jumped from the boat, the boat captains body moved up a hand, touched the top of his neck, looking for a head where one had been, then the body went slack, fell, crumpled to the deck in a pool of dark red blood.

Without a hand on the tiller the attacking boat swung rapidly, the mast boom came crashing across the deck sweeping many archers into the water, screams, the twisting boat cast its rear to the ship, with a decisive slam the bow of the ship ripped apart the light boat's hull, stuck for a second, the boat sank quickly.

Screams came from the second boat, it was now closing in, load up came the command from the ships captain, powder, balls, were slammed down barrels.

Ducking low the ships crew moved around the deck, unseen under the rails, it was a plan, let the archers fire a volley into the bow, where they had been, turn the ship quickly away from the bay, fill the ships sails with vital wind, turn her ass to the small boat, let them have a couple rounds of balls before a new flight of arrows could be sent.

All went as planned, the ship turned, wind in her sails, arrows pounded the bow, all balls from the guns ripped through the archers, sails, boat captain.

One arrow from a boat's archer that got off late skimmed over the men with smoke sticks, hit the ships captain in the back, he held on, once clear of the ambush he lay upon the deck, with treatment he lasted two days, turned over command to the first mate, all cried, told stories of his courage, a sad loss.

The rest of the run up the coast was without event, which was worse than being attacked, every second was spent on guard, loading weapons, moving around, checking the sea from all directions, nights were constantly disrupted with visions of sails in the distance that were not there.

Hunters have command of the hunt, they can pick place, angle, weather, skill, guile, while the prey must accept that they have no control over any element of being killed.

The coast along the kingdom was rough in most places, two coves offered the best places to dock, one had long docks built by King Philip to dispatch

Prince Rogan, with all the people, commons house, it was not a place for a quiet docking, just beyond that port was a secluded cove that at high tide offered a soft sand beach.

Crew members knew where to go, many times had they carried Dracon here, as the ship pulled in three riders appeared on the hill above, soldiers, tunics, helmets, approaching cautiously.

Jumping from the ship in the shallow water with two small kegs of powder Zorn was ready to get home, picking up speed the riders pulled swords, Zorn could hear a gun cock on the ship.

Turning back to the ship Zorn called for them to fire, smoke filled the air, a pike pulled from Zorn's back was thrown, all three riders crumpled in the saddle, falling, the horses bucked up, stayed, did not run.

Screams came from the ship, worried about landing they had not been watching the sea, sails of smaller boats were appearing from each side of the sheltered cove, with less draft the boats could maneuver better in the cove than the ship, being caught was a death sentence.

All canvas had been dropped on the ship, the hull scraped against the rocks as it turned hard from the shore, skill would win this battle, short handed the crew were running, jumping on ropes.

Looking down on the dead military men Zorn could see the long scraggly beard, King Harrow allowed beards, not long unkempt like this one, pulling his pike from the middle rider Zorn could see the holes from arrows that the original owner had died from.

Compared to Zorn's stallion this horse was very slow, winded easily, at the top of the hill he looked back at the cove just as the ship passed close to one of the boats, the boat tried to change direction quickly, volleys of arrows rained down on the ship, soon puffs of smoke came from ship, sound followed a moment later, the ship sounded like a full army when the crew fired their fire sticks.

The boat made a simple mistake, turned away from the ship, lost the wind, turning down wind the ship caught the wind, it was a moments mistake, the ship was spreading the gap.

Turning away Zorn prayed for those on the ship, then made his way to the castle, wanting to use his skill of riding side trails, there was no time, warnings must be early, or they provide no purpose.

Close to the castle walls more soldiers could be seen, at the gate questions that were never asked before were answered before entrance was allowed.

A captain of long riders, Madras, was waiting, Prince Rogan's approach was not new news, a couple of days, a week at most, taking on uniforms of the kingdom's military men was fresh news.

Showing the two casks of powder, combined with the fire sticks Zorn brought on his first trip, they could be valuable weapons in the war to come.

Shaking his head Madras said that would not happen, a blacksmith decided to beat one fire stick into a sword, heating it caused it to discharge, two people were hurt, all fire sticks were banned.

Offering the two casks of powder seemed useless, Madras took them, without testing there was little chance they could be used.

Asking where Madras wanted Zorn to fight was met with a laugh.

The order was, return to the field, do your job, the army would fight, the people would fight, Zorn's job was out there on a horse, his contribution to the war would not secure victory or cause a loss.

Do your duty was all the Madras would say, placing a hand on Zorn's leg the captain offered a warning, they are animals not men, trust no one, wits will be your best shield.

Zorn told the story of Dracon, burning the city, giving him the ship, staying to protect the kingdom.

Madras noted that he never considered Dracon a hero, both smiled, ordering Zorn again to do his duty Madras slapped the horses rump, waived goodbye.

17

CAPTAIN OF THE GUARD

"Perfection is a last breath taken on ones own terms."

Herzog was the captain of King Harrow's personal guard, short, dirty, smelly, walking more with a twisting on one side of the body, then twisting the other side to catch up, quickly with purpose, determination in each step, people looked away, gave room as he walked across the main square.

Herzog's arms hung like the rear legs of a prize hog off broad shoulders, hair on the powerful shoulders was matted down, the smell from far off was also like that of a old hog, unfamiliar with bathing.

From Herzog's belt hung weapons, short, thick, heavy, polished, honed sharp.

Wolf and Cozet from the hamlet stood beside King Harrow watching Herzog's each move, checking each twist, change in direction.

Calling out, King Harrow tried to gain some attention from Herzog, a greeting, pleasantry, even an acknowledgment, every step was paced, unchanged, God himself calling from the heavens could not have interfered with the journey of such a determined man.

Wolf and Cozet were sent to seek Herzog out, learn, encouraged to show obedience, respect, follow each command, each grunt of Herzog to develop the skills of scouts for the military.

Along the small row of tables filled with goods Herzog grabbed onions, ripped a few bites then threw them away, apples, fruit, none finished, skins devoured, ripped apart by brown stubbly teeth, juices ran down into the beard, not often washed, the beard was a pallet of meals eaten while walking.

No merchant asked for payment, it was better to just allow the theft, payment would have required getting close enough to smell, exchange of currency, words, it was better not to be paid.

Through the stables Wolf and Cozet followed, horses moved to the rear of the stalls, even when Herzog came close to the stall with offerings of apples in his huge hands, the horses would back away, stomp on the ground, nostrils flared, necks arched, some horses would stand on their rear legs, teeth bared, a warning, keep away.

At the last stall, the largest horse, pure black, wide, long groomed main, tail flowing in the slight breeze, Herzog's personal stallion.

The stallion ran to the gate, a nose went through the slats, Herzog petted it, the stallion ate the apples, Herzog's horse was so huge, powerful.

Herzog and the horse talked, grunts, whispers, friends, trusted secrets for the two only.

The two old friends looked up at Wolf and Cozet, laughed at the same time, the butt of a joke in a secret language, the two looked down, continued to whisper, exchange stories.

Calling to two stable boys Herzog gave orders, sent them scurrying in different directions, one went into the stallion's stall, gathering blankets, leather straps, a crude saddle was being formed on the stallion's back.

Herzog's saddle was not the full painful saddle that nobility or an army officer used, this was a web of straps with loops around it, comfort for the horse, not the rider, utility for a warrior carrying many weapons into battle.

The second stable boy had returned with a log his own height mounted with a cross bar holding small flags. Looking down the long length of a horse exercise pen Herzog's long index finger pointed.

Panting, trying with every step, the stable boy went off with the post, a test.

Wolf and Cozet looked upon each other, never had they shot at the same time, the same target, see who was best, Wolf thought he might let Cozet win, he was known remarkable, nothing more to prove.

Herzog lead the stallion from the stall, the reason for all the straps became apparent, he crawled up the animals side like a child going over boulders, grabbing straps, pulling up, foot holds, body twisting, new straps grabbed onto, footholds found, toward the front Herzog was now in the sitting position.

Black sharp eyes darted out from under the mask of hair on Herzog's face, transformed, new, powerful, a weapon made of unusable parts, oddly the horse had also gained stature, pride, power, grand, separate, broken, unusable, together, fierce, unstoppable.

At the far end of the stable the post had been placed, Herzog pointed, together in one swirl of motion the arrows gently rose from quivers, nock on bow, a slight kiss on the cheek.

Cozet upon one knee, the bow at a slight angle, pulled to her cheek, enough for the distance, no more than required.

Wolf was straight, feet separated, shoulder width, full draw for more power, impressive impact.

Five flags on each side, five arrows from each archer, five simple refined graceful movements, dancers supple limbs, arms like water, fluid, strong, unstoppable, harnessed in an instant, released, again upon the path, no hesitation, thought interrupts that flow of death, destruction, worry later, alone, archer, bow, arrow, united.

Looking to Herzog the archers expected some acknowledgment, nothing, Herzog pointed to the stable boys, they scurried off as if rats set upon fresh cheese, kneeling before of the archers a boy held out the arrows, honored to witness their skill.

Horses with full saddles were brought out, neither Wolf or Cozet had ever ridden a beast like this before, farm horses, slow, straight, steady, battle stallions were wild, aggressive, fast.

Herzog was a slow patient guide, it was obvious that suddenly being taller than his guests had improved Herzog's confidence when talking to them.

Along the road to the bays, past the channels, Herzog showed Wolf and Cozet each guard placement, how to move quickly from one area to another, the lay of the kingdom.

While Herzog was scouting placements for battle, attack, moving men through woods, Wolf and Cozet were locating animal trails, tall climbable trees, caves to offer shelter.

The three ended on a hill overlooking the only castle gate, entrance, main roads, an area anyone laying siege to the kingdom would be required to take, hold, sacrifice men for.

To think of the enemy as a herd of game a good hunter would attack where they went for water, calmed down, ate, relaxed, full, easy to attack when offered a false sense of protection, most vulnerable.

Stopping at a clearing Herzog had Wolf and Cozet stay back, kicked his stallion Herzog leaned out with a battle axe in hand, a small tree shuddered as the heavy blade cut cleanly though it, leaning out from the other side, legs hooked in the straps Herzog slashed through another tree, then jumped up into the saddle, another tree fell.

Pulling hard the stallion made a quick turn, Herzog popped up, standing on the horses back with feet locked in straps on the saddle, a kick, with hooves pounding the team launched off like a rabbit, a small stiff bow in hand, arrows snapped from the bow into the stumps.

Just before reaching the scouts the stallion made another turn, two large knives came from Herzog's belt, at a full gallop the knives were thrown into the stumps, each hitting with a thud, point first.

Turning back Herzog pulled a net from the horses back, riding at the scouts he snapped it over his head watched it spread out, a quick flick of the wrist, it went right over Wolf and Cozet enveloping them both.

Wolf and Cozet laughed and clapped, a fine display of skill.

Herzog dismounted, stood with Wolf while Cozet disappeared into the forest. Taking a few pinecones Wolf began walking the field, tossing a pine cone in the air, at the zenith of its flight an arrow appeared, grabbed it, the pine cone and arrow tumbled to the ground a foot away.

Walking a few more paces another cone was launched, another arrow, not from the direction of the first, Cozet had moved from Wolf's side to in front of him.

Next Wolf threw a pine cone hard at a tree, just as it struck the tree an arrow passed through it, sticking it to the tree, another arrow then another arrow stuck into the pinecone.

Walking from the woods Cozet bowed to Herzog who was excited by the display.

Wolf walked back to the road, handing Cozet the two remaining cones she climbed on her horse, rode, she was far when the first cone was placed upon a rock.

Wolf's muscles strained under the full arch of the bow, firing a much lighter arrow from a stronger bow allowed for longer range, the arrow now had longer in flight to be susceptible to vagaries of breeze, shadows more easily tricked the eye, moisture could make the string slightly less resilient.

While the string was propelling the arrow down the road the archer caught a glimpse of Herzog's face, concern, worry, eyes closed for an instant, the arrow struck the cone, it looked like a snake taking a mouse, they slithered along the ground kicking up a cloud of dust.

Wolf slowly fired another arrow, the cone was only about five paces before Cozet, the second arrow struck the cone and rolled it up to Cozet's feet.

Herzog was clapping, excited, both great archers, respect earned, skills needed in the coming war.

While Cozet rode back Herzog handed Wolf a sword, not Wolf's weapon of choice, useless to a hunter, Wolf had never even held a sword before.

Herzog showed Wolf how to hold the sword up, with a few mild blows from Herzog, Wolf dropped the heavy blade.

Bow's were fine tools in the forest on game, swords were for killing men in battle.

Picking up the sword Herzog handed it to Cozet, she held the sword, wanted to put it down, Herzog prepared to strike Cozet as he had Wolf, teach her, before Herzog's first swing had even started Cozet tossed the sword straight up in the air.

While Herzog was looking up at the sword Cozet stepped beside him, placed a small blade at his throat, Herzog watched the sword fall onto the ground in a clanging dust cloud.

Wolf laughed, Herzog laughed, even Herzog's stallion stomped his feet on the ground.

To each his own,

To each her own,

Artist or assassin, perhaps an artistic assassin.

Behind the castle walls that night rumors were flying, insane tales, freaky laughter muted in whispers, when the rumors reached King Harrow's ears, even Harrow had to quietly laugh.

Can you imagine, a comedy, Herzog bathed, dressed in good clothing, a guest of Wolf and Cozet for a fine dinner.

Under Harrow's laughter was a daunting question, never had King Harrow been privileged by sharing a meal with Herzog, now a bath, even a real conversation.

For some grotesque is a cloth of power, woven, fine clothing, helping to instill fear before a blow could be struck.

This friendship might destroy Herzog's reputation built on fear, a situation to be monitored when the pressure comes.

Herzog was nothing more than a tool Harrow used, each tool has its purpose, alter the tool and the tools value diminishes to the craftsman.

18

SPIES SONG

"He would move on before all those he befriended were slaughtered"

Manicured supple fingers danced on the strings, vibrations wafted in the air, hung in the breeze, blended with the harmonic pulses of the vocal chords, pushed with slight puffs of air that rose from the lungs.

In mathematical computations that became music to the ear, a smile to the lips, relaxation for the body of anyone close enough.

A smile, slight, not overt, kind, humble, inviting, not a demanding smile, avoiding the look of being so happy that the watcher must be happy also.

This smile was one of confidence, joy, acceptance of ones own skin, environment, place on this earth, a smile that accepted all around, invited them in.

Eyes were kept down, looking to the ground, just in front, never a stare, slow to move, just under the brim of the small hat. they were soft brown eyes, when no one was watching the eyes would dart about, gather information, take in all around with detail, in a blink they went down while he thought about what his eyes had just taken in.

Songs of girls, horses, far off lands, dreams of riches, humble amends, people around him with crosses upon their clothing, carriage, person would illicit songs of praise to God.

The tavern at the dock appeared to be his home, sitting on a seat at one of the tables laid out on the patio the troubadour was given small meals, a few patrons bought him drinks, his room was paid from a heavy purse, he seemed to have nowhere else to be, nowhere to go, first on the patio in the morning, last at night.

Riders came, tired, hungry, longing for rest, feet up, a good steak, many drinks, often purchased a few drinks for the singer who made them feel at ease, lips moved more frequently when lubricated with amber brew, a soft smile, kind eyes, no judgment.

Sailors long on the sea with one crew, tired of hearing the same stories, tired ears from the same lies, conjuring, dreams, fantasies, illusions of sea monsters. Telling the troubadour of ports, strengths, weapons, villains, captains cruel deeds, sailing lore.

Enlisted army men, after hours of training, working, grooming horses, running, dressing in heavy uniforms, marching in organized lines, exhausted, spending a months wages on a day at the tavern, lieutenants could afford two days, officers with better salaries and stealing a bit from each enlisted man below them could spend one or two days a week.

A good meal, some pitchers of amber brew, a couple of songs, stories with the troubadour, all heading up the trail to soft flesh for a few coins, tender words in the ear, boasts to make the dresses think them more powerful than they were, or to impress their own ego, or simply words spoken to impress themselves with their own ability to lie.

It was all in good fun, tender flesh, smiles, whispers of desire, what man would not spout some utterance, show his ability to impress, make the back more willing to arch, legs to spread apart, a groan of appreciation.

Good whores hear, let go, pay no mind, less than impressed, except these lust vessels, wanton flesh pots, legs spread, whores, they paid attention, asked questions, desired to know more, using just as they had been used.

Out the door as best the whores could, writing notes just as the troubadour had taught them, paid them for, simple symbols for boat, ship, men, a down arrow for a small army, an up arrow for a large army, many up arrows for a large well armed army.

The young troubadour named Kendal, with the wonderful voice had spent many a night in soft tender love making, great tipping, teaching note taking, question asking, somehow he had each girl convinced that when they gave him the best story Kendal would take them with him, to a large house, be his wife, make babies, tend a small garden.

Riders would stop at the tavern, eat, drink, whore, in the morning ride early with a small pouch of papers from Kendal, a pouch of songs for Prince Rogan, a desire for a throne on land, requirements of power, knowing movements in King Harrow's kingdom was power if one sought his throne.

On ships that did not land at the docks of the kingdom the riders would sail off into the horizon, chase wind, deliver news, tactics, movements, requirements for taking the throne of King Harrow.

Morning found a new merchant ship in port, broken mast, small repairs, no timber capable to make another mast here, next kingdom down had such things, craftsmen capable of pealing bark, cutting square the beam, matching rigging holes, finding knots of weakness in the wood.

From the dock came a tall man, Kendal's eyes darted around, dropped down, stared at the ground, focused on the dirt.

Redrawing the picture of what Kendal had seen in his mind as he looked away, leather clothing, very odd on a ship, if the clothing got wet it would be too heavy, uncomfortable, boots were large, high, hard to work in, impossible to climb rigging, vane, ego, demanding, beside the tall man a very small oriental woman in silk robes that shimmered in the early morning light.

Standing beside a chair the tall man just looked around, the oriental woman quickly grabbed the chair, pulled it out, head down, she did not look at him, not a servant, a slave, beaten, anything to avoid another beating, eyes that knew the sting of a lash upon her back.

The tall man sat slowly in the chair, the small woman stood behind him for a moment, then dropped to her knees waiting for the next command, a coin was flipped onto the table, she took it, scurrying off into the kitchen.

It was not the man himself that first caught Kendal's attention, in his waistband a small black handle protruded with ivory inset, a small fire stick, or a very fancy dagger handle.

The crew of the ship had not arrived, work was being done on the mast itself, perhaps the captain was with his men, this could be a master, owner, wealthy passenger, military leader in transport.

Odd, if a military leader, who already had these fire sticks, could his army be armed with them as well, would they turn the tide in a war over fast bows, arrows could be hurled a hundred lengths of a fast horse, could these kill at a further range.

The problem was, with his own woman, so early in the morning, it was unlikely he would be walking the trail to soft flesh, it was time for an enticement.

Running a tavern, inn, brothel required establishing rules, one never to be broken rule was that no whore was allowed in the establishment with normal God fearing people, they should only be screwed in private, alone, then dismissed, as it said was acceptable in the book of religious virtues.

A few coins from Kendal changed the rule for this morning, three girls were selected, angry about waking so early, yet willing to perform for money, dressed in clothing that made them look like virgins on their way to convent for an afternoon prayer, sitting at the table with Kendal they talked quietly, offered demure smiles, laughed with white gloved hands covering mouths, yet with breasts pushed up, out, soft pillows of flesh held prisoner trying to escape.

At his table the tall man paid no attention to the oriental woman on her knees beside him, when he drank from the mug the oriental woman would jump up, pour him more, he got angry the first time because the oriental woman blocked his view of the three girls with Kendal.

The tall man's food was eaten without any attention to taste or flavor, part way through Kendal realized that not only was the tall man watching the girls, he was furious at the fact someone so unworthy as a troubadour would have three lovers while all he had was one small oriental, inferior, unworthy of his strength, power, heavy purse.

Watching this show intently Kendal took a cue, one by one he kissed each woman's hand, holding it gently for a long time, on the second hand he could hear the tall man slap down his knife and fork.

The tall man stood quickly nocking over his chair, the oriental woman fell trying to catch it, he looked down at her in disgust, thought about kicking her, then realized that the other women at Kendal's table would reject him if cruel.

The tall man walked to Kendal's table, smiled, announced a name that was long, lyrical, rhymed, when the name ended came the title, important sounding, not one that Kendal had heard before, a boast followed of his power, wealth, armies that followed him, most of all the tall man looked only to the women, never did the tall man look at Kendal, it was as if the troubadour was invisible, unworthy of a glance.

Kendal asked quietly if the tall man would like to sit, partake of a drink, join them, the tall man simply looked down, took a deep breath, looked back to the women, asked that they join him at his table, improve their lot in life from that of a worthless troubadour.

Never seeing the thrust, a small spike, thin blade, pierced under the tall mans coat, up under the lower rib, into the heart sack, then, up into the heart itself. The tall man never moved.

Many things the tall man wanted to do, thrust a sword into the insignificant singer, pull the fire stick, ignite a ball into his face, even kick at him, the tall man's body never moved, muscles unable to react, slowly he slumped forward, caught by Kendal, one girl jumped up, shielded the site.

On the other end of the table a girl leapt up, grabbed the oriental woman who stood with wide eyes, maneuvered her up to Kendal's room, the small silk robes fluttered in the coastal breeze as she ran.

Over his shoulder Kendal carried the body to the waters edge, took the fire stick, a heavy purse, a couple trinkets, a large ring with a huge green carved stone kept in his breast pocket.

The kick was easy, the body fell, importance drained from the tall man just as his blood had.

All men tasted the same to the worms and maggots.

The oriental woman took her change in master without question, the whores fashioned a dress, though she was much smaller than any of them she looked fine in clothing of the new world, the soft skin upon her back had welts of a fresh beating with a hard lash, red marks of a flat hand slapped against her face covered in powder.

When Kendal entered his room the oriental woman fell to her knees, he took her hand, lifted her up, no longer a slave, she clung to his hand, this was not what Kendal wanted, his work required being unnoticeable, a woman would change that, she had to leave, go on, start a new life.

Pointing to himself, he pronounced his name slowly, the oriental woman looked confused, she pulled from her pocket a piece of paper that said only Miko.

Kendal gave each whore an extra coin, requested they bring Miko food later, the girls left, Miko sat, began crying, he cradled her face in his hands, her hands reached up to his, her hands were soft, kind, afraid.

Going to the side room Kendal removed the items from his pockets, examination was needed, new tools, things to pass on, one had a dial, twelve numbers, springs, the other, when held to the ear made a ticking sound, small, in the same rhythm, gold in color they both had purpose.

The second pouch was full of balls, metal, soft, balls just right for the opening at the end of the fire stick, a small chord was also in the canister just like the one in the lever of the fire stick, an igniter, set fire to the charge in the barrel.

When Kendal returned to the room Miko's new dress was upon the chair, perfect soft flesh, she stood beside the bed with eyes cast down, slowly she lifted her face to look at him.

Tears filled her eyes, Miko offered herself to her new master, laying with her was incredible, she offered Kendal pleasure unlike anything he had known before, love was an addictive pleasure to be feared, Kendal felt pure stimulation, power, joy, exhaustion.

When done Miko laid upon the floor beside the bed, unworthy to share the bed with the man that had saved her, Kendal took her hand, pulled her up, laid her beside him, put his arms around her, he slept soundly, she cried.

For her, pleasure was given.

For him pleasure was taken.

For her, his pleasure assured her safety.

For him, her pleasure endangered his life.

The first crewman from the tall man's ship was the captain, large, rough, he traded some very strange black long bows with baskets of arrows to the customs house for a couple bags of flour, a cage of live rabbits, the ships cook quickly grabbed up the needed food, returned to the ship, made a feast for the hard working crew.

In the tavern the ship's captain was asking about the tall man in black with the little oriental woman, language was hard at first, no one even understood the question, in the end it was the singer that was able to convey that no one matching that description had never come to the tavern.

Angry, the captain slammed his hand down on the table, a pitcher of nasty tasting grog quelled his anger, a good plate of meat, beans, bread, did wonders for his disposition, all paid by Kendal.

Language kept the captain from providing much information, something about long voyage, hard seas, damage to the ship, better port needed to finish repairs.

As the captain moved the outline of another fire stick could be seen under his shirt, they must have a stock on the ship, small, easy to use, these would be valuable weapons.

While the captain walked back to his ship Kendal quickly grabbed up a horse, rode hard, up the coast, a long ride, small bay, two boats waited, black, shallow hull, small, black sails, each carried a crew of four to deliver a payload of ten desert killers, skilled with blade, bow, hands.

Death is an art form, never admired by the canvas.

It was in the dark of night when the small boat slid into the docks, sail down, black hull made no wake, pulled up further down the dock unnoticed by the military guards on the point of land, the half awake guard on the rear of the ship heard nothing, the young alert guard on the front of the ship was eagerly trying to stab a rat with his blade.

A lone man, tall, dressed all in black, walking as if he owned the place, a small figure followed him, the master and his oriental slave were returning, very visible, eight more in the water swimming slowly were unnoticed.

When the tall man and his slave walked up the long ramp to the ship the guards came over to welcome their ships master.

Before the guards figured out it was not the master and his slave they were murdered, blades through the chest, no air, no warning, coming from the water was quick death for the ship's crew.

Four sailors came onboard from the black boat, moved quickly, as the sun first broke the ship pulled from the docks, praying for a breeze to push them out over the rolling waves escaping the cove, her new captain maneuvered for the wind.

Sadly the wind was not with them, the ship was being pushed back as the wind came down the coast unable to help.

In desperation the new captain turned the ship down the shallow coastal waters, it was being pushed from the side by the waves back into the rocky shore, the change in course got them the wind at their back, able to build up speed, turning into the waves now the captain was able to weave the boat further out to deeper water, cutting an angle the ship made a run for deep water, freedom of the open sea.

The small black boat skipped from the docks like it had come, the sail up and moving fast she was watched, she was leaving so no one paid attention.

At the tavern, a sailor who had been sent ashore was bewildered when he came to a table for breakfast, found his ship already gone, the plan had been to leave later, on a better tide, in a better wind, the ship would return in a few weeks with a new mast to collect him and the ship's master when he returned.

The exiting of his ship did not curb the sailor's appetite, given a good sum by the ship's captain the tavern owner was ordered to give the sailor room and food, the sailor was to have no hard drink or women, it was of no matter, knowing he was going ashore the sailor had pilfered a few golden coins for his pleasure needs.

On the patio Kendal found the sailor very talkative in a language they both understood, two months working down the coast, around the worst sea they had ever seen, high waves coming from all directions, many experienced sailors were ill, forced from shore they raced across an ocean that was calm as a plowed field.

A strange land found, trade for silks, fire sticks, powder, balls, the ships master was given a small princess he treated like a slave, he beat the men on the voyage down, on the way back the master beat the small woman.

The sailor was not able to say where they had come from, he had been in port drinking when offered passage on the ship, accepted, found himself working for a mean captain, beaten by a cruel master.

All sailors bore the stripes of the master's lash upon their back.

Out in deep water, on the ship, a chain was tied to each body's neck, all dumped overboard, before the last body hit the water fins of the water dragons could be seen circling, blood churned from the water, the feast invited new guests.

After the ship had passed a single body popped up, the captain's remains drifted on the tides, rolling in the waves, small fish picked at the exposed flesh, feet, face, hands were picked clean, eyes pulled from sockets.

Rolling on the high tide the body washed up onto a small bit of rocks just below the guardhouse at the docks.

Taken up for burial the body was stripped of items in the pockets, word spread quickly of the body around the commons house, tavern, whores, everyone had a theory, story or lie to tell.

Traders in the commons house quickly identified the body as the captain from his clothing, Kendal and the sailor also identified the body from his general look.

Sailors beaten by a bad captain offered blessings to the devil, for he was certain God would have nothing to do with the captain's afterlife.

Mutiny, his crew must have rebelled, tossed him overboard, the solution was simple.

Agreeing, Kendal smiled to himself, thanked God the plan worked.

The sailor stayed on for another full moon, coins ran out, he accepted passage on another ship, many times he passed the singers wife in the hall, dressed in large petty coats, hoops, hair up, a veil.

On the day the sailor left he gave Kendal's hand a hearty shake, told Kendal to treat Miko well, he pointed out that Miko was a good woman that should be treated with respect. Both smiled, the sailor had known all along, kept quite, a good man.

Spies sing sweet songs, love, valor, smiles to hold your heart.

Kendal would move on before the war started.

He would move on before all those he befriended were slaughtered.

It was a sad part of the song spies sang.

19

BITTER FRUIT

"She came to vilify—she left the villain"

Upon King Harrow's lips the taste of treachery, the bitterest fruit of all, soured the mood of the court.

One truth was the most frustrating, those who had done wrong did not deny it, they instead would look Harrow right in the eye, bold, no shame, explain in calm fixed words why they had done the most immoral, evil, nasty, disgusting things.

This gray gloomy day there were no rumors easily avoided, a disgusting act, a family matter, lords with outlying estates were often left to deal with on their own, the court, King Harrow, were best focused on issues of the entire kingdom.

Bustling through the court was a huge woman with unkempt strands of hair hanging down over her puffy white face, her clothing was amazing, the best red velvet, embroidery of gold, blues, greens with shimmering stones, yet the woman was as unkempt as a fish monger.

When she spoke it was clear, the wife of a lord, chief advisor, a family above reproach with an impeccable record of service, yet here she was storming down the center hall of the court with a small blond girl wearing only tattered rags in tow.

Screams, shrill as a demons howl came from the woman's huge red face, lips emoting anger, pain, terror, the normal assemblage of those with business before King Harrow, advisors, lords, knights, all spread before her as waves separated by the bow of a strong ship.

At the feet of King Harrow the young girl was forced to her knees, soft blue eyes, pink rosy cheeks, white skin as if chiseled from pure marble, it was hard to comprehend the screeching, something about the huge woman's husband giving the child drink, taking the drunken child to bed, adultery, evil, cruel, casting aside his wife, duty, honor.

Words were comprehended at some level, more immediate were the young girl's tears, eyes that told of pain, misunderstanding, seeking compassion, words from the shrieking demon could not outweigh the image of pain on this young innocent girls face.

Whispers in court are often the most terrifying part of procedure, words from King Harrow that were so powerful they must be kept between ones lips, another's ear, for to have the words spoken out loud might cause panic, fear enough to grip the soul, words that could rip the heart from ones chest beating.

When King Harrow's officer of the court heard the whispered words the officer immediately jumped from the king's side, grabbed the young girl's hand, off they went down the hall.

King Harrow's spoken words were strong, clear, the lady was to return to her home, fix her appearance, be a good wife for her husband, return to this court only when she represented her station in society.

She came to vilify—she left the villain

Expressing anger to King Harrow was unwise, stupid, could even get you a quick trip to the axe in the square.

Asa Foley

The anger on the woman's face quickly vanished, she knelt, bowed her head, turned, walked out much as she had come, parting the onlookers in her path with grim determination, resolute strides, bold resolve.

Again whispers, King Harrow's officer had returned, all looked at the exchange, kneeling down by Harrow's side, the powerful words caused the king to rise, stride off in a slow steady pace.

King Harrow's stride displayed his anger, frustration, bridled fury, only a fool would bring business before this king on this day. A decision was to be made, powerful decision, something Harrow would rather have avoided.

In a side room with the books, scrolls, tablets, sat the lord whose wife had just thrown the young girl at Harrow's feet, begging a private audience was bad, it meant that confessions were coming, words that would make this entire mess even worse.

A wise king learns that the most powerful words are often the ones not spoken, let the blank void fill the air with tension, the other party will feel compelled to fill in with a confession, the truth, never overt, lies, simply the reality as they see it in the twisted confusion of their own reality.

Vibrating off the walls, silence had done its work, the confession was most disturbing, the girl had been the daughter of servants, the lord tired, the girl provided him with drink at dinner, she talked softly, laughing, touching, interested in his power as a man, held his hand, he gave her drink, when she passed out he took her to his chambers.

It was here that the lord's voice changed, the first part was as if his right, not a confession, a statement of facts, the next part was spoken with regrets, a need for understanding, seeking compassion.

The lord's actions had been vial, that of an animal, the girl had come from her stupor, her fear ignited a frenzied carnal desire, the lord tried to describe in detail how he had demanded from her flesh more than sexual pleasure, this was demonic destruction of his soul, this temptress confiscated what was good in him, her tears were fertile ground for desires of the flesh a civilized man must deny himself.

Feeling compassion, remembering the condition of the lord's wife, understanding a mans needs, knowing his own demanding desires King

Harrow was about to have the lord make payment to the girl, her family, be done with it.

Sadly the lord went on, the girl was a witch, she had done this to him, he was not at fault, she commanded him, made him, forced him with her body, eyes, lips to desire her such as was not human, not within him before her spells had driven him to do this.

Silence filled the room, hung in the air, words demanding her death by painful bloody ways, in the square, so all could see, the witch punished for what she had done to him.

The lord's eyes filled with red hatred, revenge, savage, brutal, twisted.

Following what was being said King Harrow filled in, hang her by her hands, flesh bare, white, gleaming in the sun, the lash of nine strands with knots tied, soaked in lemon juice would lay upon her, rip her flesh, blood would stream down.

Jumping to his feet the lord was in a tantrum, the lash would be laid across her breasts, belly, her soft rosy cheeks would be cut, fifty, no, a hundred lashes, her limp body, blood streaming down, the blond hair matted in red blood.

While the lord was relishing the idea of the young girl's bare bleeding body being cut down, laid upon a table, opened at the belly, Harrow whispered in the ear of the officer of the court.

Praying was important to cleanse the soul, kneeling down King Harrow asked the lord to join him in deep conversations with the master of all before the taking of the witch to the square for her just, righteous, dispatch from this world, this would be done so good moral men could live in pure harmony with God.

Within a few minutes the two men rose, king and lord, walked to the square, King Harrow asked the lord to join him up on the elevated area where the headsmen did his job to more closely watch the witch be beaten with the lash.

King Harrow said how they would be able to smell the vial stench of the witches blood, taste the spray of her fluids, see the tears, demon tears, seeking sympathy, righteous men would withstand her torment.

It was a moment before the lord realized the witch was not coming, Harrow's hand on one shoulder, the headsman's hand on the lord's other, it did not take much pressure for lord to kneel down, the lord understood on some level unable to comprehend fully what was about to happen.

Head down, the lord looked to the ground, the axe lightly touched the back of his neck, in response he lifted his head slightly, then it was gone.

The crowd cheered, the mass of sweaty humanity enjoyed the show, somehow it always seemed the cheers were more for those of higher rank, perhaps the loudest cheer would be for the day King Harrow knelt down here under his own axe.

More pressing matters, the lord's estate must be given to another to run, the nasty looking wife must be dealt with, in chambers behind the throne a meeting of high officers was held, who to best take the estate, be made powerful, loyal, clever yet dogged.

Many names were tossed out, trusted leaders, those to whom debts were owed, favors were a tool, used by a craftsman they could easily build a more powerful kingdom, used carelessly they could begin unraveling the fabric which bound them all.

It was in the end a lowly army officer who was given the lord's lands to run, the decision was based on his ability to lead men, develop a strong army to defend outside the walls of the castle.

When told of his new position the officer was overcome, he would not only be given an estate, lands, servants, he was to collect taxes, soon he would be given a lady in waiting as his own.

Kneeling before the king, the new lord was grateful, humble, the king hoped all the humility, loyalty, honesty would remain, power had a way of destroying the very things that caused a man to be selected in the first place.

Sewing the seeds of discontent, others in his court who felt themselves more disserving of these lands, this power, were frustrated to see them given to an officer so young, untested. Yet the remembrance of the lord kneeling down, the kings hand on his shoulder, an axe blade, blood running down over the block, none questioned the decision in spoken words, thoughts never force the king to kill you.

That night King Harrow retired to his chamber, opened the rear door, walked the hall behind the ladies in waiting's rooms, the last room, Jaclyn, one of King Harrow's favorites, a little older, tall, straight, piercing eyes, focused on pleasing a king who had worked hard, drink, food, warm water, soft feather bed, seductions of the flesh were her specialty.

This night a small blond girl stood beside Jaclyn, hair perfumed, cleaned, scrubbed by maids, a girl in training.

When Harrow approached them the girl fell to her knees, tears streamed down from the blue eyes over red cheeks. Harrow took the girl's hand, kissed it gently, she kissed the beard of the man that saved her life.

King Harrow held the porcelain white hand of the young girl while he sat upon the bed, she stood looking down at him, her soft eyes filled with tears, intoxicating drops of fear streamed over her cheeks, down to the corner of her pink lips, just enough to moisten them.

King Harrow drank wine while Jaclyn unhooked the small robe from the girl's shoulders, it fell to the floor, blue, red, green, soft undergarments were taken off slowly.

Whispers from Jaclyn, the young girl got onto the bed, pulled Harrow to her, trembling flesh, pure, young, hungry for his power, security, wealth, terrified of what he might do to her.

While Jaclyn watched, Harrow was a tender lover, laughing, caressing, holding, soft words of encouragement to a lover so young, tender, the moment was quite sweet.

As Jaclyn leaned over, instructions whispered, gentle caresses to show, instruct, lead, the young lady was learning.

Without warning, just as the lord had described, Harrow was no longer tender, pulling at the girls tender limbs, strong hands grabbing flesh, Harrow exhausted his passion.

In that instant King Harrow became an animal, the girl did not cry, she begged for more, twisting, placing her breasts in his mouth, her eyes wide, she hungered for the pain he caused, she hungered for his pleasure, her desire was satiated by this orgy of raw animal lust.

When finished with her King Harrow looked up and down the small frail white flesh, his hand marks were visible, red now, black in the morning, a painting, a tapestry, an abomination of flesh, fear, a work of art in pain, tears, regret.

Jaclyn gave Harrow more wine, the girl was given glass of water, Harrow rose, standing beside Jaclyn, they watched as the poison in the water took effect, tender marble white flesh trembled, eyes fluttered, sadness overcame the face, the poor child went limp.

Summoned by a bell from a tug on the rope two large men carried the girl away wrapped in sheets, maids put new covers on the bed.

The lord had killed her, it was Harrow that finished the job, another bath, King Harrow made love to Jaclyn like a king, kisses, accepting the pleasure offered, admiring her skill.

During the night Jaclyn asked Harrow if he would ever do that to her.

Harrow offered to get Jaclyn a glass of water, if that was what she wanted, she laughed, some day she wanted him to take her, out of control with lust, demanding, ripping, tearing, to lay exhausted on top of her used body, giving herself to him in a way he would never forget.

Yes, someday, before Harrow married her off to another, he would make Jaclyn his slave whore for one night.

Jaclyn was not afraid, she lusted to be so used until the man she loved had nothing left to give.

Within the terrible weight of power comes a dark truth sequestered away in the hidden reaches of those in royal robes, all were human.

Each level of power required a higher level of appearance that power was wielded by those who were not human.

Flesh was the downfall of many, rumors of lust were everywhere, out of control carnal lust would spill over to a loss of control when command was needed.

King Harrow wanted the young girl to live, her death was a great loss, hours or days he would have liked to enjoy the animal desires quenched in the loins of a new flower sprung of desire, as king, Harrow was not allowed.

Her willing flesh was not a pleasure he would deny himself this once, rumors were not a price he was willing to pay.

Would Jaclyn, one of Harrow's favorites, find some day that in her bed he was an out of control animal, yes, that was why Harrow kept Jaclyn here, the lust, desire, hunger was to release that animal inside of himself, it was not controllable, it would come again, his father had slave girls, no one missed them when gone, they told their stories to the unmarked graves they occupied.

When the animal inside of Harrow was done with Jaclyn he would give her a glass of wine, without question she would drink it, there was no marriage to a lord, her life would be forfeit for the secret passion of the king, she knew it, he knew it, the lie was a more palatable answer for now.

Morning light found a tear on Jaclyn's cheek, she desired to give herself to her king just as the girl had done, when finished, there would be nothing left of Jaclyn, the greater the desire, the greater the fear, the more it consumed her.

20

CAPTAIN LOVE

*"Damn her, witch, spells, demon, the love of a woman
is the most addictive drug of all."*

Kingdoms were large intricate machines that needed constant maintenance to keep working smoothly, many in the kingdom saw themselves as powerful, necessary, even divine in the building of a well run kingdom.

Reality was quite different, it was the ones that accepted their work, function, mission as just what it was, janitors, workers, jesters, cogs in the machine, oil applied cured the squeaks, of course a little adjustment came with a twist from a large tool, here, there, the proper pressure at the right point.

When reason, logic, pressure were not enough someone had to pull out a hammer, beating on some parts kept all the parts working correctly.

The thick, ugly, short, captain of the guard, Herzog, had no illusions of himself, he was the repairman of last resort,

Sending Herzog to a village was a statement that things were not right.

Sending Herzog meant things were going to get fixed.

Sending Herzog foretold of change or death.

Limited options obtained the most permanent results.

Often just Herzog riding alone into a village brought calm order, people willing to discuss, converse, talk long into the night, the option of having Herzog reach for an axe on his belt was what legends were made of.

Truth is an odd illusion mixed in the fog of legends.

In his youth Herzog was lost, wondered into a village that had been hit by a pack of robbers, while eating, drinking, hearing tales of the evil men in the hills, sadly for the robbers they chose to attack.

It was six, eight, twenty, depending on who told the story, tale, fable, the number did seem to get bigger over the years.

The robbers moved into the village as they had done a few times before, running, half clothed, half starved, at first they had been scared, driven by hunger, after a few times, little resistance, the robbers were bolder.

One truth would never be forgotten about that night, a robber running close to Herzog's horse started the beast, it jumped clawing the air, a silver axe from Herzog's belt sailed over the fire like an avenging demon, twenty lengths of a horse the axe flew, the blade cleaved the mans head in two, right down the middle.

Looking at the down man, the other robbers decided, unwisely, to attack the little freak of nature, it is possible that in the dark they could not see Herzog's strong arms, sword, axe, blade on his belt.

If someone had asked, no one ever dared, Herzog, alone, outnumbered was trying to get to his horse, get out, leave a fight where he was outnumbered.

The robbers just happen to be between Herzog and his horse, blocking freedom was the death sentence, not some act of vengeance or justice.

First to attack Herzog was the man that had retrieved the axe from his dead comrades head, seeing the running figure in the night the robber swung with all his might, the heavy axe blade was more than he could handle, it pulled him around, from behind Herzog simply stabbed him.

Just then a second man poked Herzog with a sharp stick, the first blow with the sword broke the stick, swinging back the blade hit the robbers neck, broken, like a chicken for the pot the robber wobbled into the fire creating a cascade of sparks that in legend had grown to a lighting storm.

Other robbers ran in together, unorganized, no weapons, just farm tools, weak from hunger, all died.

The only one alive not cheering was Herzog, having never killed before the memories of that night haunted him every day of his life.

Another reality came to light that night, the village elder had tried to find a woman to please, massage, comfort their savior, hopes that if treated well he would return, protect them again.

No woman was willing to offer their savior proper comfort, back then Herzog was clean shaven, deformed, well dressed, well spoken, hoped to have a woman of his own some day.

Alone on his cot that night Herzog realized that he would be alone all of his life, the sadness of killing, the crushing sadness of not being worthy of any woman, he decided that night, if they could shun him, then he would live without their approval.

When the docks were built by King Philip to dispatch Prince Rogan, Herzog, as captain of the guard, was instrumental in getting workers to work, gathering taxes, following King Philip's orders.

During the construction Herzog also secretly regretted Philip's decision to make a port, open the kingdom to attack, no trade was needed, everyone was fed, the treasury room had enough gold, there was no good to come from these docks Herzog helped build.

It was Herzog who had insisted on the first guardhouse, fast horses to warn the kingdom, he also had constructed on the second floor his sleeping chamber, offices, storeroom, on the third floor was a lookout to the ocean.

While the first guard quarters were under construction Herzog realized the vulnerable position left open, the first guardhouse could stop any intruder with warning, if a ship slipped in under notice of the night guard enough men could overpower the first sentries.

The second guardhouse was constructed as a block at the end of the only trail from the docks, these guards were spread out along two long walls, like wings of a divine angle, Herzog called them jaws, the center of the guardhouse had every new weapon in ample supply to chew invaders into small pieces.

Stones jutted from the walls just the height of two men off the ground, flaming oil poured from the top would hit the stones, cascading like a waterfall of flame over the attackers.

In the many holes in the walls arrows were set in bows that were mounted into the walls, when attackers came they could be pulled back, cocked, held ready to fire, a single man could pull one rope, each tug would fire twenty arrows, more than two hundred arrows were ready to seek flesh.

Herzog had his only one true friend, Gaston, assigned as captain of the customs house, both had served the kingdom a long time, King Harrow, King Philip, and even King George before them.

Herzog and Gaston also shared one belief, training men to do things perfectly meant in the heat of battle they would do them correctly.

Many a captain's head ended a battle on the end of a pike when he had not properly trained his men.

Too often Herzog and Gaston had seen farmers made into soldiers, in some battles they had seen farmers fight with pitchforks, hoes, throwing clods of dirt.

Brave, always dead, a waste.

The dock met land at a central point before the road went to the kingdom. Covering that road was the customs house, goods had to go through the customs house to get to a ship or be taken from a ship.

The customs house had a unique feature designed by Gaston, the second floor, used for storage, was lifted or lowered by large winches on either side of the door exiting to the kingdom, pulling it up took twelve strong men, by pulling one hidden lever the entire thing would come crashing down crushing all within the customs house, this also served as a method of blocking the door for anyone attacking.

The second floor design had to be modified because the first attempt would require the man pulling the lever to be under the second floor when it came down, crushed by the second floor dropping on him, in practice it might make one hesitant to pull a lever that would also kill him. A small concave was placed in the wall for a man to hide in while pulling the lever, then he could escape when the carnage was done.

A smart innkeeper saw opportunity and while the docks were being built they built a tavern with rooms upstairs. Down a trail behind the tavern cabins were built for working women to ply their trade.

After the tavern, inn and brothel were built Herzog came to visit the docks, a surprise inspection, chance to relax, unwind, play some games of chance with Gaston.

Greetings were quick between the two old friends, they adjourned to the tavern, a cow had been hung for curing a few days before, ripe, tender, ready, after large steaks, good wine, Herzog winning a few coins, Gaston paid for them both to have a woman up the trail.

Protests from Herzog, objections were overcome, they walked up the trail for pleasure.

Herzog's real reason for not wanting to go was not wanting to be rejected again, turned away, even his heavy purse could not make him desirable to these women.

Girls grabbed at Gaston, none would even look Herzog in the eye, a young red head caught Gaston's eye, she took his hand, they disappeared into a cabin.

Alone, Herzog was left just looking around, the girls went into the cabins, closed the doors, walked away.

Herzog turned to walk back to the tavern, trying to humor himself, they were just sacred of how big his manhood must be, afraid of a real man.

From one of the last cabins a short blond woman ran down the path, she stopped, took Herzog's hand, she was plump, a very beautiful face, her body was like his, thick, strong, she smiled.

Herzog did not know what to do at first, he wanted to tell her it was alright, he could just go, she did not have to degrade herself like that.

Samantha was her name, no words spoken, he stood without moving while she undressed him, this was not normal, all the other girls just laid down spread their legs, pulled up the dress, men drop their pants, have at it.

With a bucket and cloth Samantha washed Herzog, he objected a little, she did not stop, she laid him on the bed, slowly she undressed.

It was the most incredible thing Herzog had ever seen, not her body, the way she looked at him, real desire, naked, Samantha laid beside him, she stroked his beard, kissed his hairy body, then climbed on top of him.

As the shudder went through Herzog, Samantha smiled, she held him, she wanted him.

That night Samantha fell asleep with her head on Herzog's shoulder, her first true sleep in a long time, safe, protected, happy.

Herzog slept little, hating the tenderness, angry that he had fallen for her prank, pretending to want him, an actress, a sorceress, furious at himself for enjoying the touch of her flesh, she must have been drunk, sober in the morning she would see him, scream, run in terror.

Samantha's breath on Herzog's skin was a wonderful feeling, a smile while sleeping cannot be an act.

Part of Herzog wanted to jump up, grab his armor, run, find a fast steed, far, far from here. He closed his eyes, slept a while longer, afraid if he moved she would awake, the feeling would end.

Herzog awoke to Samantha kissing him, rubbing her hands on his body, she aroused him, kissed his forehead, nose, cheek, her hair cascaded down on his face as she kissed his lips.

Herzog's hands moved over Samantha's body, feeling each curve, small breasts, stocky body, wonderful to the touch.

Samantha laid on her back, pulled him on top of her, Herzog did not want to hurt her, he relaxed, let it happen.

Worst of all Samantha was looking at him, not closing her eyes, pretending he was someone pretty, she looked at him.

When Herzog was done, Samantha wrapped her legs around his, her arms around him, held him close.

Herzog never said a word, dressed, walked out the door.

Samantha cried soft little tears whenever she thought of Herzog, how it felt to be safe, warm, cared for, she was a prostitute, he was a customer, this was business.

On the trail back to the kingdom Herzog prepared for a fight, there were no threats, he just wanted a fight, to beat something, to kill something, to explode in rage at something.

Even now Samantha would be spreading her legs for any guy with a coin, kissing other men, he was just one of many, a jerk, feelings, damn feelings, he was worse than just a customer, she had pretended to like him, care for him, kiss him, fall asleep next to him.

Pulling the horses head to the right Herzog charged off into a small clearing, trees were brutalized with axes, arrows, swords, his horse charged at each tree with a quick kick in the side, pulling the reigns hard they would change direction.

The partnership of horse and rider was gone, this was an angry master to be obeyed.

Back on the trail Herzog rode slowly, plodding along, visions Samantha laying on her back, a line of men, coins in hand, her smile, her kissing their lips, she was pulling at them, one after another, putting on her act, making all the men feel wanted, he was not going to fall for her game.

Through all of that anger, the feeling of soft breath on his chest, her smile while sleeping, waking to her kisses, soft touch.

Damn her, witch, spells, demon, the love of a woman is the most addictive drug of all.

Herzog knew in time, with hard work, discipline, some amber brew, he would forget Samantha, put the entire night out of his head.

Herzog had a plan, a month, thirty days of getting up before dawn, jumping from bed so that he would not lay there pondering thoughts of her.

Herzog drove the castle guard crazy with training, some said he was possessed, some said he was just insane, every man was exhausted.

Nights Herzog would stay up late inspecting weapons, sharpening those that did not meet inspection, designing new saddles, cleaning equipment.

In the darkness Herzog also drank, without being drunk he would not go to sleep quickly enough, sometimes a damn tear would break from his eye, slide down his face, absorbed into his beard.

It was not just Samantha, it was all women, destroying men, ruining strong men, changing good men, how dare that prostitute do this to him.

Just a damn whore, worthless trash, screwing other men while he lay alone, enjoying the hands placed on her by soft men that smelled good, wanting their smooth silken bodies, inside of her, taking their pleasure for a purse of coins.

It was just before sleep, when the anger and rage could not be maintained, in those moments Herzog would remember Samantha bathing him, sleeping with her flesh against his, her kiss in the morning, first his forehead, then his nose, then his lips, damn whore.

Herzog's men were most pleasantly surprised when he left to inspect the guardhouses at the docks.

Instead of training, Herzog's men had a party for his departure, a week or more of rest.

One of the men who watched Herzog ride off told him to offer greetings to Gaston, Herzog would say nothing to that evil piece of trash, then kicked his horse harder than any had ever seen him do before, he was off.

Herzog was not going to Samantha, he was not going to see Samantha, Samantha was out of his mind, he would not drink in the tavern, no steak, the meat could not be fine enough to go through that again, wine at that tavern could destroy your mind.

There was little plodding or rest on this trip, heels were kicked into sides when the pace was not fast enough, worst of all the constant muttering, talking, shouting, while the words made no sense to the stallion, the anger was well understood.

Just a day before Herzog left for the docks, late at night, a large sailor, drunk, demanding, had taken Samantha, grabbed at her face, demanded a kiss, she slapped him, he hit her hard on the cheek, forced her face down, as large hands wrapped around her throat, she passed out.

In the morning the other girls heard Samantha crying, cleaning her up they all told stories of bad things that had been done to them.

All Samantha could think of was the one night she had slept so soundly, safe, cared for, desired, she cried not for what had been done to her, she had been sold by her father to be a whore, this was her life, she wanted more.

It was early evening when Herzog entered the commons house, a warm greeting from Gaston was met with a curse, walking up to his old friend Herzog punched Gaston once, dropped him to the ground, another curse, Herzog stormed out.

Herzog walked into the tavern where army men saluted him, he did not salute back.

Up the trail Herzog went to the last cabin, forcing open the door, all he could see was a man on top of a woman pounding away, throwing the man to the floor he could see it was not Samantha.

The man jumped to his feet, doubled up his fist, that was as far as he got before a heavy right hand broke his nose.

Running outside the whores were coming to see what was going on, then Herzog saw Samantha, face bruised, eye swollen shut, was it a lie, did Samantha lie to him, she fell on her knees, tears ran down her face, no,

Samantha protested, no, she wanted him, wanted to care for him, wanted him to care for her.

Herzog grabbed Samantha by the wrist so hard it hurt, half walking, half dragging, pulled her to the tavern.

Herzog said he was taking Samantha, the tavern owner protested.

The tavern owner had paid for Samantha and wanted his money back, his protest ended at the point of a sword, a deal was struck, the tavern owner would be happy Samantha was gone, in exchange Herzog would not make this place off limits to his men.

The tavern owner started to protest again, a slight pressure on the blade allowed him to see the wisdom of the situation.

Dragging Samantha up to Herzog's rooms in the guardhouse caused muffled statements from the guards, quickly quieted by a single look from dark eyes under furrowed brow, a hand resting on the notorious axe in his belt.

Now Herzog was furious, angry, betrayed by himself, letting his emotions run wild like this, being made a laughing stock by a whore, his men would laugh at him now, they would no longer fear him, he was out of control.

Samantha grabbed Herzog, forced him into a chair, she knelt in front of him, her head bowed, she swore to serve him, care for him, love him, all the days of her life, tears streamed down, she looked him in the eyes, he fought back tears, strong men do not cry.

She wanted him.

Three disgusting little words, sold with tears, trembling lips.

A month of anger, killed with little words.

Herzog tried to get angry again, he could not look in Samantha's eyes and scream whore, or other words meant to degrade, hurt, he had no power, no plan, a wise warrior knows when the battle is lost.

Samantha went beside his bed, lowered her dress, it fell easily on the floor, Herzog stood while she undressed him, they lay upon the bed, entwined, made love, she cried until they went to sleep, both slept soundly.

Gaston arrived at the guardhouse, he was just reaching up to knock on Herzog's door when two army officers tackled him, held him down, questioned his sanity, wondered why he wanted to have his head split open by an axe.

A man with a woman is no longer your friend.

When Gaston heard which woman Herzog was with he laughed loudly, sometimes he deserved to be punched. Of course, he hoped later to be the best man.

21

SIMPLE BATTLE

"Was the enemy commander less competent than our incompetent commander."

Conscription into the army was simple, army officers rode by the field you were tending, pointed, you followed, now you were the front line in King Harrow's army, a great honor, for the remaining hour of your life.

Valdez was just getting ready to go home for dinner when conscripted for a battle the next morning, his army won that one, now he was getting ready to fight in his second battle.

Jostling, pushing, shoving, the feel of a lance tip just touching Valdez's back, slight pokes, irritating, aggravating, infuriating, he wanted to push back, push forward, find space.

Lines were important, each person with a job, just in front were the peasants, collected from farms in the surrounding valleys, they were the first wave, to soften the other army, show of strength by numbers.

Peasants had a place, most with sharpened sticks, rocks, no shield, a pitchfork, all they really became were bodies to trip over when the real fighting started.

Bloody little piles of rags that could catch a foot, cause a fall, get you killed.

The second line were the first real fighters, hardened by one or two battles, with a pike, a real iron tip on the end of their stick, small shield, cast sword, not the nice forged swords used by the officers, these were dull, heavy, often broke when hitting a better blade.

Third line were the real professional military men, veterans of ten or more battles, they had long pikes to keep pushing the first two lines forward into the weapons of the enemy, kill any of their own men that fell back, tried to run, were just not fast enough.

Motivation came from an easier death at the hands of the enemy, than your own army pushing you forward. A few crazy conscripts in the front lines thought they would be victorious, win the battle, delusional fools.

The cavalry line followed the third line, these were the baton on the conductors hand, commanding an orchestra to play faster, slower, louder, softer, hiss thunder, spit fire, drown an enemy's fear in an ear-shattering roar.

Far behind, on a slight rise, with enough room to turn, run, hide if the battle went badly were the officers, cowards of rank, idiots with a cause they were willing to get others killed for.

Army phalanx was a machine, intricate parts, motivated, driven, combined into a united will of one unqualified commander to do the impossible, or get everybody killed trying.

Was the enemy commander less competent than our incompetent commander?

Were the other peasants more afraid than our peasants, all of whom understood today they would die?

Would someone question, just one, that their God was better than the enemies God.

Would anyone question if there was a God, why would he allow this.

It started.

Shoving, bumping, small jabs from behind, the middle was the worst place to be, yet here Valdez was, most likely to kill, most likely to be killed.

The peasants were very slow this morning, no running, good formation, tight wall to protect the second row.

Calvary pushed harder in the middle, the general wanted a wedge, the center of the line was now ahead, forward, first to contact the strong enemy line.

Pokes from behind were hard, it hurt, moving more quickly put Valdez in with the peasants, out of formation, it did not matter, from this point death was assured.

From the front or back, the direction of the blow that took his life did not matter.

Screams came down the line, a roar of anger as the first lines connected, the peasants fell quickly, Valdez was alone, the third line had slowed, watching the carnage, afraid.

Hearts were pounding now, each throbbing pulse fired huge bursts of energy into tense muscles, eyes were wide, wild, penetrating, feet moved over ground, blood, bodies.

Valdez arched his back, he thrust forward, striking a shield hard.

Down the pike glanced, into an enemy foot, screaming, pain, like a fish on the line fighting for life, the pike was alive with the vibration from the wounded man.

Pulling hard, the pike would not free from the ground, Valdez grabbed at the sword in his scabbard just as an enemy pike cut at his arm, pain fired through the arm then radiated out through his body.

Valdez tugging at his sword, wild now, in the crowd he could not pull it free from the scabbard.

Another gouge into Valdez's flesh, this from behind, a peasant had gained his feet, blood over the peasants eyes, thrusting wildly, struck Valdez in the back of the leg.

Valdez fell forward, landing on a wounded man, grabbing at the wounded man's sword, Valdez finally got control of the blade, thrust up, to the side, blood sprayed, a vial stench filled the air, no scream, lungs destroyed.

Death, a personal private moment, in the thundering theater of carnage.

Swinging the stolen sword back to the other side the blade ripped into the flesh behind the knee of an enemy, severed the knee just before the man could stick a pike in Valdez's back, his enemy fell, another stab with the sword, another enemy dead.

Valdez was insane with the smell of blood, fear of death, hatred of those trying to kill him, blood pumping in huge masses of power, anger, violence, attacking anything that moved.

Pikes were now thrust at Valdez by the enemy's third line, many at once, just beyond the third line, angry, afraid horses stomped the earth, whinnied, tried to protect themselves.

It was only one pike, from the side, quick, sharp, just under Valdez's ribs, he could feel a sharp blast of pain, then nothing, a numb feeling, quickly very cold, the taste of blood in his mouth, confusion, anger, sounds of the battle went quiet, all the vision of butchery went into slow motion.

Looking at the long stick protruding from his side made no sense, it should not be there, trying to swing the blade again, it was a thought, his arm did not move.

Another pike came over the top of Valdez's shield, he watched it, could see the forge marks on the tip, it disappeared into his chest.

On a hill, far from the battle, officers, drinks in hand, sitting on fine white horses, pondered the effectiveness of the wedge, it had done well, they were winning, look how they had broken the enemy line.

Though asleep with a lady in waiting that morning King Harrow accepted praise for having won the battle.

Officers patted themselves on the back for beating the enemy.

The dead were happy to have served King Harrow, their country, their God with honor.

At least that was what the families were told.

A memorial to honor the dead served two important functions, Harrow's, officers, commanders, advisers could pat themselves on the back in public for a job well done, hard fought.

The second reason was that many a lad from the family, a brother lost, hearing stirring speeches of the glory of war, glory of death in service to the king, would sign up to fight in the place their brother that had just given his life.

The glory of war, was not really very glorious when being fought.

Beside a small creek, deep green grass dotted with lavender, golden wild flowers, two women knelt, hands clasp together, no body to burry, no last view of Valdez's gentle face, kind eyes, strong limbs, the women were empty, hollow from loss, pain, tears.

Each woman tossed a bundle of flowers into the stream, watched it drift away.

The black dresses would be washed, stored, used again, again, again.

If there was honor in being a warrior, there was little in being the mother of a warrior.

Sixteen years he was his mother's child, for only one year a warrior for the king.

All glory unto you God, for men know not what they do.

22

LONG SAND

"Fear of death becomes irrational choices, irrational choices become a fear of death."

Zorn left his homeland when it was about to be attacked, the frustration hurt him deeply, he rode up the coast looking for his ship, it took a red bead to find it on a shore north of the kingdom.

He would return, visit his hamlet, mother, father, home, all someday, not today.

Message delivered, job done, no one paid attention, it seemed Zorn was not accomplishing any of his dreams.

Dracon was fighting while Zorn was an unappreciated errand boy.

Life in need of accomplishment, purpose, desire to serve, all became nothing when it fell on deaf ears.

The wander lust of the sea became days, nights, playing with numbered cubes, losing money made the crew very happy, productive.

A stallion offers changing views, riders choice, up a hill, through a valley, along a ridge, interaction with others, the sea is a demanding mistress, she flogs you with monotony, just when your dreams have died, she tries to kill you with a storm.

The ship's crew, while on the coast waiting for Zorn, had benefited from a couple good days hunting, stealing, pilfering, commandeering, a larder full of succulent meats, cheese, wine, even two small casks of hard amber liquid that was sweet on the lips, hard on the head, stolen from a church.

For days wind did not catch canvas, progress was slow, drinking was the only option, waiting for attack, a coming army, relaxing more each day, losing discipline.

In frustration questions were asked, they were simple questions, why was the ship deliberately going slow, the answer was just as simple, Dracon told them to keep the new young owner of the ship safe.

A change in orders from the ship's new master, get back to the port city, a slight change, the sails went taught, the ship was tacking with the wind, alive with energy.

On one run, as they headed in the direction of the coast, screams came from the mast lookout to turn fast, many sails, just dots on the ocean, at least a hundred, the largest flotilla they had ever seen, moving together up the coast.

This finally got the ship captain's attention, he found more canvas, got more movement, the ship was cutting through the water, spray from the bow announced the progress.

It was a day before the captain relaxed, began normal sail techniques, turned back to the coast, long hours of sitting on deck with bows, waiting for attack, trying to catch the wind, outrun the unseen enemies, demons in the darkness.

Exhausted, frightened, wary, the first known point of land came into view, it would be a few hours now to the city, port, warm beds, good meals, soft flesh of smiling women, strong drink.

Gods of the sun moved the ball lower in the sky making a red light bounce up over the edge of the earth, it was the first contrast they had of smoke coming from the city, home port, salvation, these were strands of smoke from a fire which had gone out, large enough to have lasted days.

The plan was to keep safe, out of the harbor, not to be trapped by any lingering enemy ships. Only one boat was resting just off shore, her hull black, her sails black, no tension on her lines, she did not move, nothing in the bay moved.

Without hesitation the captain of the ship ordered her into the harbor, dead on at the black boat, crew not on a sail grabbed up fire sticks, Zorn had his back plate on, fire stick in one hand, bow in the other, ready for action.

Two small black boats burst from cover behind the ship, the crew did not see them, the sound from the boats of squeaking sails betrayed the surprise attack.

Archers on the decks of the attacking boats had short bows, like those to shoot from a horse, the ship's crew carried fire sticks or long bows, almost double the range.

From a locker the middle of the ship the captain pulled a huge long fire stick, standing beside the rail, resting the heavy weapon on a wooden stand, it belched forth fire, a huge plume of black smoke, a shudder went through the leading boat's black hull.

Breaking formation the boat with damaged hull turned to open ocean.

The second black boat turned to the ocean as if to follow, then turned back, from the boat archers let fly arrows, jumped up to see where they had gone, short, each arrow slid beneath the water without even a splash.

Waiting, focused, the ship's crew looked to the captain, he pointed at the black boat who had just shot at them, a brace of arrows flew, men tumbled over the side of the small black boat, or back onto the deck for a writhing death, out of site of those who shot them, denying them the satisfaction of watching the arrows new home pass from this earth.

Turning the ship back to the single black boat resting at harbor, arrows were ready, no motion, closing now to a few boat lengths, all was silent.

Within a few paces the ship started her turn, heads popped up from the small boat, they planned an ambush, too late, the ship rammed just in front of the bow, ripped a gaping hole in her side, the black boat dropped under the wake before the ship was fully past.

Men in the water screamed out, then one sailor bobbing on the surface, fired, no one on the ship said to shoot, all bows on the ship were unleashed, arrows looking like pins in the floating bodies, blood ran on the surface of the bay, bubbled in the waves, red, then pink, the ocean swallowed the blood, men, arrows, as if it never happened.

It was over in the blink of an eye, attention turned to shore now, the captain remembered the story of Zorn finding fake army men in the kingdom, fire sticks reloaded, there were burned out pylons to tie to.

The crew stayed aboard, alone, Zorn walked to the large barn, flat ash, nothing, empty shells of black rubble, once a fine barn.

Walking into the hills would take days, the ship would wait, another attack might come, put the ship at risk.

Zorn remembered the beach, Dracon waiting, a good spot to start a search in the hills, send the ship to sea, harder to find, not possible for the small black boats to chase her down in open ocean.

When the ship was offshore of the beach, the captain shoved Zorn over the side, with a scream Zorn hit the water, the captain threw an empty cask over the side, well that was how the captain remembered the first story of Zorn getting to the beach.

Wading ashore again, there was Dracon, two milkmaids, large smile, good food, by the fire they ate, drank, made love all night.

All from the city were in the hills cutting wood, Dracon had planned for this day, the city would be rebuilt, even now men were heading to tear down the charred timbers of the city to make room for the new buildings.

Over rough trails they went deep into the woods, there was the city, tents setup much as the city had been, taverns, small cook shacks, even the brothel was setup with tents at the edge of the camp.

Late into the day Zorn and Dracon talked of the ships that had come, a hundred at least, so many at the mouth of the bay you could have walked from one deck to the next without getting your feet wet.

Fires were set as the ships approached, timbers soaked, burned quickly, the ships moved fast on full sail, a launch of arrows on fire hit the first ships, burned some sails, a wise captain turned the ships, goods burned, nothing to plunder, this city was unworthy of losing one ship over.

In Rogan's confusion of retreat, back on course to war, three small black boats had waited, looked for anything they could attack, the first ship in was Zorn's, getting rid of the boats, Zorn's ship and her crew had served a valuable service.

Morning broke just as Zorn was ready to sleep, milk maids were in the woods taking care of the cows, on a soft cot Zorn laid down, weary, safe, he slept until he felt a body beside him, loving hands pulled him close.

It was dinner before Zorn and his dark skinned lover walked from the tent, stacks of wood were already at the edge of the tent town.

A wagon approached, Dracon was laid out in back, arrows in his back, arm, blood covered the floor of the wagon, Dracon looked weak, pale, gaunt.

Two black boats had come back, invaders were already onshore, a hunting party, out of nowhere an ambush, arrows struck before they could flee in the heavy wagon.

A chest under Dracon's arm, new orders for Zorn, a stallion in the woods, be a long rider again, the girl from last night, Fatima, dark skin, strange language, came from across the sand, eight weeks of sand, perhaps a two hundred day ride.

Fatima would be Zorn's passenger, a princess, get good favor with her father King Santoum, buy good ships in her homeland, outfit them, the chest open, gold, red, blue, white precious stones larger than any had ever seen.

Late into the night Dracon passed, just as he had lived, worried about others, everyone cried, drank, laughed, remembered a good man.

Zorn quietly put on his back plate, pulled his bows, took the two nets from Dracon's stash, mounted the stallion in the woods, he would be back by morning.

Without a command the four hounds jumped up and ran in perfect formation as if understanding a mission Zorn did not understand himself.

Along the road the team cut into the woods, approached from the edge, as expected an ambush was waiting on the road.

The old bitch was running, barking, anger, screams, Zorn and two hounds came through the woods, hooves and paws ripped up the ground, the old bitch did not have a groin, she had ripped out a throat, blood streamed down her face, she was hunting for more.

Arrows snapped from the bow as if driven by the wind, bodies fell, men were running from the burned out shell of a town, arrows loaded, Zorn leaned down as far as possible, the stallion was at full gallop.

The first sweep sent arrows through the running men, the stallion never broke stride, two arrows hit Zorn's back plate, stuck, good stories to tell.

Pulling hard the stallion whipped around, out came the swords, two running sailors were chased down, leaning from the side of the hurling beast the swords slashed through them, tips broke off, new tips for new targets.

Last of the hounds came in looking for action, a man staggered to his feet, locked eyes with a hound, started to run, the hound jumped his back, bit down through his neck, the sound of broken bones, sprawling, a cloud of dust, the hounds red eyes were all that could be seen through the dust.

Releasing the stallion Zorn rolled off to the ground, the horse ran circles creating a cloud of dust, men ran at the stallion, just in time to realize there was no rider, just in time to feel an arrow, taste a blade.

Back on the horse Zorn made a run at the city, dogs were now sprinting in front, suddenly the hounds broke right, the rider pulled left and knelt on the stallion's back, another ambush.

Archers were dressed in black, laying on the charred remains of the city they blended in.

The hounds were not running by sight, they could smell the bodies on the ground, it was a dog's game, run over a body, the sailor would stand, Zorn would shoot, on to the next.

It was almost morning when the team returned to the city in the woods, Zorn fed the hounds large cuts of meat, fed and brushed the stallion, removed the arrows from his back plate, they all slept soundly.

Afternoon came, Fatima waited to ride, everything well packed, route was set, all she needed was the team.

In the dark they left, quite, four horses, four dogs, all the next day the team moved along without a sound, no words spoken, even the dogs did not bark.

Zorn did not follow his training, they rode during the day, made fire at night, ate well, slept together in the cold, most conversations were just training Zorn in Fatima's language.

In the dark Fatima's soft flesh against Zorn's, a head on his shoulder, her soft perfumed hair filling his senses, they slept late, less miles each day, the exhausted dogs did not run as far in front scouting.

A wagon on the side of the road, a body lay on the front seat, horses had been cut away, bodies lay not far off, robbers, an attack, this was not safe territory, they started riding at night, sleeping less during the day, hounds were rested more, everyone was more alert.

Reaching the sand was a relief, helpful, safer, no place for robbers to hide, it was endless, hot, hard on the horses, Fatima talked Zorn into riding the edge of the sand to find good water, outfit for the trip.

A red bead of hard riding and there was no water, no building, tent, fire pit, not even animal tracks, roads, trails, humans did not exist in this place.

On the eighth day there was a glow, ever so slight, seen from a long distance, it looked like a fire of some kind, waiting all the next day, Zorn and Fatima approached with caution, a well, water for sale, run by a family, children, old people.

Camels, they had two fenced corrals, one for horses, one for camels, they left the good horses, took good camels, the only horse taken to cross the desert was the stallion.

Water skins were filled, animals were watered, an extra camel was purchased to carry the hounds, one hound would scout at a time.

Fatima was good with the camels, Zorn had never seen one before.

On first trying to ride a camel the only knowledge Zorn gained was that they spit, he had to clean his face after that lesson.

Days and nights blended into each other, food and water were rationed, a large cloth on stakes was just high enough to lay under, protection from the sun during the day.

They had stopped tying knots in the rope hanging on the stallion's saddle, days were not important any longer.

A herd of sheep out at a small water hole, the shepherd was seeking water while looking for something to eat. A caravan was coming, the shepherd was going to supply the caravan with additional food when they got this far.

Another two-day ride before they found the caravan, twenty tents spread out with herds of goats, sheep, many camels.

Fatima changed into flowing thin clothing, her face covered, many colors were woven into the fabric.

Zorn was to play the husband, it was an order, Fatima could be killed for travel with a man that was not her family.

Riding into camp men came from the tents looking at each camel, each weapon, others ran to the edge of camp to see if more riders were following, worried of an attacking army, assassins could be waiting in the sand to kill them all.

Fear of death becomes irrational choices, irrational choices become fear of death.

At the largest tent Zorn and Fatima stopped, waited, called out to occupants of the tent, waited, finally Fatima shouted a shrill command, her camel dropped down on its front knees, another yell, the huge beast folded it's long rear legs, she stepped elegantly to the ground.

From his camel Zorn yelled commands, the camel seemed to ignore him, an old man came from the tent, smiled, spoke softly to the camel, it dropped to the ground, Zorn was able to step off, the old man laughed at a man not being able to command a camel.

The caravan was that of a man who was an enemy of Fatima's father, King Santoum, Zorn and Fatima were treated as honored guests, animals were killed for a feast, riders were sent to bring herders together for food, music, dancing.

Daughters were revered, not equals, in one corner of the tent men were eating well, served by the girls dressed in soft silk flowing robes.

When food was over a dance started, young girls spun in circles, men drank, laughed, lied, clapped, enjoyed themselves.

The girls came back, paraded one by one before Zorn, he laughed, then it was time to make a choice.

Zorn tried to decline, marriage, take another wife, he was an honored guest, offered a daughter.

Fatima pointed to a green piece of cloth so Zorn pointed to the girl dressed in green, the girl and Fatima laughed and giggled at the same time, the other girls grabbed the girl in green, the girls all ran from the tent.

Slowly Fatima stood, bowed her head, walked out, Zorn chased after her, his marriage would be simple diplomacy, a daughter would now be in Fatima's fathers house, King Santoum's castle, their host might gain favor with the king from this marriage.

Fatima told Zorn to return to the tent so they could negotiate a dowry, payment for his new unwanted bride. Zorn at least understood negotiating, even if it was for a bride he did not want in a language he barely understood with customs that seemed to shift more than the desert sands.

Trade was simple, the old man wanted Zorn's stallion as a dowry.

Zorn said no, it was not possible, horses were tools here, his stallion was his life, friend, trusted member of his team.

Haggling went on, no one giving in, a small red stone of flawless quality was offered, declined, more stories, very late at in the morning a larger red stone for the girl, two gold coins for hides, a fire stick for three more camels.

It was very late when Zorn was walked to his tent for the night and next day, two old women were sitting by the door, a drape was hung on one side with his first wife, Fatima, behind it, a bed of pillows was laid out in the middle with his new bride on them, waiting for him, he had not seen her face, her looks were the least important problem he had now.

On either side of Zorn the two old women tried removing his clothing, he pushed them away, uncomfortable with the ceremony, then they washed every inch of his body in camel milk, honey was then spread on him, warm water washed it off, all the time he looked at the girl on the pillows who waited for him.

Zorn was escorted to the pillows, his new bride rose, slowly she danced to music without sound, her clothing dropped to the ground, one scarf at a time she was revealed to him.

When her veil was removed it struck Zorn how young she was, just a child, thin, undeveloped, she was too young to be his lover.

Zorn called out to Fatima of the girl's young age, she was a wife, paid for, insulted if he was not a man, it was his duty, take her.

Protesting again Zorn said she was too young, it came back that if he was not a real man, in the morning he would be killed for insulting her family, the two old women were there to approve, inspect, judge his performance.

Zorn's new wife moved slowly, she would not kiss him, he tried to be, she cried, tears streamed down her face, the old women came, inspected, done, approved, his new wife joined Fatima to sleep.

Men slept alone, no matter how many wives they had, both those now called wife talked, laughed cried together while Zorn slept soundly.

In the dark Zorn called out one question, a name, his new wife's name.

Quintal.

A report by the two old woman told of a good man, duty done, marriage consummated.

In the morning no one in the newlywed tent moved, exhausted, they slept.

In late morning Fatima and Quintal joined Zorn, they lay beside him, held him, the man they now trusted with their lives.

That evening all the animals, hides, people were assembled, time to travel, a large man, with a huge long sword named Hassan came from behind them and stood silently.

Hassan was to go also, given as gift by the father, guard of his daughter and new son in-law, envoy for him to King Santoum, a way to seek favor with those in power.

All night the group moved along the sand, the journey was at least a red bead, more if camp was made for pleasure of a man married to two wives. Such a man might be too tired to make long journey each night, might wish to spend longer in the tent each day.

No one spoke to Zorn, as head of the caravan he was offered quiet to think, contemplate, the two wives never seemed to stop talking, pointing at Zorn, laughing, jokes he did not understand.

After the sand came days crossing through villages of small mud huts, under fed children looked out, no one seemed happy, another day of hunger, misery, sadness.

At the capital Hassan went off ahead, the caravan followed, by the time they reached the gates of the castle guards were standing at attention, waiting for the new visitors.

King Santoum would not talk to his daughter, Fatima, married to an infidel, one of those that had come on religious crusades, killed thousands of his people without moral conviction, in the name of an evil God, worst of all the infidel was married to a daughter of his enemy, a traitor on the run across the desert.

Preparing to leave, Zorn was stopped by guards, Fatima had entered the castle, found her mother, begged that King Santoum at least talk with Zorn.

King Santoum was angry, he had sent the girl off on a caravan, to marry a prince, she was kidnapped, now returns the wife of an infidel, she had betrayed him.

Zorn and his wives were allowed to stay in the castle, given every comfort, Santoum did not see Zorn for over a week, forcing a delay was a way Santoum showed power over Zorn and his daughter.

Fatima and Quintal attended to Zorn's every need, often a third woman would join them, she was tall, very shy, when Zorn asked her name she would leave quickly, not return for hours.

Finally Fatima returned to Zorn with Quintal right behind, behind the two wives the tall woman walked slowly.

Zorn needed a third wife, this one should be his selection, she was a friend of Fatima.

Protesting loudly did nothing, Zorn did not want one wife, he did not want two wives, he did not want a third under any circumstances.

Her name is Salome

Salome's father is a ship builder, the largest in the kingdom, he would not entertain an infidel, her father would talk with his son in-law, give a new son in-law favorable terms on a fleet of ships.

Salome was her father's oldest, unmarried, she was too tall, men looked upon her as a good woman, not a good wife.

Slowly Fatima, Quintal and Salome walked forward, knelt beside Zorn, he laughed, she was as tall as his other two wives if they stood on each others shoulders.

Zorn's lips parted, softly he accepted what was inevitable, if not one, why not three, time was the only question.

Smart men only ask that one word when it comes to marriage, when, it is best to leave the rest of it to the wives.

Two days later Zorn was anointed with oils, dressed in long white cotton robes, taken to meet the new prospective father in-law.

At the door Zorn was denied entrance by two large men with huge swords.

Zorn sat, waited, the sun had moved a considerable distance across the sky, he had not moved.

A servant brought Zorn a plate of food, drink, he ate, drank, he did not move.

Night came, cold came, Zorn did not move.

Just as the dawn was breaking an old man came, sat beside Zorn, questioned why Salome would want to marry a man so stubborn as not to leave when sent away.

Zorn offered that perhaps Salome had learned from watching her father.

Weddings were elaborate affairs, seven days of planning was an event itself, food gathered, much yelling, demands, running servants, Fatima and Quintal would demand as much as they dared, then hide in their room laughing.

For the most part Zorn tried to ignore all that was going on.

For the most part everyone tried to ignore Zorn.

Everyone involved felt Zorn was so unworthy of such a prize.

The marriage itself was uneventful, quiet vows, the feast was a party that started one morning, went to the next morning, followed by a day of quiet recovery.

After the feast Zorn returned to his room, Salome lay upon the pillows, she had given the two old women strong drink, they slept soundly.

Salome knelt before Zorn, she kissed the hem of his robe, offered herself, prayed he would be kind, hoped she would please him.

From the other room Zorn could hear Fatima laugh.

Zorn held up Salome, we are equal, lovers, lips pressed against each other, soft, new, hunting, pleasing.

Fatima and Quintal had already instructed, explained, Zorn was not like them, he did not know how to be with a woman, he was not strong, knowledgeable, demanding, more gentle like a woman, Salome's new husband had to be helped.

Salome allowed Zorn to be soft, she encouraged his passion, she found with guidance he was an adequate lover, as a soggy cracker is still a cracker.

Salome encouraged more from Zorn, he apologized for being rough, she gave up and realized she had not married a real man.

Zorn was finished, softly stroked Salome's skin, softly holding her, she jumped up, ran to be with the other wives, he realized that he was simply here to service his wives, a male whore to those who now commanded his life.

Not one, not two, yes three masters, whether Zorn was fortunate or unfortunate was yet to be revealed to him.

King Santoum did not attend the wedding, his absence was noticeable, Fatima as first wife waited three days then rode to the royal palatal residence to confront her father, it turned out he was ill, was in hiding so his enemies did not know he was so sick.

With the clap of his hand King Santoum summoned ten men and ten women to the throne room, a present for Fatima's husband, she was excited, her father had accepted Zorn.

Fatima thanked her father, then begged, wait to take the servants, Zorn had no home of his own yet.

For missing the wedding, knowing it would insult to Zorn, Santoum provided a home, three days ride down the coast, on a small bay, with a dock for Zorn's new ships, vineyards were on the hill, pigs, lambs, chickens, everything the new couple would need.

Fatima ran, knelt before her father, tears streamed, be happy, make the infidel happy, King Santoum commanded, she kissed his hand, moistened his robes with her tears.

Her tears were soft, yet Santoum kept thinking that he would trust Zorn until, as was all infidel's nature, he would betray us, infidels always betray us, when he betrays us I will have him killed, take back the house and servants.

Zorn was impressed with the new home, large decks around the outside looked out over the bay, docks were spread out around the rock formations, each dock had its own road, the home was secured because all around were vineyards with impassable grape roots.

Second floor of the house were the sleeping chambers, a large circular room with six rooms off of it, Zorn guessed more wives were coming. Centered between the bedrooms a large set of doors entered the infidel's chambers, a golden dome, large balcony that looked out over the ocean, silk pillows lay upon the floor.

In the center of the room a large bed with silken covers, King Santoum had consulted with others about how to make the home comfortable for Zorn, son in-law, infidel, devil.

23

BOY

"Art is simply practicing the same task until you become part of it."

Sitting on a rock beside the small pond a half-day walk from the castle Morgan, the young boy taken by Wolf and Cozet from the hamlet sat watching the ripples on the surface from stones flung in anger.

Like the ripples, the further from the evil done to him the less power the evil had over him.

Morgan's first days after being taken were full of thought about that night, his father was killed, his mother sent him away with his father's murderer.

Each long walk came with a question, one of those life changing, hard to make, requires great thought kinds of decisions.

Return to the castle with his father's murders, or keep walking.

Each day Morgan felt less pain at the decisions of that night. His father was part of the crowd trying to kill Cozet, she cried when talking about killing him, his mother could not keep him alone, he had a better life at the castle.

Logical decisions were often more brutal than a whip ripping your flesh.

Being a guest of King Harrow there were many new things to learn, some in the castle taught reading, writing, in the barracks soldiers taught Morgan sword work, archery, horsemanship, care for the hounds.

Of all the things that caught Morgan's time, it was the days with Herzog's wife Samantha that often made him feel most welcome, accepted, trusted.

Samantha was kind to Morgan, both outcast, new to the castle life, she would bake cookies, cakes and they would eat, laugh, gossip.

Herzog, Wolf and Cozet were often off for two day trips so Morgan would sleep on a bench in Samantha's kitchen area, warm from the fires, it was easier to sleep soundly knowing someone he trusted was close.

Being only a few years older than Morgan, Samantha had accepted life as it was, a man who wanted her, treated her fairly, kissed her gently.

Despite all the good, Morgan hated those who had forced him into this life.

Often Morgan's conversations with Samantha would turn to talk of returning to the village, back to his mother's home when he was large enough to help her, how he would take a fast horse, or just start walking, it was something he must do.

Truth was that Morgan had no remembrance of where the hamlet was from here, it had no name so as to ask people, he remembered the mountains behind it, which were not viable from the castle.

Herzog had taken Morgan to the coast once, on the trip the boy had asked where his home had been, Herzog did not know, all the small hamlets were the same to him, dirty tired people trying to scrape together enough to eat, fearful of strangers, superstitious, Herzog felt life in the castle was better, Morgan was a lucky boy.

Morgan wanted to scream at Herzog, no one understood how unlucky he was, father murdered, mother forced him out, his fathers murder not punished.

Knowing Herzog was friends with Cozet, the woman that killed his father, Morgan kept quite, nothing to say, it was better to be silent.

Upon reaching the ocean Herzog billeted Morgan in his quarters, fed him well, that night Wolf and Cozet came in, shared the room with Morgan.

It was odd how Wolf and Cozet were now acting like his parents.

The relationship was uneasy, Cozet, trying to be his mother, would hug Morgan, he did not try to pull away, he did not like it, his body would get ridged every time her arms were around him.

In the morning Wolf, the one trying to be his father rose early, woke Morgan, they took the bows that Wolf had made. Walking out along the ocean they would stop, shoot at trees, Wolf offering Morgan small tips on what to do, how to hold, what to focus his eyes on.

After a time Wolf began to smile, he enjoyed teaching Morgan these skills, as if a parent, while Wolf could never replace Morgan's father, perhaps he could help the young man grow, it was a good feeling.

Then came the hard part of the conversations, a war was coming, not safe here or in the castle, Herzog was sending Samantha to another castle, away from the fighting, safer, Wolf wanted Morgan to go with Samantha and Cozet, to safety.

Sometimes those trying to help, hurt you worse than those who hate you.

Dumped again, inconvenient again, abandoned again, why take him if all you were going to do was send him away, dump him on Samantha, cheat him out of another life he had come to trust, accept, even grown a little in.

Wolf tried to put a hand on Morgan's shoulder, his fatherly friendship was brushed away.

Being a hunter, Wolf spent much of his life in the woods alone, hearing the forest, moving through it as if he was not there, the forest was a home for Wolf, a place that accepted him, he belonged to the forest.

It was clear that getting Morgan to move to safety was not going to be easy, Wolf tried again, working to explain safety to someone who had not experienced life was impossible, demanding Morgan to follow orders was impossible, wanting what was best for Morgan, when it was not what he wanted was impossible.

In the end Wolf was no match for a boy who was hurt, angry, cheated, the hunter gave up, decided to let Herzog convince Morgan of the need for the trip.

In bed with Cozet, Wolf whispered that he would let Herzog tell Morgan more about the trip, how Samantha was going to be safe, how Morgan and Cozet should go with her to safety.

It was a mistake, telling Cozet that he thought she should go with them to safety, there was no reason for her to be with him in the woods, sneaking around in the cold, in danger, like an animal, hunted, killing, perhaps being caught, raped, or worse.

Cozet had let him go to the forest once, lost him forever, she had believed him dead for a long time, she was a widow, she would not go through that again, her life was with Wolf or she would kill him this night in his deep slumber.

He lost two arguments that day, everyone wanted to stay and be killed instead of get to safety.

A smart man knows when to be quiet.

A wise man knows never to have said anything in the first place.

A crafty man has someone else explain his position.

Herzog was the best one to broach this subject again, Wolf rolled over, went to sleep.

In the morning Herzog had the reigns, beside him Morgan rode with bow in hand, ready to kill any game they spotted, in the back Wolf and Cozet laid upon the cargo being returned to the castle.

Wolf casually brought up Samantha moving to safety during the war, Cozet shot Wolf a hard stare, he ventured carefully on how Morgan and Cozet should go with Samantha to be safe.

Herzog laughed, it was a discussion he had with Samantha, right up until she hit him in the head with a rolling pin, so, no, she would not be leaving.

A blade, pulled quick from Cozet's sheath, held against Wolf's male organ, he never mentioned sending her away again.

Wolf yelled out for Herzog to be careful of bumps up ahead.

Along the road a rabbit ran, standing, drawing his bow, Morgan held still for a moment, arrow nock kissing his cheek, a little lead, far too long of a shot, the arrow hung in the air for a moment, the rabbit took a long stride, tumbled, everyone yelled, from a moving wagon, a remarkable shot.

Art is simply practicing the same task until you become part of it.

The rabbit made a fine lunch, stew over an open fire in the middle of a lush green field with a small stream flowing through it.

While all others enjoyed the feast Wolf looked at the area as if it were to be a place of battle, an area where he and Cozet would someday practice their deadly skills on others, taking life, perhaps being killed.

The hunter was being destroyed by a war that had not yet happen.

War was an art, not just in killing, also knowing how to die well.

24

FRAGILE SPY

*"Spies had the illusion of a code, without it
they were inhumane monsters."*

King Harrow was amazed by the beauty of his own kingdom, warm radiant mountains, colorful fields, crisp streams, rivers in turmoil, seas of deep blue covered in foaming waves.

Playing the part of king required being locked away in stonewalls unable to enjoy the beauty one worked so hard to protect.

Two days of riding in any direction from the castle would get the rider to the edge of his kingdom.

Mountains behind, two large rivers cascaded on either side of the kingdom separated from the monarchies north and south, the front of the kingdom laid upon the rocky cliffs constantly pounded by the ocean.

Perfect to defend, the kingdom had never really been attacked seriously by anyone in all these generations, of course, that was about to change.

The kingdom was not well fortified or known for a large fierce army, the kingdom simply did not have anything worth pillaging, kingdoms to the north and south, with large ports had a great deal more gold, silver, precious stones.

King Harrow's kingdom mainly had farmers that traded goods, paid taxes, farmers sons served terms in the service of King Harrow, most were returned quickly to harvest crops which were most important.

Taxes were paid often as a percentage of the crop, taken by ferry over the rivers to the neighboring kingdom, sold in the ports to passing ships looking for cargo.

Most of the trade money was returned to the hamlets for the purchase of more seed, tools, or a horse for plowing.

The castle was nicely outfitted with everything a king could want, not allot of jewels or gold, it was a simple place to live, a simple place to rule, an easy life with few domestic squabbles to overcome.

Spies also kept the homeland safe, King Harrow kept informed by a few spies that moved through his own kingdom and the three surrounding kingdoms looking and listening for ill intention, rumors, drifters, concerns.

It was one of these spies, Xavier, who had spotted, Kendal, a singer on the patio of the tavern by the dock during the rainy season.

Xavier realized Kendal was not just good natured, well tuned, this singer was asking too many questions.

Just as Xavier was getting ready to grab Kendal for questioning Kendal vanished, along with a small oriental woman.

During the season of heat here was Kendal, another kingdom to the south, too many questions, free with a coin for a drink, smooth on the ear, created many lose discussions that had details of how many, where, cargo, plans.

Xavier followed Kendal at a distance, a very small cove, there was Kendal, a black boat, black sails, well armed crew, too well armed, any of those sailors falling overboard with so many knives would be dragged under the water fast, these were killers on a quick shallow boat for land attack.

This small black boat would be useless attacking a kingdom with a large port like the one Kendal was now singing in.

A boat this small could only be for attacking a kingdom without a large port, a kingdom Prince Rogan was building a fleet to attack.

Just before dawn Xavier and two men entered Kendal's room, the singer was on the patio regaling sailors all around with good song, free drinks.

Xavier and his men moved fast, quiet, Miko, the small oriental woman was bound, gagged, hauled out before she could make a sound.

As dawn spread on the land, reports from the whores had danced in the singers ears, a good night of stories, boasts, conjecture, sifted, mixed, tested, the lies would wash out, a nugget of valuable truth would be found.

Xavier sat quietly, in the shadows, simple choice for Kendal, information for the life of Miko, the truth for her continued ability to draw a breath.

A simple exchange of information, man-to-man, spy-to-spy, trained liar to experienced liar.

Kendal pulled a blade, perhaps the trade should be Xavier's life for the girl.

Xavier did not fight, no one would trade, kill Xavier and the singer would get Miko back in pieces, small pieces cut from her flesh over hours of torture, rape, horror, her face frozen in a scream of such inhuman fear.

Kendal placed his blade against Xavier's throat, the singer understood men better than anyone, he watched for his blade to instill fear, reaction, mistake.

There was no reaction from Xavier, he sat in the shadows quite, calm, waiting for answers, Kendal's knowledge of men told him Xavier would die before showing any fear.

Fabricate a story, knit truth and lie into a believable fabric of almost truth, Miko's life in the balance, Kendal's mind raced for answers, his cover blown, that was bad, worst of all it came to him in a wave of rancid anger, he cared for Miko, breaking the first code of spies, passion, compassion, trust, understanding, all the rules he knew never to break, yet he had, payment for his careless, foolish, stupid emotions had come.

Kendal chose a demand, bring Miko to the room before he would talk, perhaps shes dead already, how could a man who had lost command of the battle make such demands, Xavier showed a slight grin, assurance, she was safe, bringing her to the room would not make her safe.

Truths spoken with respect can destroy bluster, confuse the brain, eat away at confidence.

If Miko were brought to the room she would be killed along with Kendal, no way out, he had to die, it was required, letting the singer live could allow more information to flow to ones enemies, the singer's life would end this night.

Kendal went to a hole in the wall and looked out on his last morning light.

One more demand from a condemned man, Kendal's pouch filled with gold be given to Miko, it was hidden, Kendal gave it to Xavier because in some odd why the singer respected the fact that Xavier did not lie about taking Kendal's life when the information was gone.

Hard truths honestly spoken create respect.

The information flowed, most of it already known, what was not known was the timing, when would the attack come, Kendal claimed he just sent information, he received no news from the fleet.

From the shadows came Xavier's disappointed hollow voice, with Miko's life in the balance Kendal had told a lie, exposed, naked truth was now given, three weeks, perhaps a month.

Xavier nodded, Miko had been taken to the castle, the same castle Kendal's men would attack, the same kingdom Captain Rogan was trying to retake.

Kendal's lies might have caused Miko to be in a castle that would fall, she would be killed, ravaged, taken as a slave again.

When Xavier moved from the shadows, a blade hidden in the darkness flashed out, a cut on Kendal's cheek.

Kendal had not mentioned the black boats, how many, where were they, what were they doing, lies, illusion, partial stories, all these would end her life in the worst of ways.

Just one, Kendal protested, he gave out another story, he was just out for a ride, accidently happened upon it.

Another flash from Xavier's blade, the other cheek cut, lies, the black boat had been attacked, destroyed, the black boat's captain told of the spies work, Xavier knew of the others, confirmation was the only course of action.

Kendal offered information quickly now, ten or twelve traveled with the fleet, ahead, scouts, this one was the only one he knew of.

This time the tip of the blade went into Kendal's left leg, deep, to the bone, so sharp it made no pain at first, blood sprayed from the wound, then a wave of heat, ran up, filled Kendal's face with fear, searing his mind, tears filled his eyes, he fell on the floor without a scream.

Xavier was now visible, tall, well armed, a long thin blade in one hand, fire stick in the other, ready for a fight, yet he had not moved when Kendal placed a blade at his throat.

Stories must match, or this will end badly for you, very badly for Miko.

The black boats were taking the coast, the customs house, the black boats captain was cruel, his men were a patchwork of thieves, villains, killers.

Captain Rogan had a plan, use the docks then spread the men out through the kingdom like weeds in a field, killing at will, until the castle was under siege, unable to sustain itself, the kingdom would fail, Rogan would replace Harrow on the throne.

Without any visible motion Xavier's blade sliced through Xavier's vest, into the singers heart.

Honor among men with no honor was all that Xavier could offer, Miko would have her pouch of gold, be taken to live with Xavier inside the castle walls.

The truth had one regrettable understanding, there was no way to defend against it, the kingdom would be in turmoil, killers everywhere would escalate fear.

An army could be fought, surrendered, negotiated, weeds, killer weeds, there was no strategy for killer weeds.

Back in the royal chamber telling King Harrow of Kendal, Xavier reported on the war he knew was coming, storm clouds told of coming rain, thunder, lightening, it was only a fool who looked at the clouds in the sky and did not prepare, bundle in warm clothing, get under cover.

Those that discredited Xavier's report in public were removed or discredited themselves as traitors, fear was a creative tool that King Harrow would use to repel this storm, tax more, bolster what army he could.

In Xavier's quarters Miko sat quietly, breathing deeply, trying not to be afraid.

When Xavier entered Miko spoke not one word, watched his every move, a bird in the cage with the cat.

Xavier handed Miko the pouch of gold coins, there was no need to tell of the singer's death, the pouch told the story, she knew the profession had no other outcome.

Xavier took Miko to his bed, they simply lay together, he did not try to take her, they lay upon the covers, dressed, he slept soundly, a quite man, he required nothing from her.

When Xavier woke he touched his lips to Miko's, there was no emotion, while he expected fear, passion, rage, there was nothing.

Taking Miko to the market, Xavier held her hand, it was soft, gentle, the only thing they shared was the man he had absolved through death, he was trying to be kind, understanding of her situation.

Spies had a code, odd that a profession of lies, illusion, treachery could have such a code of honor, respect, integrity.

Spies had the illusion of a code, without it they were inhumane monsters.

Miko had become part of that code, her singer had loved her, she loved her singer with all her heart, now Xavier would care for her as part of the code, she accepted that.

A spy is an illusion, which truly destroys what one believes about themselves, the seeker tries to uncover the humanity locked within, a jewel, guarded, sacred, is the real spy.

Upon Miko's new lovers bed she satisfied Xavier, he was allowed to use her body, her heart would never be given again, acceptance of reality came with surrender.

Upon Xavier's bed he accepted her, all of her body was taken, used, embraced, caressed, he had no heart to offer, he accepted her body as a lover should, love was not within him.

It is the lover's illusion that must be held sacred, when the curtain is pulled back love is a prison of one's own making.

The subtle breeze along the ocean carried sails pushing the black wooden hulls of boats, death, men, warriors, murders, killers for a price that would try to end both Xavier and Miko's lives.

A fruit that is fragile carries more flavor, savory deep colors that embrace the senses in each intoxicating bite making the season of such a fruit more valuable, intoxicating, sensual.

So it is with life, a succulent fruit that often is most cherished just before our last breath.

25

WIFE'S SHIPS

*"It is only scoundrels and royalty that can take pride
in their treachery."*

Zorn was shaken awake early in the morning by his third wife, Salome, a plate of food, small dates, tea, toasted bread with garlic. Time to select the ships, her father would build them, it was time for the master of the house to make decisions.

Along the coast in a carriage that had been sent for them, a small bay, the shipyard was alive with work, men in robes carried large timbers from ships that brought them to port over to a partial hull sitting upon runners.

Much as a baby in the womb, cells building function, form, power, ready to slide into the bay when finished, a shell to carry a crew, a dream realized.

Salome sat in the carriage while Zorn and Hassan walked the yard, a small man approached, hesitant smile, bending down to Zorn, offered greetings.

The small man took them to the shore, pointed to a small ship, square hull that looked very stout, very unremarkable, not fast or maneuverable.

Hassan told Zorn to not accept the ship, it was of an old design, not fast, newer designs were faster, held more sail, able to carry more men, weapons, plunder, decline now, a better ship would be offered later.

Zorn thanked the small man offering the ship, rejected the first offer, asked about more modern designs, the small man looked at Hassan in disgust.

Hassan put a hand on his large sword, looked back at the small man and growled.

A new plan, build sleek new ships, Hassan ran to the carriage, soon returned, a list of requirements.

Payment would be done well, the ships must be done well, fast, shallow for coastal work, large sails, comfortable captain's quarters, galley.

Cargo ships were in far off lands as they spoke getting black wood for masts, hard, strong, able to be thin, not break under heavy loads.

Hassan asked for the flaming of arrows, Zorn questioned, the small man from the yard walked off, all followed, at the edge of the water a long stick with a tube on top.

A small stick from a fire was touched to a string on the tube, a blaze ran across the sky as the tube hurled the stick out over the bay, how many on each ship, ten times his fingers on each side, so be it, a warship, they would give life to a assassin ship.

Two hulls, a stiff outside hull, a thinner inside hull to protect from ramming, the builder asked what else would be required.

Looking to Hassan, Zorn was willing to listen, Hassan ran for the carriage, the boatman lit another tube, it flew much further than the first had.

Upon returning Hassan was having a hard time breathing, three ships, one large, two smaller, each with a complement of a ten, times ten, then times ten again of the fire tubes.

Laughing, the ship builder said it could not be done, Zorn simply turned, walked away, just before reaching the carriage the small man caught them, three months at least, not a moment earlier, the cost would be high.

It took a moment for Zorn to accept, Hassan was about to enter the carriage when Salome yelled at him, his head dropped down.

Hassan agreed that he would stay with the builder to look out for his masters best interest.

For three months Zorn was kept well in the house, it seemed Salome had taken charge of everything, each afternoon the three wives would leave for about three hours, the story was the same, the bizarre for shopping, woman's work.

Worst of all Zorn was kept from the boat yard, he wanted to see the progress, view the workmanship of his new prize ships, Salome said her father owned the yard, everything was on time, it would be an insult not to trust him.

A man in a cage is nothing, no matter the bars are of gold, smiles from the servants, pleasurable touch of a wife, or three, a cage is still a cage.

Horses and hounds were Zorn's life, new roads, people, exploring, this was not a cage, it was a casket for the undead.

It was more than Zorn could take, boredom was an enemy he could not shoot, kick, fight, escape was the only possible alternative.

Letting the carriage leave, Zorn tried to follow, his path was blocked by servants, he could not get his stallion, his saddle was gone, riding gear stored.

Casually Zorn walked to a farm down the road, finding the owner he persuaded as best he could to borrow a horse, likely the man thought that he was stealing it.

First Zorn rode to the boat yard where the workers were running, the yelling was very excited, ships were in the bay, heavy to the gunnels with goods, three were on the docks being unloaded of large timbers, in the runners sat three hulls, long, thin, almost sexy, they looked fast just sitting ready to slide down to freedom.

Spotting his master, Hassan ran up with a report, all would be done soon, a month at most, weapons were being loaded now, a tour was given, small holes carried fire arrows, they could reach a long way, explode on impact, a hundred loaded, a thousand on each ship, food stored deep in the hull, a cooking area covered, the captains quarters aft, protected.

Spotting the carriage approaching Hassan was nervous, Zorn swore him to secrecy, the long rider rode off along the coast, then turned back up to the road, from the hill Zorn could see Salome pointing, she struck Hassan.

Something was very wrong with this, Zorn's first plan was to ride down, confront Salome, it seemed the plan was too simple to work, slowly, use her trust of him to find her plan.

A loyal wife, or cunning enemy, often one in the same.

Zorn waited until night, talked quietly in his bed chamber with Quintal, the youngest wife, a plan, she knew nothing, she was just happy to be shopping, spending so much time at market.

Then Quintal asked an odd question, why he was not a strong man, were all men weak where he came from.

Placing his face beside her ear he asked softly what Quintal meant, she laughed, she explained that a strong man would have struck her for even asking the question.

Zorn told Quintal how he wanted her to be his partner, she stood, looked down at him, walked off to be with other wives.

When Quintal had left Zorn's sleeping chamber Salome came to him, questions about the boat yard, her job, not his, he should just wait in the house, the ships would be ready soon.

Zorn pretended to accept Salome's statements, her anger, her forceful statements, the ships were under construction, something was very wrong.

A soft body at night for pleasure, a devious mind during the day for betrayal.

As Salome was leaving Zorn asked about assembling crews for the ships, a ship needs a crew, captains, first mates, all loyal to the ships master.

Salome's head spun around so fast Zorn thought her neck would break, it was taken care of, nothing he should worry about.

Taking a sword from his back plate Zorn walked out of the bedroom, down the staircase, through the door, each step getting more angry, out to the servants quarters above the stables.

Salome's personal driver was surprised when the blade poked into his chest, lies are simple truths as the teller wishes them to be, the steel of a blade can often make the truth of a man much more meaningful if one listens.

Pressing the blade harder, another lie, fear was winning, blood covered the front of the man's nightshirt.

The wives driver looked for compassion in eyes that had none, the truth will set you free, more torture or perhaps forfeit of your life, truth.

The confession poured forth, sailing, a ship down the coast, in a bay, the three wives were sailing each day, learning, they talked of tactics, weapons, reading maps.

Tossing the man a coin Zorn ordered him gone from the property, never to return.

Walking back into the house Salome stood at the top of the stairs, Zorn showed her the blood on his blade, placing the tip at her throat he asked if the blood of two liars should be mixed on this night.

Zorn had no need for a wife he could not trust.

Not a word from Salome, she looked upon him with disgust.

Fatima and Quintal came running, falling upon their knees at Zorn's feet they begged he not kill Salome.

The truth can be like a sharp edge on a blade, in your hands it is valuable, in an enemy's hand it is dangerous, at this point Zorn worried that he was his own enemy.

Turning as if Zorn was not there Salome walked back to the wives room with Fatima and Quintal following her like puppy dogs.

Zorn had lost a war to himself, he was weak, he should have killed her.

Standing alone at the top of the stair, Zorn realized the worst wars were ones you lost before you even knew they had started.

In the morning all three wives were gone, the servants would not speak to Zorn, he was alone in his beautiful prison.

Walking to the neighbors farm Zorn intended to borrow the horse again, the farmer protested, Zorn entered the barn anyway, the horse lay with a cut neck, a large man, big sword, watched by his three wives, killed his horse, rode off in the carriage.

Walking out to a small fence Zorn realized just how out of control all of this was, his stallion, he needed to ride.

Returning to his own stables Zorn pulled the stallion from the stall, there was a small blade stuck in its rump, the same handle as Hassan had carried in his belt.

Zorn was no longer master of his house, wives, servants, guards were his jailers.

Working for an hour Zorn sewed the flesh back together in crude stitches that caused the stallion pain, all of the riding gear was gone, Zorn tied a rope around the stallions mouth, it was miles before the two felt as one, he had control of something again.

Servants were shocked to see the master of the house ride his stallion out. Salome would exact retribution upon them for allowing Zorn his freedom.

Nursing the horse along slowly Zorn worked his way up the coast, there were many small alcoves, a few scattered docks, no carriage or ship to be found.

Turning back Zorn rode slowly to the shipyard, it was getting dark, every other night the wives had returned before dark.

There it was, the carriage sitting just inside the entrance to the working area of the shipyard, as Zorn approached Hassan came forward blocking the only way through.

Stepping down Zorn let the stallion stand, instead it reared up as it caught the pungent smell of Hassan, the man who had stabbed him earlier.

Zorn pulled his sword, Hassan was afraid, killing his master would mean his own death, Hassan had orders from Salome that Zorn was not to pass.

Zorn pulled the small blade that he had removed from the stallion's rump, tossed it on the ground at Hassan's feet.

Treachery done by an honest man will be his undoing, no matter the reason.

It is only scoundrels and royalty that can take pride in their treachery.

The fight was quick, Hassan made one failed swing, Zorn stepped back, Hassan made another swing, Zorn stepped back again.

Hassan made a third swing, Zorn stepped forward sticking his blade through Hassan's belly.

Pulling the bloody blade Zorn did not watch Hassan die, there was no point, hurting his stallion could not go unanswered in this culture.

Walking to the docks Fatima and Quintal ran to meet Zorn, stop him, persuade him, plead with him.

Behind them Salome stood beside the largest ship, defiant, no remorse, confident.

The first two wives clung to Zorn's clothing, begged that he listen, it was all for his own good.

They were going to sail with Zorn, it was only that they did not want him to leave them, they loved him, were afraid of losing him.

Zorn ordered his third wife to kneel before him, she did not move.

Yelling in rage at Salome, Zorn demanded she kneel down, she did not move.

The shipyard master came running, he pleaded for the killing to stop, the ships were almost done, the best on the sea, unstoppable in war, able to ride the heaviest seas.

Then the shipyard master pointed to Salome, she demanded only the best for you on these ships, she required these ships keep you safe.

The ships would be done in a week, final work was being done now.

Zorn ordered Salome to stay on the ship, she was not to return to the house, his house, under any circumstances.

Salome said nothing, turned, walked away.

Somehow it was a great victory when Zorn gave the orders, now he realized he had just lost.

To the victor goes the pain.

Fatima and Quintal pleaded, this was an insult, Salome may kill herself.

Zorn was in no mood to listen.

Finally Fatima asked if Zorn knew how to captain a ship like this.

The ship Zorn had sailed on was nothing like this, he would hire a crew, a crew he could trust to run this ship, he would learn.

Fatima explained how Salome had taught them to sail, to captain such a ship, she could train him as well, it was best for all if he forgave her, brought her back to the house, did not shame her in public in her fathers shipyard.

Even Zorn's anger, righteous anger, was his own enemy.

Zorn allowed it, for the next two weeks Salome taught Zorn to sail during the day, names of the parts of his ships, how much to lean it over in the wind, how to light the fire arrows, what a sail could do, how far to go before the mast broke.

Finally Zorn was ready, in his heart he knew there was no way to trust Salome, it was the three wives over dinner that described their plan, Fatima and Quintal would command one ship, Salome a second ship, as husband Zorn would command the largest ship, most powerful, they would follow him.

Crews had been selected, were ready to go, it was all out of his hands.

Zorn hated it, felt that Salome would betray him, she had the least respect for him.

That night it was Salome that came to Zorn's bed chamber, undressed, offered herself, asked that if he could no longer trust her to take her life now, end her suffering, it was too painful to love him with his suspicious mind.

Within Salome's humble apology came a feeling of arrogance, strength, defiance.

Zorn accepted Salome, made love with her, took her hand when she went to leave, made her lay beside him that night, no wife had ever slept with him after he was done with her.

Some acts of kindness, love, passion can cause the deepest of wounds.

A woman can be a cunning enemy until she is in your arms, then her truth will be unbearable to control, her true evil nature will surface or die.

They lived in an uneasy truce, each day training on a ship, learning winds, tides, reading weather, turning quickly, leaning hard on the wind for speed, slowing for an easy voyage.

Finally a beautiful morning came, launch day, the four proceeded to the dock of the ship yard, watched as the three ships slipped into the water, each with a small wake they cut the water like knives, sleek, fast, powerful.

The yardmaster came, congratulated the ship's new master, told how it could not have been done without the direction of Salome, Zorn was a lucky husband to have such a woman with him.

Chests of gold and jewels get empty quickly when living such a life, about half of what Zorn had left was paid for the ships, which included all of his outfitting of fire arrows, food and stores.

War ships were ready for war, battle, conquest, assassinations.

A line of men assembled to get work on the ships, while most of the crew had been selected by Salome, Zorn sat at the interview table, he was there in name only, it was Salome who interviewed, selected, placed them on the correct ship.

There was one man, small, dirty, he spoke Zorn's native language yet was turned away, Zorn caught up with him, he had sailed from other countries, knew of the land Zorn came from.

Zorn assigned him to his own ship, Salome was angry, the man could not be trusted, only her selections should be taken.

As the sun broke over the mountains Salome pulled herself from under her husbands arm, the four ate together that morning in silence. A first trip on the ships, working apart, yet together, seeing who was fastest, there was a tension that had not existed before.

Zorn thought that it might be a good time to order all three wives to stay at home, a wise choice, a good choice, not the choice he wanted, with untested men on untested ships it would be foolish to leave his wives at home.

Moving from the harbor the ships were slow, the sorting out was hard at first, these ships were nothing like those they had trained on.

Faster ships also got into trouble faster.

The wind and ocean seemed to be communicating which would cause another problem.

Fatima and Quintal could not keep up, Zorn and Salome had organized their ships more quickly, leaned them against the wind for faster runs up and down the coast.

Returning to harbor that night they found an emissary from the court of King Santoum there with a greeting. A request from the king, Fatima's father, the ships were requested the next morning to be sailed up to the main harbor for inspection by the navy.

One curious man from the court was asking questions, too many questions, he seemed to be concerned about the fire sticks, how the hulls were doubled, making them stronger from attack.

A man would build a cargo ship for trade, a war ship was for war, heavy armor, a mast that would not break under heavy load, there was talk that these three ships were deadly assassin ships, killers on the waves.

Perhaps these ships could be used to overthrow a king, an infidel with no loyalty to King Santoum who had such ships would be a danger.

Protesting, Zorn told the man how he had only loyalty for King Santoum, no intention of doing anything other than sailing home, back to King Harrow, the ships would never be used against King Santoum, his father in-law, his benefactor.

Between the accusations of King Santoum, distrust of his wives, Zorn was getting very agitated, he remembered the old days of horses, hounds, long days alone, no intrigue or treachery to fill his mind.

That night Zorn kept all three wives on his ship with him, they were nervous, seemed to be casting hard looks at each other, he could feel the tension, he enjoyed that they could not hatch new conspiracies against him.

During the night servants took needle and thread to the remaining stones from Dracon, sewing each into the fabric of his clothing, each wife had sewn into her clothing a few stones as a precaution if something happened.

Leaving port with the first breaking of the sun Zorn quietly let his crew do what they knew to do best, only making decisions when needed, setting course, speed, requirements.

On the ship just behind Zorn Salome was screaming orders that could be heard across the water, each move of each man was an order, command, establishing her dominance from the start.

On the last ship Fatima and Quintal were not even visible, telling the crew to follow the other two ships, Zorn's first two wives had gone below deck for rest, away from the sun, hidden from the waves, the only orders they issued were for food, wine, pleasure.

26

BATTLE STARTS

"Courage is often just not understanding how afraid one should be."

Prince Rogan's small black boats slid up the coast before the fleet, fast, light, maneuverable in the shallow costal waterways, a pack of jackals on the prowl hunting for weak targets of opportunity.

Planning was a good leaders job, kings, generals, commanders seeking victory, willing to watch their own men die to have it, detached, impersonal, pawns on the chess board, expendable layers of protection.

Taking King Harrow's kingdom with a normal army would have been a logistics problem of placing men, weapons, ships on unfamiliar soil, customs, languages.

Rogan knew this kingdom as a lad, felt warmth for the people once, tasted their betrayal of him each night in his dreams, willing to destroy what he wanted to possess it. It was the land and castle Rogan wanted, the people were just in the way of his dream.

The fleet under Price Rogan was no army, because of all the different languages, fighting skills, weapons, most of all the motivations of his men had no cohesive faction.

Desires become needs, a wanton lust for plunder, gold, wine, women, food, warm bed, solid ground they could call their own.

First of the black boats was a decoy, it ran past the guard houses above the commons house just within eyesight, close enough to be noticed, planned for.

It was clear from the information the spy Kendal had given before his death that a black boat working for the Prince Rogan was in these waters, this time Rogan let the guards catch just a glimpse of her.

Army men were pulled immediately, extra patrols of guards moved up the coast, the boat may have landed, be plying its deadly trade, catch it in the act, blunt the tip of the spear.

A runner was sent to Gaston, riders left to inform King Harrow of the sighting, men and arms would be needed to repel the invaders back into the sea.

It was Gaston that realized the ruse right from the start.

No more patrols were sent north, a certain ambush, it was better to send two patrols south with scouts out front, patrols in the rear hanging back, the scouts could flush the enemy, the patrol could destroy them.

The first of the patrols found the black boat, it was smashed at the base of a large cliff, driven into the rocks by a relentless sea, no survivors, waves, rocks, cliff claimed the prize, invaders must have all died, no more threat, time to relax.

The first of the patrols south found nothing, no armada, no boats, it was just a big hunt for ghosts, illusion, flesh could be killed, ghosts killed a man from within.

Prince Rogan's sailors were working their way inland from where the black boat had landed, after unloading the killers, the black boat had been skillfully sailed into the cliff, a great show to keep the guards attention.

Trained in the art of killing from birth the sailors were heading for villages to be brutal, brutality creates rumors which creates fear, in return fear fed more rumors, shadows, illusion, those were the most powerful weapons.

Fifty well armed fighting men swept through the first village, a small collective of farmers, tillers of the land, working in dirt to gather enough to stay alive.

Men and old women were killed first, dragged to the center of the village to be stabbed, beheaded, it was a gruesome, the pile was set afire, any that tried to crawl out were stabbed again, screams came from the pyre, black smoke rose into the air.

There was no resistance, women dragged to their beds which had been shared with husbands a few minutes ago were now ravaged by men from the sea that did not speak their language, the sailors understood the cries for mercy, they just did not care.

What food the monsters could gather was taken, more sailors would come that needed pleasure, so the women were left alive, only a handful of sailors stayed in the village to watch, wait, dominate.

After the initial carnage some young boys were allowed to escape so that the rumors could start, tales told, seeds fertilized in horror would grow a bountiful crop of confusion.

Wolf and Cozet were scouting in the woods only a half days walk away, on foot it took them most of the night to reach the village.

As the sailors arose at first light they were greeted with arrows for breakfast, the first was the boat's captain, he had taken a mother and daughter for the night, placing the blade upon the mothers chest had made the daughter a compliant lover.

When the captain exited the hut at the edge of the village a single arrow slipped through his ribs, exploded his heart. Crumpled in a heap on the doorstep, from conqueror to corpse in an instant.

The captain's men raced to the door, looked at the fallen leader, one started to enter the cabin, an arrow hit square in his back with enough force to tumble him inside.

Sailors were running now, seeking cover, shelter, a sailor hid behind a wall, only to be cut down by an arrow from another direction.

A woman, half naked ran from the cabin, pulled a sword from the captain's belt, stabbed the corpse with it, extracting vengeance for his sadistic brutality was the only thing her mind could process.

With his bow in hand a sailor rose to kill the woman defiling his captain's body, before the arrow even kissed his cheek a small arrow smashed into his spin, death was not quick, laying paralyzed all the sailor could do was watch as his shipmates started to run from the village, looking for a way out, thinking an army was behind them.

Cozet watched as Wolf readied himself on the main trail, when he was set she moved to the herding position, as the sailors ran she would pick off the ones in the back, motivating the herd into Wolf's trap.

Running, screaming, terrified, the sailors saw the trail was their only salvation, moving just ahead of them Wolf was taking them one at a time, they never saw him, rock tipped arrows sheared through clothing, protection, armor, as if it was not there.

Stopping on the road the last five knew to continue running was futile, they took cover in a ditch.

Wolf had moved on, waiting for his final shots, Cozet ran down the trail, she was almost upon the sailors when the first jumped from the ditch to attack her.

Without breaking stride Cozet jabbed the arrow in her hand up, the sailor's eye exploded, the sailor grabbed his face, fell to the ground screaming.

Another arrow rose from her quiver, before she could place it upon the bow another sailor jumped from the ditch, an arrow from Wolf's bow smashed the mans leg, sending him tumbling, both wounded sailors screamed in agony on the ground.

The remaining three sailors were no longer in the ditch, scurrying into the brush like rabbits from the talons of the eagle, they were too dangerous to hunt on their own, Wolf and Cozet moved back into the forest.

From up the trail came the women of the village with pitchforks, sharp sticks, stones, the lives of the two sailors on the ground ended quickly.

The three escaped sailors split up, their stories of arrows flying from thin air to end lives, torture, were spread through the other marauding bands.

Kingdoms can be won, armies defeated, peasants slaughtered, illusion is a powerful weapon. Rumors of Wolf and Cozet killing so many sailors spread quickly the boat captains put a priority on finding the two and delivering them to Prince Rogan.

That night in the limbs of a huge tree where Wolf and Cozet had made a bed they lay in silence, it was he who broke with the first words. It was clear that the war was starting, it was clear in small groups with luck, skill, cunning, they could defeat some small groups of sailors.

What would happen when a large army was moving through these woods, how would they survive killing only a few, when the few were followed by a hundred or more.

Worst of all, when the war ended, if Rogan was on the throne, they would not be treated as enemy soldiers, they would be put to death, a horrid death in the square to make an example of defiant ones.

Cozet kissed Wolf's ear, touched his neck softly, what was to be done, the war had come, strings drawn, death sent, like an arrow that has left the bow their destiny had been set.

Fight the edges, when all is lost move over the mountains, slip into a village, another kingdom, die of old age, loyalty was something King Harrow needed, Wolf would not be loyal at the expense of their lives.

We have cast the ship from this shore, upon her deck we make our voyage, if this be a long journey or a short venture, it is beside you that I will be till safe on land we toil.

When my eyes close at last, from old age, an arrow, in the square, there will be no regret, your love is the only passage that will keep me warm when my body is cold in the grave.

Slowly, with great reverence, Wolf placed his lips to Cozet's, this night was theirs, morning would bring another chapter.

At the docks the first of Rogan's ships were just coming into sight, archers from the fortifications were scattered in the hills above the docks, holes in the ranks, too many patrols had been sent out after the black boats.

On the road from the kingdom a flank of archers were in wagons running at full speed to fortify the archers at the commons house, loss of the docks meant an open door to the kingdom.

There were less than two hundred of Rogan's sailors moving from the north down to the fortifications.

While all fortifications were prepared for a frontal attack from the sea, the soldiers were not ready for groups of two or three sailors with bows moving silently through the woods from behind.

King Harrow's lookouts stationed along the tree line were cut down before air could move from their lungs to warn anyone.

Sailors coming from the rear were not like any the soldiers had seen before, sort, stocky, light of feet, wearing animal skins, able to move quickly without sound, stop, become part of the forest, lost to the eye among the leaves, branches, underbrush.

Expecting a flank of riders on armored horses the lookouts from the top of the fortifications never noticed the brush move, grass bending, nor did they hear the muffled sounds of those within the fortifications as the sailors simply knocked, killed those that opened the doors for them.

On the roof top only one mistake was made, a young officer running to the edge trying to shout a warning was tumbled over the side by an arrow in the back.

The archers on the side of the hill realized too late the situation, ships in front of them, archers behind them in their fortification. No place to hide, no place to survive, death was inevitable.

Courage is often just not understanding how afraid one should be.

Terror is understanding the fear, incapable of changing it.

Gaston had become an official in the commons house, without training, discipline, physical work, he was no longer an army man, except at heart.

Grabbing up his sword Gaston started trying to work his way to the fortifications, the sailors on the roof were more concerned with the military archers on the hill, they paid no attention to one man sneaking through the brush along the path.

First Gaston pushed against the gate, it was blocked, the sailors must have understood the need to protect this area, he moved to the side, a stable door, small, worked his way through the feed, tack, ropes, in the armor room he grabbed up a long pike with a steel tip.

Gaston took off his boots, only wearing his chest plate for protection he moved through the halls quietly, then he heard orders, another language, barked in anger, he could see down the hall two sailors dressed in animal skins poking at one of his men with arrows, his man was rolling around in pain, trying not to die.

Running from hiding to certain death was a hard choice, Gaston hesitated, then made his move, past bodies of his men, warm blood on his feet, out of shape, it was a long hall.

One of the sailors looked at Gaston for a moment in confusion, the other was putting an arrow on his bow, the bow was snapped into place, for a moment Gaston thought about stopping, surrendering, being killed anyway, out of instinct he ran harder.

Crouching just as the sailor fired, the arrow past Gaston's ear so close he could hear the hiss of the feathers, the pike went through the sailor who had fired the arrow, from front to back in a huge explosion of blood, guts, pain.

The second sailor looked on, startled, then poked Gaston in the arm with an arrow, a boot from the man on the floor sent the remaining sailor tumbling back against the wall, Gaston fell upon him, hands locked on the sailor's throat.

As the sailor and Gaston slid to the floor the army officer on the ground rolled onto the sailor's legs pinning them, the sailor fought for his life, Gaston fought for his, the sailor's eyes were bulging out, in the end the sailor took his last breath, Gaston rose slowly trying to catch his breath.

The army officer on the sailor's legs had died, given all that he had, two down, too many more to go.

From hiding Gaston killed two more with the pike, he was searching for a good vantage point to get more. It was upon the stairs, Gaston was tired, breathing hard, a sailor heard him coming up, knowing it was not another sailor, the sailor fired an arrow.

The arrow slid down Gaston's breast plate, into his leg, limping, Gaston was able to turn, make his way back as he had come, at the gate he released the bar, able to open the main entrance.

Standing outside the fortification Gaston held up his arms, screamed to his men on the hill, exposed, vulnerable, without hesitation they started to run for the open gate, arrows slammed down on them from the roof of their own fortification.

Gaston ran for the customs house, arrows hit beside him, just as he crossed the path to the customs house an arrow hit his arm sending him tumbling into the bushes.

The sailors on the roof took him for dead, focus fire came to the army archers running for the gate, most made it through the fortifications gates, many wounded, stumbled through, still outnumbered.

Once inside the large stonewalls the fighting was difficult, designed to be defended from the outside the small alcoves became hiding places for the sailors waiting for army men to run past, shot in the back, the soldiers were easy targets.

The last of Rogan's sailors were seen running through the fields, disappearing into the bushes, soldiers had taken the roof, tried to fire down on escaping sailors with little luck because the roof was designed to fight from the ocean side, not the rear.

All Prince Rogan's ships were now in sight, over a hundred large sails of many colors billowed in the soft breeze as they started moving toward the docks.

The plan was simple, five larger ships hit the docks at full speed, men began jumping from them immediately attacking the customs house, many would die from the archers remaining on the hill, expendable pawns in the chess game of war.

Other ships and smaller boats tied off to the ships tied to the dock, other boats would crash into the shore to be abandoned, their deadly mission complete.

There was a mass of confusion, like rats the sailors spread out, covered the land.

27

WORTHY WAR

"Drawing the last breath, death on ones own terms,
glory be such a man."

Wagons of King Harrow's arches on the run to the docks were driving the horses until they dropped.

Captains of the archers kept quietly in their hearts that this was a ride to certain death, King Harrow, a coward, had kept most of the troops inside the castle, this small force was just a flower in the storm, a sacrifice to be made for no purpose other than royal show.

They were only half way along the road to the docks when it started, archers from the woods shot the drivers, horses thundered on as the drivers slumped over, sacrifice was expected, desired, praised.

The first driver collapsed from his seat, the horses slowed, the wagon slowed, the driver tumbled forward, his body hitting the rear of the horses which caused them to bolt, the heavy wagon rolled over the drivers body.

It was too late, the second team of horses thundered over the first drivers body, the second driver tried to apply the brakes, two arrows ended his life during the futile effort, the third wagon was too close, in trying to stop the horses all tried to run left, pulling the wagon sideways.

Men were sprayed from the third wagon as it careened out of control then flipped.

A forth wagon, slower horses, back far enough to react, brakes applied, archers jumped, ran for the woods, it was like hounds to the hare, the small number of sailors were chased, shot, killed quickly.

The captains were furious, if Harrow had wanted success there would have been riders out in front to sniff out the attack, scouts would have cleared the road.

This war had been coming for twenty years, it was old King Philip, long dead, that had sent Rogan to sea, it was now weak King Harrow, commander, general of the army that had done nothing to prepare, good men died for weakness of the crown.

Wagons were put back on their wheels, archers piled in, wounded were left on the side of the road to fend for themselves, a cloud of dust was all the comfort they got. Those left behind cheered on their comrades, or perhaps the cheer was from those that would live to those that would die.

In the customs house sailors came running from the ships, the exit door was blocked, sailors piled in the customs house while more tried to open the far door.

A small alcove was paid no attention, the dark man in the shadows of the alcove was not of concern, Gaston pulled the lever as he fell forward from a loss of blood.

Pins holding the second floor up were released, the timbers quaked just long enough for the sailors below to look up, the entire floor, all the goods stored on it, everything crashed down.

Gaston perished with them, the last act of a brave man.

Drawing the last breath, death on ones own terms, glory be such a man.

Sailors jumping from the ships to the dock were blocked by the customs house, it was the only path from the docks up to the fortifications, sailors began jumping from the docks as more sailors tried to push forward.

Some sailors tried to climb the hill up to the fortifications, the slippery hill claimed many with broken legs, crushed hands, some were drowned as others fell on them from the crowded docks.

Rogan watched the confusion of war from the bow of his ship, not a word, an army of misfits was doing exactly what it was capable of, dying in disarray, confusion, the lack of professionalism made up by the brute strength of numbers.

Below decks of the large ships the elite troops waited, heavy with fire sticks, armor of chain, heavy leather, they were saved from the vagaries, confusion, wasted death of the masses.

When all was settled the elite would move into the sunlight, take control, secure the area for Prince Rogan.

After breaking down doors, tearing apart timbers, the sailors were able to get a path through the customs house, running over the second floor, hearing the cries for help of their shipmates crushed beneath it did not cause them to slow, help was not coming for those in the way.

Camaraderie, gallantry, compassion are illusions of war, when the battle is over valiant deeds were a fable to tell in taverns when no one is trying to kill you.

With his last breath, under the second floor, Gaston thought of his friends, lovers, parents, King Harrow who he died for no longer mattered, a kingdom, after all was not land, stone, building, a kingdom was just her people.

The flank of Harrow's archers arrived from the kingdom just as the sailors cleared the customs house, arrows reigned down from the fortifications onto the docks, no shot was aimed, any arrow in that direction found flesh, took life, wounded, blood flowed.

First of the wagons did not stop in time, before the arrows could be launched sailors were able to shoot the horses, tumbling steeds blocked the front wheels of the wagon, King Harrow's archers were launched in all directions, most landed with broken bows or crushed quivers.

The next two wagons turned quickly heading for the fortifications, the forth wagon was too late, it turned sideways, archers on the wagon fired, fired, fired, bodies of sailors piled up.

The forth wagon's archers pulled bows with every ounce of energy they could muster, soon arrows were being fired by the sailors, without cover it became a simple matter of numbers, the archers of King Harrow were taken.

Sailors forced captured archers from the wagons to the walls of the fortifications, each sailor held a blade to an archer's throat, a simple demand, open the gates or watch them die.

The captain from the first wagon screamed out to not open the gate, an arrow from the wall passed through the captain, just far enough to pierce the sailor holding him, when the captain dropped a second arrow took the sailor from this life.

Other archers of the kingdom watching this knew their lives were forfeit, some froze in place while the blades spilled their blood, some fought before the blade made its cut, a few made it free, ran a few steps before being cut down by arrows in the back.

The hope of using the compassion to get the gates opened had only given those inside resolve to win at all cost.

From behind the fortifications the two wagons of archers scurried inside carrying bundles of arrows, long bows, ready for a siege.

Sacrifice is often not understood in the heat of the moment, discussions of bravery were honed for generations as legend long after the dead were buried.

The elite troops Rogan kept below decks became restless, wanting to fight, gain glory, it was Captain Rogan's choice to leave them far in reserve.

A keg was handed over by Rogan, taken to the fortification gate, a fuse lit, before it could explode a young officer on the roof released a basket of rocks down to stop the attack at the gate, the rocks covered the cask.

The explosion sent the rocks spraying like birds scattered from a tree, sailors were cut in two, the gate was blown from its hinges, a metal bar holding the gate was bent like a sapling.

Discipline and training of the military men sent many a sailor to hell during the attack, in the close halls, small alcoves, on the roof, numbers prevailed, savage brute force overcame discipline and tactics.

When sailors took the fortifications roof Rogan marched the elite troops up the docks, with clean uniforms the elite troops talked as if they had won the battle.

Viewing the death of his sailors Rogan felt no compassion, offered the wounded no assistance, orders were barked for numbers, how many were left, get into formation.

Prince Rogan needed these men to become King Rogan, he did not want to share the kingdom with his sailors, their death now was convenient, as long as enough were left to take the castle.

While fighting at the docks was raging Herzog was pacing in the castle, short, hard, axes hanging from his belt, he had tried to leave with the archers wagons, go defend the commons house, fight with Gaston and his men.

Herzog had been stopped, order of King Harrow, he was not to leave the castle.

Word was sent that Herzog was heading for the throne room, many chose to leave so he could have a private audience with Harrow.

Harrow tried to explain calmly that Herzog was too valuable, as the captain of the guard he needed to protect the castle and all within.

Herzog yelled back, he belonged in the battle with his men.

King Harrow spoke quietly, this was not a war that could be won, the kingdom's army was small, resources were small, rabble could not be beaten, if the attackers were only an army, a leader that was not bent on vengeance, the fight would be different, this battle would be fought with diplomacy.

A commander seeking glory, pillage, plunder would be easy to force into quitting by mounting an attack, attrition, Prince Rogan was rightful heir to the throne that he had been denied, Rogan would not quit because some of his men had died.

This war was for a capitulation, negotiation would not work, all Harrow could do was hang on until reason prevailed.

Harrow needed to keep a valuable resource like Herzog close in the castle walls to show force and keep the people in line, it would be best for all.

Herzog looked at King Harrow in disgust, Herzog had never fought for any king, he fought for the kingdom, the people, farmers, his brothers in arms, craftsmen, children.

King Harrow saw himself as the kingdom, it was impossible to tell Harrow he was expendable, replaceable, unnecessary.

At the fortification above the docks twenty soldiers had been captured by the sailors, two officers were taken from the men, the remaining soldiers were lined against the wall, a line of elite troops shot them with fire sticks, metal balls cut through their bodies spraying blood upon the wall behind.

Rogan ordered the two officers to report what they had seen to the castle, there was no hope, with powder and fire sticks King Harrow should not allow the slaughter of his army when fighting was futile.

In the morning Wolf and Cozet moved slowly from the tree, working up the trails they arrived at another hamlet, only ten or so huts, few cattle were walking around, they watched for half an hour, no one moved.

Slowly Wolf and Cozet moved in, hiding, watching, looking for life, there was nothing, it was far too quiet.

Making Cozet wait at the edge of the huts Wolf moved in the hamlet square, he was crouching behind a wall when the first shutters opened, an arrow hit Wolf's quiver, just piercing under the skin on his back, Wolf tumbled, other shutters open, arrows came from other directions, it was an ambush.

Running through a stall Wolf was able to hide behind a cow for just a moment before a burst of arrows dropped the screaming bovine.

Shouts, orders, sounds of men running were coming from the far side of the hamlet.

Bow in hand Wolf ran for cover, just before reaching it sailors with bows stood from behind it, Wolf kept running, they fired, he rolled, arrows flashed just above him, coming up on one knee Wolf was able to shoot one sailor, other sailors were ready to fire again.

An arrow slammed into one of the sailors from behind, the sailor screamed, for an instant the other sailors stopped to looked their downed comrade, the arrow was in his back, the remaining sailors ducked, tried to move for cover, another sailor was hit, they were no longer running from Wolf, now they ran from the new attacker, Wolf ran as fast as he could to cover.

A door open just to Wolf's right, an arrow from the woods sliced through the door, a scream came, Wolf fired another arrow into the cabin door, another scream, a sailor ran out, a huge sword in his hand, another arrow from the woods hit the sailor's belly.

Wolf ran for the woods, a large group of sailors with swords ran from the huts chasing him, he was faster than they were, the gap opened slightly.

Arrows flashed from all sides, the sailors chasing Wolf were falling, screaming, more arrows flew, targets dropped, sailors were on the ground.

Reaching the spot where Wolf had left Cozet he panicked, she was gone.

An arrow struck at Wolf's feet, he looked up, back into the woods a man was waiving a bow, it took Wolf a second to realize that beside the huge man was Cozet.

Sailors with bows were now running from the huts to chase Wolf, the prize, a bounty was on his head, from places all over the woods arrows flew, the sailors retreated back to the huts.

Women from the village that was destroyed the day before had gone to surrounding villages, found hunters, archers, not fighters, not warriors, men capable of killing from long range no matter the game.

The hunters wanted to work with Wolf and Cozet, learn from them, the sailors had killed wantonly, this was the time to fight in unison.

Wolf declined, work in small groups, avoid the hamlets, villages, take sailors where the hunters could slip back into the woods, ambush, surprise, they were vulnerable to armies.

As they talked a scream would come from the hamlet every now and then, archers in the woods finding targets of opportunity.

Finally Wolf asked the hard question, yes, all in the hamlet were dead, a young boy had watched, men killed first, women raped then tied to stakes in the back of the hamlet, shot randomly as target practice.

Wolf and Cozet moved back into the forest, slipped away.

Slowly the hunters were starting to move from the woods, finish the remaining sailors sheltered in the hamlet, women were moving up the trail, many of them, pitchforks in hand, before the hunters could clear the huts the women moved in clearing vermin of the sea from their homes.

When all you care for has been taken—you can take all without remorse, regret, contemplation.

The women had abandon their huts, chosen weapons to vent rage, anger, hatred upon the enemy.

Those dead were buried in a mass grave, prayers were said, then the hunters and women formed a pact, make this hamlet an easy target for the sailors to attack, combined they would bring the sailors in, then kill the sea dogs without mercy.

Moving to a cave in the mountains Wolf and Cozet discussed options, in the end it was decided that they had no options, they washed in the pond beside a small waterfall, dried each other, blessed living another day, made love as if it was their last day.

When the fire was just embers tears leaked slowly from Cozet's eyes upon Wolf's back, she remembered feeling so hopeless in the woods when she realized he was trapped, her arrows were not enough, she fired, moved, then a hand on her shoulder, others helped her husband, this war was beyond her control, she hated it.

Without those men Wolf would have died, his flesh would not be with her now, his spirit would not fill her, his blood would be running in the dirt.

If only morning would not come.

If only there were no war.

If only she could protect him.

Wolf rolled over, kissed the tears from Cozet's eyes, wrapped his big arms around her, warm, safe, she slept soundly.

This moment was the gift, embrace it, cherish it, there may be no other.

Perhaps alone they were more vulnerable, in a team they would be a bigger target, they had skills to help the hunters be more effective, alone they could wage their own war on their own terms.

It was impossible to tell what the future held, there were many options, too few good options.

28

FINAL SHIP

"Power is speed, speed is survival."

It was Zorn's first real voyage on his new ships, they were entering the harbor for inspection at King Santoum's docks, it was a disappointing start to a very long journey home.

As Zorn's ship crossed into the bay he realized Salome's ship had dropped back, she was turning hard against the wind, her ship laid over as the wind caught it, she was tacking down the coast away from the bay.

At first he thought that she was just changing angle to get the best wind heading into the harbor. Now it was clear she had no intention of following him in.

Feeling betrayed when you can only watch is an emptiness that is quickly filled in with anger from deep within your belly, betrayal destroys ones confidence, crushing all hope.

Just as Zorn was starting to understand what Salome was doing his ship's men began screaming, it was an ambush, Santoum's navy had ships hidden in coves just inside the bay, twenty ships were trying to pull out from hiding on either side of them.

The navy ships had full sails up, the wind inside the bay had not made it around the inlets where the navy ships were hiding.

Most navy ships had oars out, they were rowing to the wind, once in the wind it was just a matter of speed and position.

Power is speed, speed is survival.

Pushing the tiller over hard Zorn was getting ready for a true battle, willing to trade position for speed he brought his ship around closer to the far bank where the wind would be weakest.

Zorn ordered the crew to get all the sails up, setup the fire arrows, none of his crew moved.

Swords came off Zorn's back plate, clearly Salome had created a crew for him that would not fight King Santoum, his men would not fight their real master, spies to make sure the powerful ships were surrendered to the king.

An easy plan, Zorn would die accidentally in battle, a big funeral was already being prepared, a stone mausoleum was being built for his body.

It was the small man Zorn had hired who ran aft, grabbed the rudder, brought the riders ship back into the wind.

Zorn's ship was under heavy sail from the ocean breeze, he had no intention of losing the wind, power, maneuverability, his very life hung in the balance.

From Zorn's training by Salome he remembered the rule, he who moves too fast simply makes the first mistake. He who makes the first mistake dies.

Navy ships were now getting more wind, their sails were filling, building speed, they would be upon him soon. Like hounds on the hare, death was inevitable if his crew would not fight.

Zorn ordered his men to pull fire arrows from below again, not one moved, he stabbed the crewman closest to him in the arm, the crew did not move.

Enraged, screaming, Zorn grabbed the man he had stabbed and threw him overboard, the man in the water screamed, it was motivational.

Water dogs were not in the bay, Zorn wanted the men to think when thrown in the water dogs would rip them to shreds.

The small man on the rudder called out to the other men of the crew, die from Zorn's blade or your master, King Santoum, sinking your ship, even if you turn this ship over to your king he will kill you, do not fight for the infidel, fight for your own life.

Silence was the only response, no one moved, Zorn contemplated killing another crewman.

A shout came from the bow, one of Santoum's ships, small, under heavy oar, closing quick, each stroke produced a huge surge of speed on the navy ship that the wind could not match.

Hard right, broadside now, Zorn ordered the fire arrows lit, no one moved.

When Zorn stepped forward to light the fuses, men stood in his way.

Shouting erupted from the men, some wanting Zorn's ship to fire, save their lives, others wanted to remain loyal to King Santoum.

As if by some silent consensus the men moved from Zorn's path.

Zorn ran with a small stick from the fire, setting off the first three tubes, they all flew right over the approaching ship.

Too close, these fire arrows were only good at a set distance.

Crew members grabbed small sticks from the fire, lighting the fuses they held up the rear of the fire arrows, down the arrows slammed on the small navy ship that was getting ready to attack them.

Men on the oars of the navy ship scattered, another set of fire arrows were lit and blasted off, smoke poured from the small ship, men jumped overboard, the navy ship turned, limped out of the battle.

King Santoum's small ship lost, the attack was successful in delaying Zorn from getting to the wind, every second lost allowed the navy ships to find better wind, gain valuable speed.

Closing from all sides, out of range, one of the attacking ships erupted in smoke, the ship had fired, early, or had a longer range.

Men dove for cover on Zorn's ship, the streams of smoke came in, all missed except two which hit the sails setting them on fire, Zorn's men ran for the mast, pulling cloth down, gain control, Zorn's ship was slowing.

Ten of Zorn's men moved to the rail, two men ran for more fire arrows, it was oblivion for a few moments as smoke rolled across the deck, the fire arrows were tested for range, short of the ship that had fired on them.

Zorn ordered his men to hold fire, less distance, closer, judgment, do not waste fire arrows, the distances would close quickly, reloading could be the difference between success and failure.

Wind caught the new sails, it was Zorn's turn to maneuver, alone, the one with the wind controlled the war.

Zorn's ships bow set at the closest approaching ship, a very large heavy slow beast that appeared to be well armed. On the navy ships deck a flaming catapult was being readied.

As Zorn pulled the tiller hard to get broadside he could hear the other captain yell to fire the catapult.

Zorn responded, yelling to fire all of the arrows on the right side of his ship, ten at a time the arrows flew, luck, luck was all Zorn needed.

Two arrows struck the fire used to ignite the flaming ball on the catapult. The explosion sent sparks flying into the rigging, more fires started instantly, the large old ship began breaking away, from the side another ten fire arrows struck the navy ship, one went through the captains leg, pinned him to the mast, exploded, cutting him in half.

These skirmishes were child's play, the real war was coming, ships so close together that they could almost touch each other, moving in formation to cut off any escape to the ocean, all of this for a son in-law who had been betrayed by his wives.

All Zorn's men ran to the far side of the ship, this gave them a weight advantage and the ability to use the wind.

Another navy oar ship was closing, her sails up, without enough wind to hold her she had the oar's fully deployed, the old navy ship was getting ready for a run to ram, Zorn's ship's armor was light, unable to withstand a full force stab in the side.

Zorn had only one choice, he maneuvered his ship to run from the ocean, collect wind, speed, position lost.

The navy ship's turn was sharp, a gust caught them just right, before the attacking ship could use her new speed, Zorn used his ship to slide down the side of the attacker, breaking off her oars right at the hull, broken oars floated on the wake as Zorn passed.

Toward the end of her pass Zorn's ship fired five close fire arrows, each landed on the sails, quickly they caught fire, burning fabric fell on the ships deck, another of King Santoum's ships, was out of commission.

Through the smoke from the fire arrows Zorn could see a sail from one of his wife's ships, he could not tell which one, they were in the trap, or perhaps this was more of their plan help King Santoum kill him.

Before Zorn decided to trust or run from his wives ship, the wives ship fired a full fifty arrows at the closest attacker, King Santoum's navy ship burst into flames almost instantly, the deck was on fire, the sails were starting to burn, worst of all the smoke was impossible to see through, another navy ship disabled, the smoke made great cover for his wife's ship to change direction for a better position.

A yell came from Zorn's crew, two ships now in the fight, they had a chance to survive this day.

Four navy ships closing from the other side, Zorn turned hard and passed his ship between the four navy ships running abreast of each other almost hitting two.

At amidships, Zorn's crew fired two hundred arrows from both sides of his ship, some were held up to strike the closer navy ships, some left down to land in the sails of the farther navy ships.

The captains of the four navy ships realized their error too late, an arrow that missed Zorn's ship might hit one of their own ships so they hesitated to fire until Zorn was past.

A brash young navy captain of an outside ship made a brilliant move, he dropped all sails, his ship stopped dead in the water, just as the ship beside him passed he turned hard exposing one side to Zorn's escaping ship.

The navy ship was dead in the water so her aim was off, she fired one bank of fire arrows, most missed Zorn's slim ship, a few struck the rear setting the captain's quarters on fire.

A single fire arrow hit the little man holding the tiller killing him instantly, Zorn's ship turned sharply, almost went over on its side.

Zorn ran to the tiller, took control of his ship. It was too late, they had lost the wind, it was impossible to keep her straight, the young navy captain had his ships fire tubes almost reloaded, once the navy ship fired Zorn's ship would be destroyed, it was the way of war.

Just as the navy captain gave the order to fire he looked back to the far side of his ship, a bow was just ramming into the opposite side of his ship.

Under full sail Fatima and Quintal's ship had enough power to force the navy ship onto its side. The fire arrows all lit in a blaze of smoke, all splashed harmlessly into the water in front of the navy ship.

Another shout went up from Zorn's men, another ship far to the left of them was about to fire, smoke roared from the deck of the attacking ship, Zorn's men had boxes of fire arrows on the deck, one arrow struck a sailor, passed through his body smashed into a box of fire arrows setting it on fire.

Screaming, a sailor grabbed the burning box, pulling with all his might, the sailor staggered to the rail, then vanished over the side with the burning box.

Zorn froze as the war took one event filled turn after another, he was not able to see what was going on in the smoke, at least his crew was focused and working hard to stay alive.

Screams of wounded men came up through the smoke on Zorn's ship, another navy ship was about to fire on them.

The fire arrows looked like angels in the air, thin trails of smoke followed behind them, it was clearly Salome's ship, sails were full, moving with the wind, her ship cut through the water like a dancer, making small moves, precise timing, unleashing a torrent of death, changing direction to get a better position.

Zorn was hasty, his crew untrained, worst of all he had no plan, he just reacted to the next crisis.

Salome was the ultimate captain, thinking about her next maneuver before this one was complete, this was a chess game on the water for her.

Shouting clear precise orders Salome was in full command of her crew, her ship, the ability to fire arrows at the proper range for the most damage.

Rallying his crew again Zorn was getting ready for more battle, as he moved the attackers moved, he was the target, loaded, moving under full sail, he crossed between Salome's ship and the line of navy ships moving to block an escape back to the sea.

Like Salome, Zorn waited for the right time to fire, placement, planning, Fatima and Quintal's ship was just pulling away from the navy ship they had rammed.

Fatima was lighting fire arrows with her crew, point blank they hit the navy ship they had just rammed, the fire arrows struck just above the water line.

Even before Fatima and Quintal had sailed fully past the arrows were exploding along the navy ships rear section, water was entered the hull, it was out of the battle.

Zorn wanted to try and help Fatima and Quintal, their ship had been badly damaged during the ramming, now leaning in the water at a steep angle, their sails were up, the crew was running in all directions trying to gain control again.

Moving to a better position was critical for Zorn's survival, also to be able to help his wives survive the battle.

Zorn began issuing orders the crew understood, all sails were up, all tubes reloaded, all enemy ships must be hit in the sails to slow them down.

Sailing at an angle to the opening of the ocean Zorn had speed up, King Santoum's ships from the left were finally up to speed, ready for attack.

Waiting this time, no rush, distance was critical, at the proper moment Zorn turned his ship hard, fifty fire arrows were unleashed, his heart stopped, too far, not far enough, better judgment, should he have, too many questions in the his mind.

The thoughts trailed off in Zorn's head as the fire arrows began to land, sails were on fire, the decks of the navy ships were full of scurrying bodies, in turning away the navy ships he lost the wind.

Inside of Santoum's fleet Zorn used them against each other, navy ships were unwilling to fire if too close so he sailed his ship hard at them, smashing the side of a ship with oars scattering men all over the deck, removing half of their power.

As navy ships sailed past Zorn made a hard turn to the right, then left, this lowered the left side of his ship to the water, ten fire arrows struck the rear of Zorn's ship.

Only a few boat lengths away Salome was maneuvering for a shot, at high speed she cut between Zorn and the line of navy ships, five arrows at each ship, many navy ships were on fire, most arrows precisely aimed by Salome's crew hit in the masts and sails.

Another navy ship further off fired a salvo of fire arrows at Salome's ship, just as they were lighting the fuses Salome caught the wind, she was out of the way when the fire arrows landed.

Then it came, one large fire arrow, not like the others, ten times the size, fired from the cliffs above, it struck high in the rigging of Zorn's ship, caught in the ropes it dropped to the deck, exploded, made a hole as wood fragments flew, men bled, screams came from the deck.

The large rocket was a test, the hills came alive with smoke, streaming fire arrows raced through the sky, not enough wind to outrun them all.

Overboard, Zorn screamed at his men to get overboard, even before he landed in the water the huge fire arrows were tearing holes in his new ship, the mast held, the sails were gone, a few arrows hit directly on the deck, when it was gone they hit below deck, when it was gone they hit the inside hull.

Navy ships were closing from all sides now, finally finding the wind, hampered by the smoke, unable to target Zorn like the men on the hill had done from their stable platform.

From nowhere a rope slapped the water beside Zorn, he grabbed on, orders were coming again, fast from the deck of Salome's ship.

Salome's ship stuck on sunken rigging while trying to escape, she was angry, demanding, ordering the crew in precise steps to get free.

A salvo came from the shore again, her ship was just behind the last ship Zorn had disabled, only one large arrow hit harmlessly on the bow, slid past, exploded just under the water, the fire arrow missed damaging her ship, the arrow did push the bow away from the submerged rigging that held it.

As Zorn climbed aboard Salome's ship she yelled at him to light fuses, fire on her command only.

Where Salome found wind was a mystery, her ship danced above the water turning her side to the attackers, a hundred fire arrows were launched at four approaching navy ships.

Navy captains broke pattern to avoid her fire arrows, at the prefect range the arrows were deadly to sails, rigging, men, young navy captain's courage failed.

Turning her ships aft to the attackers Salome sailed toward the opening of the bay, Fatima and Quintal's ship was heading from the opposite direction, all sought to find the open ocean and freedom.

Six attackers abreast were chasing Salome's ship.

From the deck Zorn could see Fatima at the helm turning her ship to the side, Quintal ran down the line of fire arrows lighting fuses, a hundred arrows, the sky was ablaze, their crew chased behind Quintal placing new arrows in the holders.

As Salome's ship past Fatima and Quintal's ship Zorn could see the bow was broken open, they were sinking, they rammed to save his life, now their ship was damaged beyond repair.

Fatima and Quintal were sacrificing their lives for him, all he could do was watch helplessly.

Zorn ordered Salome to turn, help, pick Fatima and Quintal up.

Salome said nothing, they continued on to open ocean.

Fire arrows flew from the deck of Fatima and Quintal's ship. Both sides now, they were blocking the bay entrance.

Zorn screamed at Salome to turn back, save Fatima and Quintal.

Salome looked down on her weak infidel husband, Zorn must understand, accept the gift of their lives that they give you willingly, embrace the gift of your own life, a strong man would know this, a true warrior would know this, her weak husband dishonored the gift he had been given by Fatima and Quintal.

Then it came, the hills were covered in smoke, it looked like a thick blanket of fog swirling around, how many hit Fatima and Quintal's ship would be impossible to tell, the only thing Zorn was certain of was that everyone was dead.

Upon hitting the ocean Salome did not relax, Zorn took the tiller from her, she set the direction, gave him orders.

Zorn apologized, he was sorry to not have trusted her, he admitted he was wrong.

Salome laughed, walked away, Zorn was weak, a hollow shell of a man, unworthy of her, unworthy of this ship.

Salome had full sails set for the open ocean when Zorn turned to the harbor, she knew he was sailing into a trap.

Fatima, Quintal and Salome all knew the bay was a trap, they were the ones that had set it.

It was Salome that had told King Santoum the infidel would use the new assassin ships to kill him, take over his kingdom, make them all follow the false son of God, not the real teachings of God.

Both the wives ships were letting Zorn lead into the bay, it was Fatima and Quintal that betrayed Salome, stole her freedom, by entering the bay to die with their husband, stupid weak women, ungrateful for all Salome had taught them.

Salome had no choice, follow Fatima and Quintal, or her treachery would have been uncovered.

The ships laid out by King Santoum were no match for the fast ships Salome had designed.

It was Salome that told the generals to use the larger fire arrows from the cliffs to sink Zorn's ship, she even trained them how to judge the distance.

Loading Zorn's ship with men loyal to King Santoum, Salome's men were loyal only to her, obeyed every command.

Now Salome was stuck, married to this pail, weak, disgusting husband that was so unworthy of her.

That night as the stars guided Zorn and Salome further out to the open ocean, she walked to the bow, took a piece of chain, slowly moved to the rail, stood silent, listened to the wind, felt the full sails.

Truth comes on the mighty ocean at night, our own insignificance, forbidden desires, haunting memories, misguided lust, a need to end what is wrong, a betrayal of our own heart comes on the black waves at night.

Salome placed her foot on the rail, it would be so easy, no more playing the weak woman to inferior men, hearing their boasts caused her such pain.

Just step over the side and let the ocean solve all of her problems.

Replacing the chain Salome returned to her husbands bed, being so weak, unworthy, his life span would be short, it was a hardship to wait for his death, a burden she would tolerate until his lifeless body was put overboard, then she would master her own ship again, hold his remaining precious stones, take command of her men.

As morning came Zorn kissed Salome's neck, put his arms around her, held her close to him, it disgusted her, a strong man would have taken her, used her, fulfilled his needs.

Zorn was no man, no husband, no captain, most of all no lover for a strong woman of passion, desire, animal longing must wait until her husband was dead and a strong husband found.

29

SIEGE

"Dignity was the worst casualty of war."

It took almost two weeks for Prince Rogan's sailors to move from the shore to the castle.

Food stolen, women violated, lands destroyed, smoke could be seen from the castle walls in almost every direction, new debauchery each day, all in the castle could only watch, hope, pray.

Villagers running for shelter in the castle had come before the sailors arrived, King Harrow took in his people to a point, then the gates were closed, those inside would live, those outside would face less palatable fates, if all were allowed in the castle then surely all would die during a long siege.

Those denied entrance moved back into the mountains, refugees when they reached the next kingdom, from farmers and tradesmen to lost souls with nothing to show for years of toil, muscle to toil again so they could build a new life.

Some of the men in the villages offered to fight King Harrow instead of immediate death at the hands of the sailors, others were told if they did not fight Harrow then their wives or children would pay the price of death, torture, rape.

Women were taken as camp servants, cook, clean, wash during the day, service other needs in the dark, at night a river of tears washed into the dirt from violated women.

Dignity was the worst casualty of war.

No plunder was found in the small hamlets, gold, jewels, those would have to wait for the castle to be taken, what Prince Rogan would not tell the sailors was that King Harrow had a small treasury, not worth the gamble of their lives to fight for.

When Rogan and his sailors arrived at the castle walls some of the villagers who had resisted were tied in small groups, around the neck, like cords of wood.

Each morning started with a ritual, a group villagers tied at the neck were taken to the field between the castle walls and the sailor's encampment, just out of arrow range, a stake was placed in the ground, villagers tied to it, wood stacked, then Prince Rogan himself would walk down, laughing, waive to the castle, set the fire.

Some days the screaming would last beyond understanding of those in the castle, each day an arrow was fired into the castle with a note demanding surrender so the slaughter could stop.

Each day an arrow was shot back demanding the invaders leave or all would be killed.

Death was not the worst of it, those tied, waiting, knowing they could be selected the next day had lost all hope. Those to be executed anyway did not get food or water, they lived in their own filth.

King Harrow and Prince Rogan cared nothing for the people. Power was the intoxicating brew they fed upon, their only reward came in more power, people could be replaced.

From the parapet of the castle walls Herzog watched the sacrifice each morning, looked on as the archer shot the note demanding surrender over the castle walls, beside Herzog, Morgan, the boy Wolf and Cozet were helping, in anger, frustration, sadness, each day the two would leave, show over.

It was the third day that Morgan began looking at Wolf's old bows, ones Wolf had made in the woods when exiled from the hamlet of his birth.

One bow in particular was very long, almost half an arm longer than Morgan's height with stout limbs, slowly he started scraping down the limbs until he could bend them, shaving small pieced from the sides, careful to keep the same curve at each end so that one side was not pulling harder than the other.

That night at Herzog's dinner table Morgan was asked what he was working on, he offered no information, not a secret, just private.

Next Morgan made arrows, long, sturdy, of a kind of wood he had never seen before, stiff with a light grain that ran straight along the arrow, no knots, no blemish, one shot must be perfect.

In the end Morgan realized his mistake, he was making a conventional bow that was too long of a pull for him to make with his young arms, no man in the kingdom had arms long enough to pull this bow.

In frustration Morgan was going to give up, a waste of time, fantasy of a young mind not mature enough to understand the function of a bow.

Before Morgan left the shop he put his foot on the bow just to try pulling the sinew string with both hands. He was able to pull it almost all the way back. So he changed position, put both feet on the bow, pulled back with both hands. It was very hard to pull at first, he could almost reach his chin with the string.

Then Morgan lay upon his back, placed his feet on the bow, placed the arrow between his toes, pulled back with all his might, it took too much strength to pull it back.

On the next try Morgan bent his legs, held the string by his chin and then pushed his legs forward, this did not require his arm strength, he was pushing with his much stronger legs.

Morgan had done it, an arrow was under full force of the powerful bow, while this was fun it had a great flaw, no one could aim such a bow.

In the horse paddock that night Morgan snuck down and practiced, long hours of shooting arrow after arrow from his back in the candlelight.

At first he fired over the fence, out into the walls around the stables, later he had enough control to hit the fence, just not where he had aimed.

The next morning Herzog commented on Morgan's fingers being bandaged, he made the boy remove the wraps, seeing the blisters, torn flesh, concerned, he asked.

Reluctantly Morgan showed Herzog the massive bow, long arrows, almost his full length, a light rock tip just like Wolf had taught Morgan to make.

Herzog laughed at Morgan, told how they all sought answers, this one could not work, the men on the pointed end of the arrow were safer than those shooting such a silly bow.

Dismayed Morgan walked away, he did not eat with the Herzog and Samantha, later the captain came to the boy's room in the castle.

Herzog told Morgan that in the morning they would shoot his bow, take his shot, see the folly of this wasted effort.

Early fog was in, on the highest parapet Morgan lay on his back, Herzog guided the aim, the distance was too far, when Rogan lit the fire there was no way to reach him.

On this day the sailors had placed the stake slightly closer to the castle walls because the bodies were starting to pile up, there were less guards, there was turmoil because a man had broken free from the rope, caught, tied back up to be burned properly.

Finally Prince Rogan stepped from his tent, walked down to the villagers tied to the stake, stood talking with his sailors for a moment.

Herzog made Morgan wait until Rogan was holding the torch so they were sure to shoot the right man.

Standing behind Morgan, Herzog lined up the arrow with those tied to the stakes so that he could have Morgan fire when Rogan stood still while placing the torch in the kindling.

The arrow was released on Herzog's command, all that could be seen were the feathers moving up into the air, far from their sight the arrow was lost.

Morgan loaded again, held the string and arrow against his chin, forced his legs forward, strained to hold, when Herzog whispered to fire the arrow was released.

Hitting the ground between the parapet and the target the first arrow had gone into the ground without notice.

The second arrow had a slight flaw in the feathers, when out of sight it began to move to the left, hitting harmlessly in the trees.

Herzog said not to fire the third arrow, it was too much effort and the arrows were not getting anywhere close.

Morgan already had the third arrow on the bow, the boy did not listen to Herzog.

Pushing the bow forward with his legs Morgan whispered to God for this to work.

Herzog laughed at the exuberance of youth, grabbing Morgan's shoulders he turned the boy to point in the direction that Prince Rogan was walking away from the fire.

Exhausted, unable to hold the bowstring any longer, Morgan let the arrow fly.

The third arrow had long departed the bow, Morgan had stood, Herzog was about to turn away.

Prince Rogan dropped to one knee.

Herzog said how Rogan must have tripped, it was too long of a shot, and too long of a time between the shot and the fall, surely Rogan had just tripped on uneven ground.

Sailors ran around Rogan, he was up again, being helped from the field. This was no sprained ankle.

That day the note demanding surrender from Rogan was more direct, it described the slaughter of peasants, destruction of the lands, it seemed to be a rant of anger more than a demand for surrender, Herzog was sure of it, the arrow had hit its mark.

Morning next Prince Rogan did not light the fire, the stake was further back from the castle wall, lit by a regular sailor who was very nervous.

Morgan was laying in wait, three more arrows had been made during the night, each with great care. It was frustrating to not have a target, these arrows were made to kill one man, Rogan, killing a sailor would not do for such fine arrows.

That day's note from Rogan was not a demand for surrender, this note was disturbing, a trade, the archer who shot the long arrow would be placed outside the castle or a hundred peasants would be killed in his place.

King Harrow called Herzog to his chambers, who was the archer, what had gone on, the archers along the castle wall thought the shot had come from the parapet where Herzog and Morgan were standing.

At first Herzog was going to tell the tale, brag for Morgan of ingenuity, fantasy, determination that was youth, great accomplishment, bold deeds.

Honor was an illusion in the court of King Harrow, the throne was built on tales of wise judgment, hero was a term used, often, not after a twist of fate had sullied the process.

Herzog looked at King Harrow in disbelief, there was no tale to tell, no great archer, Herzog had simply watched like everyone else, no reason to think that he had some knowledge of the hero or where such a person would have came from.

Picking up a small purse of coins Harrow threw it at Herzog, find the archer with the long bow, keep the purse or give it as a prize, Harrow demanded Herzog provide that name tonight.

It shattered Herzog to think what this proved, King Harrow was a going to capitulate to Prince Rogan, turn Morgan over to Rogan to be killed, evil flesh inhabited the royal robes, royal desperate acts often staggered the imagination.

Hustling off to find the Morgan, Herzog knew that he had to get to the boy before Morgan told the tale to anyone, bragging of the deed could be a death sentence.

In the stables Morgan was on his back, three new arrows, working on a solution to the power of the bow, making it draw farther with even better arrows, longer, the arrows were now taller than Morgan.

Morgan jumped up to show his craftsmanship, Herzog grabbed the bow and arrows, threw them under a table, Herzog was just starting to tell the boy to be quiet when the stall was filled with guards from the walls.

The wall guards had seen Morgan carry a huge bow, witnessed the arrows, one even saw Herzog point at Rogan just before an arrow was fired.

Herzog, as their captain ordered the guards back on the wall, out of the stables.

Turning to leave all of the guards were filing out, one stopped suddenly, turned, pointed under the table. Herzog reached for an axe on his belt, all the men from the wall filed out, no one was willing for a confrontation.

Night fell, Herzog had the boy sleep on the bench in his warm kitchen, it was very late when the knock came, King Harrow himself, leading twenty men, before Herzog could start to protect Morgan the boy was grabbed, taken.

Risking his life Harrow went close to Herzog, trying to make the captain understand the power of this situation, a young boy's life was not important when it could be traded for a hundred people.

Harrow smiled, once Morgan was delivered, Prince Rogan had promised to board his boats, head to sea, never set foot in the kingdom again.

King Harrow tried to explain, he was turning over Morgan for the people of the kingdom, not himself, there was no glory, diplomacy would settle this conflict.

When Harrow had left Herzog spit on the ground where Harrow had stood, in his house, lied so boldly to him, Samantha held Herzog, she cried, he got more angry.

An hour later there was a ruckus in the stables, Herzog had woken the stable boys, his own stallion was saddled, along with two of the long riders stallions.

Walking the horses through the streets quietly Herzog stopped at the long rider's headquarters, two of the old long rider captains were sleeping soundly.

Herzog woke Madras and Balder, started to explain, they stopped him, whatever he wanted would be done.

Rank required reason before orders were followed, trusted friends required no reason.

When the three reached the gate guards asked about the purpose of the journey, where could they be going, leaving the castle meant certain death, cold steel against the guards throats ended the questions, the gate was let down.

From outside the gate sailors on watch could see movement, black horses, riders dressed in black, startled, the guards did not call what they could not identify, the gate closed, no alarm sounded.

Heading to the coast Herzog had turned away from his companions, they went inland, back to the mountains, each knew secret trails, not covered, slipping past guards that heard, yet never understood what they had not seen.

As morning broke Herzog was unsure if he was doing the right thing, Wolf and Cozet could be anywhere doing anything, it was possible he could ride right past them and never even know it.

Worst of all Herzog could not ride the road fearing ambush by the sailors, it was morning before he could even see where he was going, the stallion was running on instinct through the darkness, a wrong foot fall, a misstep could ruin the plan, many would die in vain.

A village up ahead, one of the larger ones, Herzog looked from a distance, a woman washing clothing could be seen, then a young boy went to the waters edge with a bucket.

Herzog moved in slowly, hoped to find everything ok, hoped to find word of Wolf and Cozet, a direction to go so he could find them.

Herzog was almost to the far side of the river when the young boy with the bucket looked up, realizing who it was the boy tried to warn Herzog off, an arrow came from a village wall, the young boy fell face first into the water, the feathers of the arrow sticking from his small back.

Sailors were running now, Herzog could hear horses starting to run, it was too late for escape, leaning down he whispered in the stallion's ear, the large horse dropped to the ground on its knees, Herzog slid off, lay on the ground beside the stallion whispering softly to his trusted partner.

From the village horses and riders were flying, some pointed at the horse laying on the ground, others thought an attack was coming from up the road, only a few came to check out the dead horse without a rider, the rest were heading up the road to defend.

When the approaching riders were only a few lengths away Herzog stepped on the stallions back, in one bold leap the horse jumped from the ground, charged the oncoming riders.

The first rider swung high, aiming at Herzog's head, the captain ducked, an axe from Herzog's belt cut the sailors leg off just below the hip, the sailor tumbled from his mount screaming, grabbing at the stump.

The rear rider was directly in line with Herzog, just before reaching the sailor Herzog's large stallion reared up, charged, the sailors horse tried to turn away, the sharp move of the horse sent the rider to the ground, Herzog's axe hit the sailor square on top of the head.

Turning sharply one of the sailors had stopped his horse, bow ready, Herzog threw a blade, just as the man pulled the bow, Herzog's blade shattered the bow, then shattered the sailors ribs, slowly the sailor faded from his horse, gently he lay upon the ground holding the handle of the heavy blade.

The last riders were side by side, looked at each other, one wanted to run, the other fight, swords swinging wildly over their heads the two sailors charged, Herzog did not move, a length of net in his hand, it was a flip more than a throw, the net spread, a circle wider than a man, it was not at the men, the horses, just over their heads.

Startled, the first horse hit by the net ran to the side, started bucking, the second sailor kept coming, Herzog pulled up his large axe, charging at the sailor.

The sailor swung his sword, Herzog brought the axe up, the sailors sword hit the axe square, stopped, broke, the axe kept going through the sailor's arm.

Screaming from the side the first sailor had just pulled the net from his horses head, tried to swing the net, instead hit his horse in the face, the horse bucked again, the sailor was thrown to the ground, a blade from Herzog hit the sailor in the center of the chest, riding past Herzog pulled the blade and retrieved the net in one move.

From up the road shouts were coming, those on the road were heading back to help their comrades.

Herzog leaned over and yelled, the stallion stomped on the ground, like the wind they were gone, a small cloud of dust could be seen, Herzog seemed to vanish in the middle of the open field.

In the hills above the village Herzog watched as the sailors searched for him, riding to the far hill he was able to have a clear view of the huts.

A pile at the edge of the village, at first it looked like old firewood, it was people, a pile, burned. Women were now being pushed from huts, blades put to their throats, killed, because Herzog had come this way they paid with their lives.

Herzog and his stallion rode on, this must stop, his mission was too important.

One sailor had caught a glimpse of Herzog up on the hill, a magnificent stallion under him, all that they had were large slow farm horses, the sailors would never be able to catch Herzog this way.

On the other hand, the large stallion would have to come down from the hills, there was a way, trap Herzog when he dropped down, take him when he could no longer ride the hills.

The sailors remounted their horses, some went to the base of the hills to track Herzog, some rode fast to get other sailors from other villages to help take the captain.

The sun had moved far across the sky when Herzog realized the hills were too steep ahead, he had to drop down, stopping for a long time he watched, no movement in the valley below, no horse, rider, cart, no one even in the fields to harvest the crops.

Herzog kept the pace slow, moving down the trail, stopping to look every few lengths, a feeling that the trap was close made him nervous, just a second before the stallion stepped on the last plateau the trap was sprung.

Sailors on horseback closed from both sides covering the ground quickly, ahead was an opening, Herzog kicked the stallion and they started to run for it, the only way out, he could keep going like this until they gave up, their horses were too slow to catch his fine stallion.

Half the distance to the main trail down Herzog realized why it had been left open, a perfect ambush, these riders were pushing him into a small cut in the rocks, if that were cut off he would have no way out.

Turning the stallion hard Herzog charged the men herding him, greatly outnumbered, one man did not have a chance, yet he did not stop, jumping up on the stallions back Herzog screamed as if the bowels of hell were leaping from his chest.

Axes and knives from Herzog's belt flew, some hit, some did not, even those who missed the mark caused the horses and sailors, confidence to waiver.

That hesitation was all Herzog needed, pulling hard left Herzog rode to the edge of the plateau, grabbing the stallions main he shouted in his partners ear, it would be a dance, each graceful stride, each placed step, down they went over the edge, Herzog threw himself to the rear of the saddle for balance, grabbed onto the straps.

Reigns lay flat on the stallions back as it found foothold after foothold on the steep hill, missing boulders, small trees, each step a leap of faith, Herzog gave all control to the stallion, the stallion knew its purpose, was up for the challenge.

As the ground began to level Herzog could see riders coming from the far left, riding hard, the trap had been sprung, not where the sailors had planned.

With only one axe and one knife left the battle would be short, futile, Herzog would make the battle to the death, if not for himself, for Morgan.

The stallion was breathing hard when it hit the flat ground, Herzog jumped off, pulled two apples from his pocket, at least they would die after eating well.

Herzog could hear the horses coming, not in site yet, moving fast, much faster than the stallion could go after that hill.

When the horses and sailors came into view there was only one rider with three horses, the single rider was bent down over his horse, Herzog had seen a rider on each horse when he saw them from the hill.

Mounting up Herzog went back up the road from the direction of the three sailors, there in the rocks hunters with bows waived to him, it took him a second to realize they were telling him to get back, slowly Herzog backed the stallion up, just enough so the captain could see the road down from the plateau.

It was the same trap the sailors were trying to spring on Herzog, now the archers were going to spring it on the sailors, the first horses appeared, running at full speed, the archers did not shoot, next came a pack of riders, waiting until they were all clear of the hill arrows came from all sides, thundering hooves stopped in mid stride, horses tried to go left or right on the thin trail, pushing other riders off their mounts.

Of the first riders through two came in Herzog's direction, grabbing his axe in one hand, the big knife in the other Herzog was hunting for revenge.

The first sailor passed to Herzog's left with a mighty swing of his sword, Herzog leaned back and the sword missed by inches, the sailor made it a few strides past Herzog when the large knife from his belt found its mark square in the sailor's back.

The second rider was now changing direction, making a run for it, leaning over the stallion's back Herzog spurred him on. It took a few minutes to catch up, dodging, weaving, the sailor was going to die when caught.

Bringing up the net a flick sent it into the air, as the sailor changed direction again the net caught just enough of him to wrap around, throw him off balance, turning sharply the man had given up running, it was time for a charge.

The sailor pulled a second large sword, spurred his horse on, with the swords swinging over his head the sailor charged Herzog, with a nudge the stallion was in full flight, the captain held his axe high.

At first it looked easy, as Herzog approached the sailor had the two swords at different levels, just a second before impact Herzog pulled the stallion wide, the sailor was not able to match the turn, missed the attack.

Lining up again the sailor was riding against Herzog, this time the captain was ready, hooking his feet on the opposite side of the saddle he let the rider come past and make his swings, easily Herzog ducked the swords, when the rider was just past the captain threw the axe at the man, both swords hitting the axe at once sent the axe to the ground without harm.

With no weapons left Herzog wisely made a run for the archers, the sailor stayed behind trying to catch up, the stallion was in full stride, it was just after the turn that Herzog saw her, a thin figure, dressed in fur on the side of the road, her bow in hand, a smile on her sweet lips.

Dropping to one knee Cozet pulled, fired, three rapid arrows, each on target, the sailor following Herzog rode past, three arrows sticking from his chest, when the horse turned the sailor fell off, making a cloud of dust in the road.

Jumping from the stallion's back Herzog ran to Cozet, knelt, kissed the hem of her clothing, Wolf walked from the woods laughing.

Herzog started shouting orders, all assembled at the bottom of the hill grabbed horses from dead sailors, rode hard.

Acceptance of the fact hunters could not fight an army.

Acceptance of the fact hunters were not trained warriors.

Acceptance of the fact that victory was not possible.

Acceptance that it was better to follow Herzog than be slaughtered one at a time by the invaders of their land, most had lost children, wives, mothers, fathers, all of the archers would willingly die for revenge.

30

EACH END A BEGINING

"In love one must follow their heart—to kill one must trust their heart."

It was midday in the castle when Morgan was brought before King Harrow, the knots on the ropes around Morgan's wrists were tight.

Harrow accused Morgan of not following orders, endangering the kingdom.

When King Harrow finished it sounded like the entire war was Morgan's fault.

Normally advisors to King Harrow would have shouted insults at the accused, spat at anyone the king held in low regard.

On this day the advisers just hung their heads, it was understood, anyone that spoke up for Morgan would be taken to the square for a slow death, lands forfeit, families made slaves.

Never wavering, Morgan looked at King Harrow with a solemn expression, finally, when the king had stopped talking, Morgan simply spat on the floor, the prisoner was led away to the front gate.

Removing fine robes the advisors threw them in a pile on Morgan's spit, one by one they walked out, Harrow screamed at the advisers to stop, they did not.

King Harrow watched the advisers, there was no changing treason, the advisers walked out the door.

One advisor stayed, a wealthy landholder who had lost most of his crops, he asked Harrow where the money was spent for the army, the army that was to fight this war, the money from all the extra taxes, money from every person in the kingdom.

King Harrow tried to explain, taxes were saved so that he could bribe Rogan into leaving, now things were out of hand, now the money was to be used to make the kingdom stronger.

Harrow's last advisor turned, with a sweeping stroke the adviser's cloak was thrown upon the others.

Alone King Harrow cursed them all, he would make them all pay, when this conflict with Rogan was over the court would know vengeance for these traitors who did not support their king.

An hour later a hundred farmers were lined up by Prince Rogan just outside of arrow range of the castle walls. A hundred sailors with swords were lined up behind the peasants.

There was a small door in the gate, it was open slowly, cautiously, walking out with his hands bound Morgan moved slowly, accepting his fate.

Grabbed up quickly by the sailors, Morgan was taken to the tent of Prince Rogan, the two brothers looked very similar in height, stature, most of all the anger each carried within was clearly upon their faces.

The night before a surgeon had cut off part of Rogan's leg, with bones shattered at the knee, the bleeding was too strong, there was no way to save the leg once the large arrow had ripped through it.

Rogan laughed when he first saw how young Morgan was, asked why the boy had shot him, Morgan asked why Rogan burned the people of his kingdom.

Laughing, Rogan felt the concepts of fighting wars were beyond the understanding of a peasant youth.

Pointing to his missing leg Rogan screamed at Morgan, accused, cursed, swore vengeance, the boy calmly explained, it was an accident, he was aiming at Rogan's heart.

Rogan realized the strength within Morgan, a boy he must now kill.

Morgan was taken out of the tent, moved to another tent until a feast had been prepared.

Killing one that a commander respects is often the price of the crown.

A tall pole was being planted in the ground in the sailors camp, Morgan would be hung from it, sailors would throw stones at Morgan until dead, sometimes it went on for hours, Rogan wondered if Morgan would scream, yell out, beg.

No, Rogan realized Morgan would stay up on the pole until dead without a whimper, for that Rogan respected Morgan even more.

The deal had been that King Harrow would turn over the archer, then the hundred peasants would be allowed to go free, instead Rogan kept the hundred kneeling on the ground with his sailors behind them waiting for a command to kill them all.

It was not an attack from the castle Rogan feared, there were many people loyal to King Harrow in his camp, knowing if they interfered with the execution then a hundred of their comrades would die was a way to ensure they acted properly.

Cows were killed in Rogan's camp, a feast was underway, when the food was gone Morgan would be hoisted, stoned, it would be a grand party, with this capitulation King Harrow showed his weakness, having lived soft while Rogan had lived a hard life.

As sailors cut pieces of burnt meat from the cows, laughed, joked, drank, a single flaming arrow arched into the sky above the invaders camp, only one lookout on the castle walls could see it, they thought the sailors must be shooting them for fun at the party.

Off in the woods Madras and Balder watched the flaming arrow arch across the path of the moon, reaching out the tips of their swords touched, behind the two long rider captains the woods came alive, hounds, more than a hundred, on the command of the old man that had whelped them, loved them, cared for them, hidden them in the mountains when the war started, allowed them to fight this night.

As Madras and Balder took off at full speed, hounds did what they were trained to do, spreading though the woods on both sides the hounds were clearing a path for the riders.

Scuffling could be heard from both sides of the riders, lookouts, centuries, sailors, hounds thought of them as toys, rag dolls to be ripped limb from limb, to stop the sailors screaming the hounds pulled out their throats.

Passing before the riders the hounds led them to the left side while other hounds cleaned out sailors found in the woods to the right.

The old man that brought the hounds wanted to stay back, unable to control himself he road behind Madras and Balder, he watched his children work, the beauty of his life's joy caused small tears to form, run down over his cheeks.

Pride was a tactless villain, evil sorceress, she fed on a man's desire, made him weak.

From the hills behind the sailors came hunters, moving in small groups down to the edge of the camp, Wolf and Cozet waited on the hill, they would be last in, grab Morgan in the confusion, head back up the hill.

Herzog started the attack, running into the camp he fired twenty arrows from his small bows, on his belt he carried only one axe, three swords, swinging wildly Herzog ran through tents, over sailors at rest, killing any in his way.

Later Wolf and Cozet moved through the camp, many sailors had left their swords and weapons in their tents or by the fires, they never carried them on the ships and felt them heavy, cumbersome to carry in the camp where they were not needed.

Running for their lives the sailors began moving to the far end of camp, from the darkness came the hounds, most of the bites were not fatal, many hounds just took a piece of leg or chunk of flesh from an arm, then ran to the next sailor.

Madras and Balder looked like Gods avenging angles, long black cloaks fluttered out behind them like wings, silver swords glinted in the night as tips were inserted then broken off in screaming sailors.

Many sailors running from the hounds ended up under the hooves of Madras and Balder's stallions, years of work, training, breading, the stallions did not to stop when bones were crushed under hooves on the run.

Some of the hounds went for the hundred peasants, the owner of the hounds rode to the peasants, stopped the hounds, the hundred sailors with knives were ready to attack, no order had been given, the fight was on, the peasants could not hurt them, as a bargaining chip the peasants could die.

As the hundred sailors turned to attack the hounds, archers arrows flew from the sailors camp, Wolf's long reach was useful here.

Moving down the hill unnoticed Wolf and Cozet were selectively taking targets on their way to the tent of Rogan.

Herzog had figured that Rogan would have Morgan.

Cozet prayed Morgan was alive in the madness of war.

Entering Rogan's tent Cozet caught him loading fire sticks, Rogan got off one shot up in the air before Wolf put an arrow through his remaining leg.

Wolf's arrow dropped Rogan to the floor screaming in anger.

A blast of smoke filled the tent, the fire stick Rogan had been loading discharged.

Cozet spun, she looked, blood on the tent wall just behind her, at first she did not understand, then she realized, it was her blood, she could feel it, soft warm blood running down her leg, the shot had gone right through her side, out the back.

Falling down Cozet looked up at Wolf, his soft eyes carried tears, anger, fear, she begged Wolf to get Morgan.

Wolf refused to leave Cozet. She grabbed at Wolf's arm, now, fast, get Morgan.

Wolf turned to Rogan, grabbed the arrow in his good leg, twisted, screaming in agony Rogan told him Morgan was two tents down, the boy was alive as far as he knew.

Stepping from the tent the sounds of hounds on one side, the hunters on the other, men screaming in all directions, Wolf ran for Morgan.

A large sailor with a knife was standing in Wolf's way, just as Wolf's knife was clearing its sheath, an arrow from nowhere took the sailor down.

From behind him Wolf could hear Herzog running, together they went to the second tent, Herzog entered first, a guard, huge with a long pike poked at Herzog, he brought the axe down, the pikes' wooden handle exploded, the sailor dropped on his knees, begged for mercy.

Loyalty pails in the face of death holding an axe.

At the edge of the tent Morgan was tied, hands and neck, Wolf cut him lose with quick swipes of his small blade, Wolf held Morgan first, Herzog held him next, the arms around him were so tight that Morgan worried this show of affection would take his last breath.

By the time the three got to Rogan's tent there was no sound, both were dead, Rogan from a small blade in his gut cutting him open, he must have said something Cozet did not like.

Cozet died from the wound taking vital blood from her body.

War is a dance of death, it is a sad dance for lovers.

Screams came from Madras and Balder, the hound's master called the hounds back, yelling for them all to pull back.

Sailors stopped fighting, swords were laid down, the heart of the attack was gone.

The revenge that fueled the sailors had died with Rogan.

The sailors were marched to a clearing by the castle, eagerly the army officers in the castle took charge of them, for all the stories it sounded like the army thought they had captured the sailors without any help.

Wolf carried Cozet's body from Rogan's tent, as Wolf passed men stopped, placed a hand over their hearts, mourned with him the passing of a gallant warrior.

In the morning the doors to the throne room were opened, King Harrow sat with his ceremonial crown upon his head, huge, large facets in the jewels reflected the morning sun, a statement of the power Harrow felt would set the kingdom right.

Harrow was about to commend Herzog for bravery when Wolf appeared at the door, in his arms the lifeless body of his wife, Cozet, Morgan followed, head down.

King Harrow had to be made to understand the cost of his treachery, the price that had been paid.

Harrow held up his hand, he was about to speak, a flutter beside him caught his attention, he turned to look, nothing was there.

Proclaiming the kingdom safe, proclaiming the kingdom protected under his command, proclaiming that the kingdom would be made right again, another flutter beside Harrow, he looked around, nothing, no one.

Brushing his hand on the goblet of wine beside him King Harrow picked it up, took a long drink, lies were fertilized with strong drink.

Turning back to the assembled crowd Harrow tried to speak, no words came out, the hostile room watched as he sat with a hand up, no words came from his mouth, a hollow look in his eyes.

Rushing to his side Herzog held an ear beside King Harrow's mouth, no air moved, down the hall Herzog could see one of Harrow's best ladies in waiting, Jaclyn, holding a small vile up, she smiled at Herzog, then turned, walked slowly away.

In love one must follow their heart—to kill one must trust their heart.

Suddenly Herzog appeared to be able to hear Harrow speak.

Herzog screamed out his very words, abdication, yes King Harrow was abdicating the throne.

Herzog held his ear close to the Harrow's mouth again, another proclamation, appoint Morgan to take the throne, a brave boy to take the throne, the boy that saved the kingdom should be king of the kingdom.

The lords, advisors, court officers, looked on in silence, one shouted, another shouted, soon all were shouting, shouting praise of King Morgan.

Hoisted upon their shoulders they carried the boy up to the throne, Herzog removed King Harrow's crown, placed it on Morgan's head.

With his last breath Harrow knew treachery, no better or worse than his own.

This was after all a monarchy in all of its treacherous glory.

Carrying Morgan upon their shoulders through the streets a celebration was held, together the people of the kingdom screamed out:

"THE KING IS DEAD—LONG LIVE THE KING"

Made in the USA
Lexington, KY
11 June 2014